# THE DEVILISH MR. DANVERS

By Vivienne Lorret

**The Rakes of Fallow Hall Series**

*The Elusive Lord Everhart*
*The Devilish Mr. Danvers*

**The Wallflower Wedding Series**

*Tempting Mr. Weatherstone* (novella)
*Daring Miss Danvers*
*Winning Miss Wakefield*
*Finding Miss McFarland*

# THE DEVILISH
# MR. DANVERS

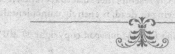

## The Rakes of Fallow Hall Series

### VIVIENNE LORRET

**AVON**IMPULSE
*An Imprint of HarperCollinsPublishers*

Excerpt from *The Maddening Lord Montwood* copyright © 2015 by Vivienne Lorret.

Excerpt from *Changing Everything* copyright © 2015 by Molly McAdams.

Excerpt from *Chase Me* copyright © 2015 by Tessa Bailey.

Excerpt from *Yours to Hold* copyright © 2015 by Darcy Burke.

Excerpt from *The Elusive Lord Everhart* copyright © 2015 by Vivienne Lorret.

EPub Edition APRIL 2015 ISBN: 9780062380524

Print Edition ISBN: 9780062380517

AM 10 9 8 7 6 5 4 3 2 1

*To old friends and new—*
*You have an uncanny ability to pop into my life*
*at the perfect moments.*
*I cherish you.*

# CHAPTER ONE

Hedley Sinclair chafed her icy hands together. The holes in the worn kid gloves snagged, expanding bit by bit. It couldn't be helped. Most of her older sister's cast-offs were threadbare now. This pink muslin dress had once been trimmed in a border of rosettes, but that had long since torn away. The petticoats had grayed from too many washings and frayed from too many mendings. The stockings were warm but only if layered by fours.

Beneath two woolen shawls, Hedley shivered. Her teeth chattered together. It had been six years since her sister had married and sailed to the colonies with her husband. Six years since Hedley had received any cast-offs or any wardrobe at all. For most of those years, she'd been confined to her attic rooms. Not forgotten, but invisible all the same.

Yet that was all behind her now. She'd inherited Greyson Park. The walls around her were her very own, and no one would ever lock her away out of shame again.

Then again, perhaps Mother was hoping she would freeze to death, or starve. Although, upon seeing her home for the first time two days ago, Hedley had realized there was a greater chance that the dilapidated roof would cave in on her instead.

Standing in the parlor, she glanced up to the ceiling. Missing hunks of horsehair plaster exposed the lath beneath. In certain places, and with the morning light filtering through the milky residue on the windows, she could see the room upstairs.

Nonetheless, Greyson Park was hers. That thought caused her frozen lips to smile. The family solicitor had informed her of her inheritance weeks after Grandfather's death, which was nearly two months ago. From Mother's incensed response, Hedley hadn't been meant to find out either.

When the time had come for her to leave, they'd exchanged no parting words with each other. However, the solicitor had imparted the "unhappy" news that she would be given no allowance, no servants, and no escort for her twenty-mile journey on foot. Which had been fine with Hedley. All she needed was right here—her own home. And now that she was here, she was determined to make the best of it.

With that thought, she opened the tarnished brass tinderbox on the mantel. Only a small circle of char cloth remained, and her piece of flint was little more than a sliver. She hoped it would be enough.

Kneeling down, she placed the tinderbox on the fieldstone ledge of the hearth and hunched over to ward off the chilly wind that blew down through the chimney. The last feral bite of winter, gnawing on the end of March, was fearsome indeed. Steel in hand, she struck the flint toward the cloth and—

The shard sliced right through her glove. Her hand jerked back. Instantly, a thin line of blood appeared on her knuckle.

Pressing the wound to her lips, her eyes narrowed at the flint. The sliver had broken in half. *"Lucifer's talons!"*

Her late grandfather's favorite oath didn't help, but saying it made her feel better.

She tried again, striking the flint to the steel. And again. "If you don't light, I'll…I'll throw you into the chamber pot. No noble calling for you. Oh, no. Instead, you'll end up as a—"

A tiny spark ignited. Nothing more than a pinpoint of orange. Still, it was something.

Pursing her lips, she blew the spark to life. Quickly, she lit the spunk stick and moved it to the kindling bundle in the hearth. After another moment of nurturing the flame, the dried bits of twig ignited.

Hedley sat back on her heels with a sigh of relief. The meager fire already began to warm her cheeks. Since that was the last of her flint until the caretaker, Mr. Tims, returned in a day or so, she needed to be more conservative. Tonight, she would do well to remember to place the curfew over the coals in the kitchen so the embers wouldn't die out.

Standing and humming to herself, she brushed off her hands and put the damper over the tinderbox. Then, moving to the woodbox, she stopped short. It was completely empty. If she didn't add a log to the kindling immediately, she'd have no fire at all.

She only had herself to blame. She'd burned too many logs yesterday, trying to keep warm. A frigid wind had come straight through the pale brick façade of Greyson Park. Then soon after, a fog had settled in and lingered. By the looks of the heavy gray clouds outside the window, today wasn't faring much better.

Used to relying on herself, Hedley lifted one of the shawls from her shoulders and draped it over her hair. Tying it at her neck like a little old woman, she made her way through the house and outside by way of the kitchen.

A steady drizzle greeted her. Sort of. The truth was, the rain felt more like tiny, frozen shards of glass. Already, the hard clay path to the woodpile was slick, covered with a fine sheen of ice. The soles of her shoes slid over the crackling ground. Fog as thick as pillow stuffing obscured her view of the shrubs, trees, and outbuildings. She didn't mind that, however. Not having a glimpse of the carriage house suited her nerves. Just thinking of it, in fact, sent an icy shudder through her, making her grateful that she lived apart from those who knew her shameful secret.

A dog howled, startling her away from her thoughts. The nearness of the mournful bay stole the breath from her body. She only hoped the animal was friendly.

"Boris!" A man's voice quickly followed a second howl. The sounds echoed around her, making it impossible to note the direction from which they originated. "Come here, you foolish beast!"

Though the words were harsh, the tone was not. It was edged with amusement in a way that was somewhat familiar.

Even though she'd always had a keen ear for sounds, Hedley quickly shook her head in disagreement with herself. It couldn't be *him*. It had been six years since she'd last heard *that* voice. Her mind was obviously playing tricks on her. Perhaps her mother was right after all, and Hedley was the family lunatic.

A shadow passed in front of her, sleek and gray, along with the steady *thump, thu-thump* of paws crunching over the icy ground.

She turned, squinting as it disappeared into the fog.

A high, musical whistle followed, merging with the thick expanse surrounding her. Then, a low *woof* answered. The dog was definitely closer, but what about the man?

The methodical march of heavy footsteps over the ice-covered grass grew louder. *Closer.* She knew that if she were unable to see the man, then it was unlikely he could see her either. Therefore, if she stood perfectly still, he might never know she was here...

*No!* Hedley rebelled against that idea immediately. She was tired of being invisible. She wasn't going to spend any more of her life that way. Gathering her courage, she peered down at the toes of her red shoes. Anyone who wore red shoes surely could never be invisible.

She drew in a breath. "Good day?"

The heavy footsteps halted. The dog gave another *woof.*

"*Good day* to you too," the man replied, his tone less amused and more wary. "I thought I'd seen smoke coming from the chimneys of Greyson Park yesterday."

A neighbor visiting, then? If that was true, then he could not be the man she thought he sounded like. For an instant, disappointment washed through her. Hedley didn't know any of the neighbors. Mr. Tims, however, had told her that Fallow Hall down the lane was owned by the Marquess of Knightswold, who'd let the property to three gentlemen tenants recently. "It was quite cold yesterday."

"Aye," the stranger said, and the crunch of footsteps began again. "As is today. And with the rain freezing over, it's no time for a traveler to be out of doors."

Wasn't *he* a traveler? If he was indeed a neighbor, the nearest house—Fallow Hall—was two miles away. Before she could ask, a dark shape started to form not too far from her.

She swallowed, suddenly nervous and wondering why she'd announced herself. She was alone at Greyson Park with no one to save her, should this man choose to strangle her and use her corpse for *his* fire.

"Very true, sir. I was merely airing out some of my grandmother's bandages," she lied. If the stranger thought the house was full of illness, then he wouldn't come closer. It seemed a plausible assumption to her. "Wouldn't want the infection to spread to the rest of us. Of course, my four older brothers all have hearty constitutions and will likely be coming outside to check on me any moment."

"Infection?" The man's steps didn't falter, and the dark shape continued to take form.

"It's dreadful. Open sores, coughing blood, and whatnot." She could have sworn she heard a low laugh.

Then, suddenly the man emerged on the path in front of her. The fog separated, sluicing away from his body as if he'd risen from a milk bath. Hedley drew in a breath, not believing her eyes. She blinked, wishing rain droplets weren't clinging to her lashes, obscuring her view.

*It couldn't be him.*

Tall and handsome as ever, he walked with a swagger. Raising his hand, he raked the unruly mane of dark hair off his forehead. The result left his features without softness.

His hard jawline and high cheekbones were only accentuated by the sharp, angular cut of his side whiskers. Dark brows arched over even darker eyes. Yet beneath his aquiline nose, his lips formed—what she could only describe as—a pout. Not a pout in the petulant sense but more so in the kissing sense.

Of course, Hedley knew nothing about kissing. Although, once upon a time, the only person she had thought about kissing was the man now walking toward her.

*Rafe Danvers.* The man who'd almost married her sister. The man Ursa had left standing at the altar.

"It's the *whatnot* that frightens me the most," he said, a smirk toying with those lips.

She waited for recognition to show on his features. For that half smile to diminish into a firm line of disapproval. After all, she knew he hated the Sinclairs for what Ursa had done. Yet as he approached, his gaze remained steady, assessing.

"What about the four older brothers?" she asked, continuing the lie and giving him another chance to remember her. Surely she hadn't changed that much. She still had the same oddly shaped face with blue eyes that were noticeably too large, in addition to a distinct dimple—more like a rut—in her too-small chin.

Then again, he'd only had eyes for Ursa all those years ago. In fact, he never even called Hedley by name. Instead, he'd given her a nickname.

"*Hey there, armless girl,*" he'd once called her. His reason, he'd explained, had been because she'd walked with her arms behind her back, and with the way her shawl had draped from her shoulders, she'd appeared armless.

Six years ago, Hedley had been dazzled that he'd even spoken to her, let alone given her a different name. It was as if they'd shared a secret. A secret that had kept her sighing for months. His nickname had meant that she wasn't invisible after all.

Yet that all changed when Ursa left him at the altar.

Soon after, Hedley had become invisible again.

"I would ask why your brothers weren't out here helping you," Rafe said, stopping only two strides from her. "Or Mr. Tims, for that matter."

Those acquainted with Mr. Timstonbury enough to call him by a shortened version of his name were usually friends of his. She, however, never would have guessed that Rafe Danvers would have kept track of Greyson Park after all these years. Especially when this house had once been part of Ursa's dowry. At one time, this house would have belonged to Rafe.

"Mr. Tims is out of town, which is why my brothers are here," she said, still watching for any signs of recognition. If he remembered her, then he would call her bluff. She had no brothers. A fact that might have made all the difference in her life.

"Terribly informal to meet a *stranger*"—Rafe hesitated as his gaze drifted down to her chin. Those dark eyes sharpened for an instant before he shook his head—"this way. Formality prohibits making my own introduction. Though, perhaps I know your brothers?"

She exhaled the bitter taste of disappointment and peeked once more at the toes of her shoes. He *didn't* recognize her. Then again, why would he?

"No, sir. I'm certain you don't." When she looked up again, she saw that he, too, glanced down at her feet, his brow furrowed. "And they wouldn't be pleased to find me out here speaking with you. Good day."

She turned to head back into the house. Then, in the same moment, she heard another low howl from the dog. Only this time, it was accompanied by the rush of paws over the crisp grass. The sound grew louder. *Closer.* The dark shadow appeared to her right, moving swiftly just as a large gray beast emerged from the clearing, charging forward, ears flapping, tongue lolling off to the side—

And barreled into her.

Hedley slipped on the ice. Arms wide, her feet shot into the air. Suspended for an infinitesimal moment, she still had plenty of time for full-fledged embarrassment to hit her. And then she hit the hard-packed ground. *Twice.* First her bum and then her head.

"Careful there, sweeting," Rafe said, appearing above her, holding out his hand.

Blinking up at him, she suddenly couldn't breathe. Although the lack of air in her lungs had less to do with the fall and more to do with the way he'd called her *sweeting.*

And all these years, she'd thought *armless girl* sounded magical.

Lying there on the icy ground, she took an accounting of her entire person. For the most part, she was unharmed, but there was a strange, slushy *pwum-pum-pum* of her heartbeat. Not only that, but her stomach bobbled, like a toy on the end of a string.

The dog howled and once again she heard the rhythmic crunch of his paws on the frozen grass, but she paid little mind to it. Putting her gloved hand into Rafe's, she allowed him to assist her to her feet. Covered in sleet or not, she felt warm all over.

"If you're going to be out of doors in weather like this, you should tread more carefully. Ice can be tricky," Rafe said, his mouth curling up on one side. Clearly, he was trying not to laugh at her—and *not* doing a very good job.

Her warmth abruptly vanished. Incredulous, Hedley glared at him. "Ice? You don't say."

Then, just when the sound of his laugh began, the dog barreled into Rafe too.

He slipped. His amusement—and that smirk—slipped as well. Hedley would have felt immense satisfaction to see him land flat on his back. Yet the more he tried to right himself, the closer he came to taking her down with him.

The soles of Rafe Danvers's boots slid on the path. His left leg shot out from beneath him, stretching him farther than any man dare. And when his foot collided with the stranger's, he catapulted her into the air.

Still holding her hand, he tried to save her. Arms locked, outstretched, he caught her—or more so, she crashed into him. Sideways. Her elbow glanced off his nose. Her bottom collided with his stomach. Wind barreled from his lungs. And before he knew it, he was flat on his back.

The woman landed hard on top of him. A curvy bit of baggage. Sprawled over him, she was soft and plump in all the places that a man enjoyed.

"Your dog is an idiot," she grumbled, shifting her body to disentangle their limbs. Her arm—the one that had struck his nose—was above his shoulder. One of her legs moved between his, her hip nestling into his groin. Her lush breasts pressed against his chest.

Rafe tried not to notice. *But…* being a man, he couldn't seem to help himself.

"I cannot argue that point." Boris, the dog in question, gave the side of his face a sloppy lick before proceeding to prance around, tail wagging, clearly pleased by what he'd done.

Lifting up, the stranger looked around as if to assess the damage. In the fall, she'd lost the shawl tied around her head, revealing a widow's peak of golden hair with threads of copper woven throughout and knotted at her crown. Her wide forehead was smooth, marked only by wispy brows. With her gaze down at her limbs, a thick fan of dark brown lashes rested on her cheeks. And beneath a rather pert nose, plump, berry-stained lips drew his attention. Against her pale flesh, those lips stood out in sharp contrast. Even more because of the unforgiving dimple in her small chin.

It wasn't necessarily a beautiful face. In a family of artists, he knew how to recognize beauty. Hers was an appealing sort of… odd face. Odd, but pretty all the same. It intrigued him. With that wide forehead and narrow jaw, it formed the shape of a heart. Her mouth did too. A tiny, berry-stained heart inside a pale moon heart.

"Are you hurt?" she asked, lifting that heart-shaped face.

Cloudy, cornflower blue eyes alighted on his gaze. Peculiarly, he felt as if she'd crashed into him all over again. He *knew* those eyes. Yet the memory wouldn't form. He'd seen her before, but whatever recollection he might have didn't match up with the lush woman on top of him.

"Hurt," he parroted, dumbstruck for the moment. Who *was* she?

Those lips parted. Then she raked her bottom teeth over her top lip in a way that turned his blood molten, like the glass he used in his art. A flame of lust ignited.

Suddenly, almost too soon—and yet, too late—she scrambled off him, taking away her pleasant soft weight and warmth.

She struggled to get to her feet but slipped again. *"Lucifer's talons!"*

At the sound of her oath, he went still. Paralyzed. The flame within him was extinguished. There was only one person he knew who'd ever used that oath and that person had been a *Sinclair*.

In Rafe's opinion, that surname was the vilest oath any man could swear.

The cold seeped into his bones, making him shudder. He hated the Sinclairs. Every…last…one.

Yet the woman before him didn't look like a Sinclair. Both Ursa and her mother, Lady Claudia Sinclair, had been renowned beauties, willowy and dark featured, with eyes that tilted up at the corners.

This woman looked nothing like them. So then, perhaps she was a distant relative. A cousin? But to his mind, a Sinclair was a Sinclair, and therefore the enemy.

Boris sidled up to the stranger, standing tall and nearly reaching her elbow. It was as if the dog were offering support without taking one iota of responsibility for what he'd done.

"Fool dog," Rafe said with a glare into those ghostly yellow canine eyes. Somewhere along the way, it had stopped drizzling, but ice covered the ground nonetheless. How long had he lain there with her on top of him?

He sat up, propping a hand behind his back. His nose throbbed, and he lifted a hand to assess the damage. Not broken. No blood.

"First he blames me for not knowing how to walk on the ice, and then he blames you," the woman said to Boris, giving him a scratch behind the ears. "It isn't quite fair, is it?"

Apparently approving, Boris licked her hand, his tail wagging. "*Woof.*" Which translated into, "Not fair at all."

This close, Rafe could see that the hem of her dress was torn. Fine threads fringed at the edge in a way that suggested the damage had been done a long while ago. The pink muslin was nearly transparent, like gauze, and lacked any luster of new cloth. Bending down, she snatched her errant shawl from the ground beside him. He took note of the holes in her gloves and the red stain across one of her knuckles.

The Sinclair women he knew were too vain to don such rags.

Perhaps he was mistaken. The thought offered him a modicum of relief over his purely male response to her.

Rafe stood and brushed the ice from his greatcoat. The black wool was already damp. Thankfully, the rest of him was dry, aside from his hair. He couldn't say the same for her, though.

Just then, Boris nabbed an end of her shawl with his teeth and began a slow backward march, likely thinking that this was his favorite game.

"Oh no, you don't," the stranger said. Wrapping the wool around her wrist, she gave it a sharp tug. This only encouraged Boris.

Rafe moved forward to aid her. When she turned and bent at the waist, however, his step faltered. Her dress was drenched on one side. Wet and plastered to the enticing curves of her hips, thighs, and calves. The delineation of her form, from the round swell of her bottom to the lean musculature of her legs, suggested she enjoyed a bit of exercise. He did as well. And since he considered himself a connoisseur of the female leg, he readily declared hers very fine indeed.

Admiring the view for a second longer, he nearly forgot that his purpose of walking here this morning was to remove this trespasser from *his* house. She didn't belong here.

Although, graciously, he was willing to offer her the benefit of the doubt. It was possible that she'd been walking near Greyson Park when the weather had turned cold. She may have drifted close to the house and, seeing that no one was here, merely sought shelter for the night.

He couldn't fault her for that, especially if she truly did have an ailing grandmother and four older brothers. Although instinct told him that she didn't. Her brothers, if she had any, would have seen to the firewood.

Yesterday, when Rafe had seen smoke rising from the chimneys, he'd felt compelled to check things out, just in case. Now, he was glad he had. Cold or not—and luscious curves not withstanding—he couldn't allow her to stay.

Greyson Park and the treasure it held belonged to him.

# CHAPTER TWO

Hedley pulled harder on the fringed brown wool and glared at the dog. Normally, she would love to continue playing his game of tug-of-war but not with her warmest shawl. She was tired of mending every bit of clothing she possessed. This was the very last item still fully intact—

In the same instant, an unmistakable ripping sound destroyed that dream. She released the shawl on a gasp.

"*Boris*," Rafe scolded. "That was ungentlemanly of you." The low authoritative tone gained the dog's attention, and he dropped the shawl immediately. Boris lowered his head but lifted his eyes in a way that made her almost want to forgive him. Almost. His tail ceased thumping and instead curled around his back leg.

Rafe bent to retrieve her next mending project and handed it to her with his apologies.

Disappointed with all aspects of her morning—the broken flint, the cut on her hand, the lack of firewood, the man standing before her having no idea who she was, and now *this*—Hedley took the shawl in her fist and left it to hang at her side. "Thank you."

Her curtness must have amused him, because one corner of his kissable pout lifted. "Gratitude with a razor's edge."

"I'm certain I don't need to point out the fact that if you'd acted sooner, *this*"—she shook her wounded shawl at him—"wouldn't have happened. He is your dog, after all."

"Actually, he isn't my dog." Rafe lifted one shoulder in an absent shrug before he reached into his greatcoat and withdrew a silver case. Without a care, he flicked open the latch to expose a row of thin cheroots nestled together. "He merely wandered into Fallow Hall one evening and never left."

Fallow Hall? *So then, Rafe is one of the three tenants,* she thought distractedly.

Absorbed by his every action, she watched him clench the cheroot between his teeth. When his lips pressed against the slim brown paper, it made her want to do the same. "Then how do you know his name?"

"I don't." He snapped the case closed and tucked it away. "None of us have managed to pin it down to something that will make him heel."

Reluctantly, she tore her gaze away from Rafe's mouth when he used the cheroot to point toward the dog.

"He looks like a Boris, don't you think?" Rafe didn't seem concerned that there was no fire nearby to light the cheroot.

This, of course, reminded her of her lack of fire. Already, she felt colder. The truth was, she'd been feeling decidedly colder since she forced herself to move from on top of him. Even with his coat covered in rain droplets, he'd been impossibly warm. "Regardless, I should like both of you to leave. As I said, I'm taking care of my ailing grandmother."

His mouth curled at both ends, his dark brows faintly arched. It was a decidedly devilish grin. "Then I should be glad to see you home."

"*This*"—she gestured with her free hand to the manor—"is my home."

"At the risk of behaving rather ungentlemanly myself, I must disagree. Greyson Park is *my* home. In fact, I recently paid an exorbitant sum for this ramshackle manor."

*He had?* A terrible, sinking suspicion settled inside her heart, weighing it down.

Hedley had known that it was Rafe who'd wanted this estate added to Ursa's dowry. She'd even heard whispers that he'd approached Grandfather on a few occasions to buy it outright, even after Ursa had left him at the altar. Each attempt had been refused, however.

While Grandfather had simply said he would not sell it, her mother was a different matter altogether. Mother's greed knew no bounds. Only Grandfather had managed to keep her in check. Now that he was gone, her mother was capable of anything.

Hedley hated to admit it, but she didn't doubt that Lady Claudia Sinclair would resort to thievery to get what she wanted. And promising to sell a property when it was no longer hers sounded exactly like Mother.

*Oh, Mother, what have you done?* "I am sorry to inform you that you were cheated," Hedley said, awash in shame. "You see, I inherited Greyson Park upon my grandfather's recent death."

It still surprised her. Grandfather had never been particularly warm to her. He'd been gruff whenever she'd crossed his path, the same way he was with everyone. But at least he'd seen her.

Rafe's grin faded. "Your grandfather..." he murmured, slowly catching on. "So then you *are* a Sinclair."

In name only, but she needn't get into the particulars. "Quite."

His dark eyes hardened, puckering the flesh above his nose. "No. It isn't possible. I have a signed contract."

"I have a contract as well." The greed of her family exhausted her. She nearly felt sorry for Rafe. But *really*, he should have known better by now than to make any sort of deal with the Sinclairs. "It is called *the deed*, and it resides with the family solicitor."

"Do you know who I am?"

"Of course, Mr. Danvers. Though I am surprised that you would want Greyson Park or any association with my family. Especially when it was to be yours upon your marriage to my sister...before she ran off with another man."

"*Sister?*" Rafe recoiled. Glancing down at his greatcoat, he brushed at the dark wool as if to remove any trace of her from his person. "I didn't know she had a sister. She never once mentioned a sister, and I don't recall you attending the family dinners."

Because she'd never been allowed to attend. "I am a well-kept family secret."

"I don't believe it." He shook his head. Reaching inside his greatcoat, he put the unlit cheroot back inside the case with a firm snap. "You're inventing all this in order to fabricate ownership of Greyson Park."

"You don't remember me at all." Why was she surprised? Her own parents barely remembered her and then only to point out a flaw. *Yet one more lovely advantage of being completely invisible.* She tucked her hands behind her back so that the thin, damp shawl draped over her shoulders. "Perhaps this will spark a memory. You once said that I appeared *armless* when I walked the garden this way."

His gaze drifted down to her bosom and lingered for a fraction of time. Long enough for her to blush. Long enough for her to wonder if...perhaps...she wasn't entirely invisible after all. In fact, Hedley had never felt so noticed in all her life.

His brow furrowed as his gaze homed in on hers. "You. *You're* Ursa's sister?"

Well, he certainly didn't need to put it that way. She knew she was no great beauty, but she didn't have warts all over her face either.

"I was seventeen when you last saw me and rather gangly at the time." Her breasts hadn't begun to show until she was past her eighteenth birthday. Then, all at once, her body had transformed. Her mother, who'd typically ignored her, had been disgusted by the change and referred to it as *cowish.* All of the women in her mother's family were slender, tall, and graceful. While Hedley wasn't short, her plump curves made her appear frumpy.

She recalled a time, many years ago, when her mother had been kind to her. At least, until Ursa had started asking why Hedley didn't look like her. *"You said her eyes would turn dark like mine, but they never did,"* a younger but no-less-terrifying Ursa had remarked. *"And you said her hair would darken too, but it doesn't look anything like mine, or yours, or even father's."*

Soon after, Ursa's doll collection had multiplied.

Rafe squinted as though still in shock over her announcement. "When I saw you at the house, I assumed you were one of the servant's daughters."

A hollow laugh escaped her. That was what her father had thought as well before he'd left to live with his mistress. "Yes, well, none of that matters now. Greyson Park is mine, and I would appreciate it if you would leave. I have much to do today, in addition to a shawl to mend."

"Wait a moment." He took a step toward her. "You claimed to have four older brothers and an ailing grandmother in there. Ursa had no brothers, and both her grandmothers had passed away before she ever knew them."

Rafe had hung upon Ursa's every word. Of course, he would recall the minutest detail, once he started to compare the two of them. Hedley wondered what it would be like to hold a man's heart and soul captive. She felt an annoying jolt of envy. "After all she has done, you still remember everything about her. Everything...*except* for her younger sister."

Rafe crossed his arms over his chest. "What is your name?"

"Hedley Sinclair." Earlier he'd said that introductions weren't made directly. Therefore, she concluded that he must have determined she was not part of society. Since she wasn't, she didn't allow herself to be bothered. Not much anyway.

"Hedley is a man's name."

She crossed her arms as well. "My father wanted a son."

"Who is your mother?" he asked, testing her with an accusatory arch of a brow.

"Lady Claudia Sinclair, daughter of the Earl of Linford. My father is Sir Richard Sinclair, who has lived in Brighton for the past twelve years. You already know who my sister is…and apparently you are still pining for her."

His dark gaze narrowed. "Hold your tongue."

"Stop asking questions."

Rafe shook his head. Turning away, he unfolded his arms. "I cannot believe this. I refuse! If what you say is true then I have just handed over two thousand pounds to your mother—along with a promise to pay an additional sum of eight thousand pounds by year's end—for an estate that no longer belongs to her."

"It's vulgar to speak of money," she chided, knowing that much at least. "But why ever would you pay so much for Greyson Park?" Even the solicitor had informed her grandfather that it wasn't worth more than seven hundred pounds.

"That is my concern. Not yours," he said, gritting his teeth. "The vulgarity in all of this is the fact that I actually trusted a *Sinclair* to keep her word. Yet all the while—and looking straight into my eyes without flinching—she set out to rob me."

Then he dared to glare at her—*her!*—as if she was to blame.

Hedley opened her mouth to tell him what he could do with his accusation, but just then a pained howl rolled through the fog. She looked around for the dog, but didn't see him.

The sound came again. From *inside* the house. She'd left the kitchen door ajar. Before she could blink, Rafe Danvers ran inside Greyson Park.

Rushing through the kitchen, up the stairs, and down a narrow hall, Rafe spotted Boris through the parlor doorway. He looked none the worse for wear. In fact, the beast appeared content, sitting in front of the hearth, head tilted, tongue lolling.

If Rafe didn't know any better, he'd almost believe that Boris's disappearance and falsely pained howl was a trick. Perhaps even an excuse to get out of the cold. But of course, the dog was not that clever.

Rafe crossed his arms. "Proud of yourself, are you?"

"*Woof.*" Boris panted, his tail thumping against the field-stone ledge surrounding the hearth.

Behind him, Rafe heard the interloper's footsteps stop abruptly. Then, she released an exasperated sigh. She too must have determined that their companion had played them both for fools. "Now that you have found the trickster, please leave."

Instead of doing as she bade, Rafe stepped into the parlor. "Wouldn't you like to introduce me to your *four* brothers?"

"You know very well that I only said that because I didn't want you to know that I am here alone. However, now you know everything. Most important of all, that Greyson Park belongs to me."

He wasn't certain of that fact. Such confirmation required a trip to London to inquire with the family's solicitor. It would be only a matter of a few days before he would return with sufficient proof to remove this unwanted bit of baggage from *his* house.

"You mean," he clarified, examining the layer of dust coating the mantel, "that you are alone but with your maid."

"I have no maid, Mr. Danvers."

The *Mr. Danvers* grated on his nerves, clawing up his back. Ursa Sinclair had always called him *Mr. Danvers*, even after they were betrothed. Just as he had been permitted to call her *Miss Sinclair* and nothing else.

Lady Sinclair, her mother, had encouraged the match soon after his family acquired wealth through inheritance and at the height of his father's popularity as an artist. Now, he realized Ursa had always thought him as beneath her, because he would never hold a title. She'd been ashamed of the familiarity of his address. Ashamed of him and his family—especially when scandal had removed his parents from society during their betrothal. He should have known she'd never intended to marry him.

Casting aside his distaste for the moment, he studied Hedley to see if this was another fabrication, like the mention of her four brothers. "No maid? Surely you do not expect me to believe that as well."

"Oh, how right you are." She gestured with a wave toward the rear of the house. "We passed my maid by way of the kitchen. As we speak, she is preparing my breakfast on the piping hot stove. Can you not smell the porridge from here? Buttery eggs? Currant scones from the oven?"

He smelled none of that, though his stomach gave a mournful grumble all the same. He hadn't had a decent breakfast since he'd moved to Fallow Hall. As for Greyson Park, there had been no person standing at the stove in the kitchen. And no fire in the oven, for that matter. There wasn't one in here, either. Just a pile of ash beneath the grate.

Rafe remembered her well enough. Those haunting eyes and that pale face. She used to walk in the garden, as she'd mentioned, with her arms clasped behind her back. He also remembered giving her a nickname on one of the many days he'd spent at Sinclair House.

But what had remained in his memory from their encounter, even after all these years, was the way her gaze had locked onto his. It had been direct and almost startled, as if she hadn't expected to see anyone that day. Or perhaps, it was more that she hadn't expected to be seen.

Of course, that would only be true if he believed the rest of her tale, about her being a family secret. Experience warned him against believing anything from a Sinclair.

"More and more, I'm beginning to think that you've run away from your true home and thought to hide out here."

"My *true home* is right here." She pursed those lips.

The action made him crave a puff of the cheroot in his pocket. "Why have you not lit a fire?"

She exhaled slowly and pressed her fingers to her temples. "I would have a fire if not for you. Your presence kept me out of doors too long to fetch logs for the woodbox."

"The logs would have been too wet." The wood she'd have chosen—likely from the top of the stack—would have been exposed to a day's worth of drizzle. "You would have gained a room filled with smoke but no warmth."

With the way she squinted her eyes at him, he guessed she didn't appreciate the obvious logic of his statement. Moreover, he decided she wouldn't appreciate it if he told her that when she pursed her lips, it appeared as though she were kissing the air in his direction.

"Had I a choice," she spat, "I'd have preferred a room filled with smoke to unwanted company."

This was *his* house, yet she was speaking of unwanted company? "Very well, Miss Sinclair"—as the name left his tongue, it caused an automatic shudder of revulsion—"we'll live in your fantasy for a moment and pretend that you've inherited this *noble* estate. Therefore, you must allow me to make recompense by building you a proper fire."

She tossed her shawl onto the edge of a moldering rust-colored sofa. Aside from a round side table, it was the only furniture yet uncovered from dusty sheets. "I do not need your assistance."

He knew she would say that. Somewhere along the way, he'd trod upon her ego as one would a cat's tail. Now, she had her claws at the ready. And those eyes looked less haunting and more like pools of ice. Good. He'd wanted to pay her back for her earlier comment about his *pining* for Ursa.

"Not *my* assistance? Well, then accompany me to Fallow Hall," he said, all politeness. Yet all the same, he was prepared to hoist her over his shoulder and carry her out of Greyson Park and bar the door from her returning. "Mrs. Swan will serve you breakfast, though I cannot promise it will be edible. I can promise, however, that the house is warm and not falling into ruin. Then, when you are suitably fed and warmed, I'll escort you home. To your *real* home, that is."

"Out!" Cheeks in high color—an extraordinary shade of pink—she advanced on him and snatched him by the sleeve. When he didn't budge, she stepped behind him and shoved. "Out, you boorish man! I've had quite enough from you, and I'll not let you ruin any more of my day."

"Ah, yes. When it was promising to be so *warm* and *snug*," he said, looking at her flustered face from over his shoulder. Then, he made the mistake of looking too closely.

*Damn*. Those eyes weren't ice after all. They were holding tears at bay.

Sobered, he allowed her to move him to the door. He left without argument, Boris loping at his heels. The kitchen door closed soundly behind him. Likely, she would have slammed it, had it not been for the tilted frame preventing her. As it was, it banged against the casing and then scraped into place.

Rafe stood there for a moment and drew in a breath. The fog was thinning, turning into floating islands of vapor. Scant rays of sunlight peered through, here and there, glistening on ice-covered branches and turning frozen heaps of last year's leaves into glasswork art. Directly ahead at the opposite end of the path, the woodpile waited against the carriage house.

Logs, seven hands high, listed to one side. There was no more than a week's worth of fuel. Perched precariously, many had rolled to the ground and were now completely saturated with dampness. There were a few, however, tucked into the middle that appeared dry enough.

Having already made up his mind, Rafe removed his greatcoat and got to work.

A quarter hour had passed before he stepped into the parlor of Greyson Park once more.

Hedley was not in the room, though he saw the tinder-box waiting near the hearth. Carrying his greatcoat bundle of wood to the box in the corner, he proceeded to fill it, overfill it, and then stack the driest pieces on the iron grate.

Boris ambled over and dropped the slender sticks he held between his teeth. They were slightly soggy, but his intentions were honorable. Both of them had ungentlemanly behavior to atone for, warranted or not.

Rafe heard her footsteps on the stairs in the hall before he heard her gasp.

"I thought I told you to leave."

Not bothering to turn around, he searched the tinderbox for flint but found only a small sliver. Instantly, he recalled the cut on her finger. A rush of guilt and something else churned in his gut.

"Aye, you did." He stood and moved toward the wood-box where he'd left his greatcoat. Fishing into one of the pockets, he withdrew a slender bundle wrapped in oilskin. "But what kind of man would I be to leave you to freeze to death?"

"You're more demon than man," she said, carrying her own bundle. Leaves and twigs poked out from the side of that torn shawl of hers. She'd removed the wet shawl from her shoulders. The threadbare pink muslin pulled taut over her breasts. Even through the gauzy fichu, he could see the creamy swells spilling over the top. Clearly, the dress hadn't been made for a woman with her form.

He was a man who appreciated a lush figure on a woman. Or at least, on any woman who wasn't a Sinclair.

"The devil comes in many disguises. I am only one of them." *She* was another. He would do well to remember that. "Though demon that I am, I cannot create a fire without flint. Is this how you cut your hand?" He held up the sliver.

She shifted her hold on the shawl, hiding her worn, stained gloves. "I would have made do."

"Of that I have no doubt." He knelt by the fire and withdrew his own flint and steel. "As I recall, the Sinclair women are resourceful in getting what they want."

"Which should be ample warning to you," she said. "Greyson Park is mine."

Hedley bent beside him and piled her dried goods beneath the grate. The fact that she'd found perfectly dried kindling inside the house proved his point about her resourcefulness.

*Inside the house... Wait.* Rafe's blood chilled. "Did you find those leaves and twigs in the attic?"

Years ago, he'd taken precautionary measures to seal the attic entrance. His treasure, his family legacy, remained hidden there. At the time, he'd never imagined anyone living here—other than him—and having the opportunity to explore each room, discovering what he'd carefully concealed. Of course, it would take a great deal of effort to enter the room. Although knowing how little he could trust a Sinclair, the precautions he'd taken did little to ease his mind.

"I don't make a habit of venturing into attics," Hedley answered, her voice frayed around the edges like the hem of her dress. Her eyes had that haunted look again, just before she turned away from him. "A bedroom window at the far corner of the house was broken. I merely haven't had time to sweep out the debris yet."

Rafe relaxed. The attic was still safe. And from the look he'd witnessed, it would remain so. Part of him was curious about her reasons. Yet a much greater part of him was even more determined to finally make Greyson Park his. He was running out of time. The Sinclairs had allowed it to fall into ruin. If he didn't work fast, there would be nothing left of his legacy and no way to restore his family name.

"Make no mistake," he said, "I fully intend to remove you from here. I will draw up the proper papers on my trip to London."

Toting the spark to the leaf pile, Rafe blew a thin stream of air to encourage it to light. Flames crackled over the leaves, outlining their veins and pointed tips in a thin line of glowing orange before combusting. Then, leaving his flint on the lid of her tinderbox, he stood. Automatically, he held out his hand to assist her but wasn't surprised by her refusal.

Those plump lips curled, exposing a row of white teeth and two sharp canines on either side. "You will not succeed."

That smile held his gaze captive for a moment. She was far too self-assured for his liking. "It will be my pleasure to prove you wrong."

## CHAPTER THREE

Gritting his teeth, Rafe strode out of the solicitor's office in Cheapside. Black clouds filled with soot and rain rumbled overhead. A fierce storm brewed. Both outside *and* within him.

"I refuse to believe it!" He'd thought coming to London would bring him better news.

Beside him, his longtime friend, Ethan Weatherstone, secured his brown top hat against a gust of wind. "I'm afraid it's true. Miss Hedley Sinclair inherited Greyson Park."

"And the contract I signed with Lady Claudia Sinclair—as it was overseen by a steward in her own employ—is essentially worthless."

Weatherstone shook his head in sympathy. "I'm sorry, my friend."

That witch had stolen two thousand pounds from him! Not only that, but she'd demanded eight thousand more by year's end before he could occupy the house. The worst part—he'd been willing to do it!

Disgusted and angry, Rafe climbed into the carriage and tapped against the roof for the driver. "Hawthorne Manor," he instructed but quickly changed his mind. "Better make that Danbury Lane instead."

In his current temper, it wouldn't be wise to visit his brother-in-law and sister. Especially not when Emma was due to give birth to her first child at any moment.

"I could offer a rather excellent scotch to...lessen the blow," Weatherstone said. It was generous of him not to mock Rafe for being such an idiot.

He accepted with a nod.

All along, Lady Sinclair had known how badly Rafe wanted Greyson Park, and she'd used his blind desire to her own advantage. "I should have known better."

"You could always bring the matter before the courts."

When nearly half the members of Parliament had been part of his father's ostracism? Rafe doubted any Danvers would get a fair trial. While he had lofty connections through his friend and brother-in-law, Viscount Rathburn, and even his friend and fellow housemate, Viscount Everhart, he refused to place his burden on their shoulders. "There must be something else I can do. Something I missed."

"I thought the clauses were odd," Weatherstone said, stroking his chin. "The first one, stating that Hedley Sinclair holds no authority to sell the property. Even more puzzling was the following one, stating that if Miss Sinclair were to marry, then Greyson Park would revert to the Sinclair estate. Why wouldn't her inheritance remain with her and become her husband's property?"

Rafe glared out the window as they passed the streets of town. "I'm certain the Sinclairs mean to protect their investment."

"Yet by all accounts, the property itself is worthless. You even said so yourself," Weatherstone added. "They would not share *your* reason for wanting it."

True. It wasn't *their* family legacy moldering into ruin. It was Rafe's. And they'd been holding it ransom for years. Thankfully, he'd had foresight enough to reinforce the structure of the attic during his betrothal, when he'd been able to come and go as he pleased. Adding braces, he'd thought, would have allowed him time to garner the support from the Royal Antiquarian Society. Unfortunately, he'd run into a few snags on that front as well. He was running out of time. "I still cannot get over the fact that a Sinclair, whom I'd never heard of before, holds the rights—without any true right—to *my* house."

The flesh around Weatherstone's eyes creased as if he were sorting out a puzzle. "You told me she admitted that her existence was a family secret. Therefore, if you take into account the peculiar clauses, the fact that she has no servants, in addition to the state of her attire, one *could* assume madness."

"*Madness?*" Rafe shook his head at the possibility. "The woman I met had no trouble keeping her wits about her."

And yet…there had been that peculiar haunted look when he'd mentioned the attic.

"Not that I agree with the practice," Weatherstone said, "but some hide their less sound-minded family members from society. Some even lock them away in an attic."

The bitter wind seemed to permeate the walls of the carriage. Rafe shifted beneath his greatcoat, shrugging off the disturbing thoughts that came to mind of a young woman wearing rags and kept behind locked doors.

"*I don't make a habit of venturing into attics…*"

Weatherstone shook his head. "I cannot say if that is what has occurred, but even you admitted to never having met her or even to hearing about her during the entirety of your—and forgive me for mentioning this—*betrothal* to the elder Miss Sinclair."

The reminder of Ursa's actions had already returned, full force, in the past week. Thankfully, the humiliation he'd once felt had worn away in the same manner that seashells and rocks gradually turn into sand.

Rafe wondered if Ursa—*Mrs. Nathan Cole* these past six years—was just as vain and overreaching as she'd always been. Once upon a time, he'd been blind to those particular Sinclair traits as well. Something he'd never expected, however, was that she would leave him at the altar in disgrace, instead of confessing her desire to marry another. He'd actually thought fate had brought them together. Fate and a mutual tie to Greyson Park.

"The house was once part of *her* dowry," Rafe said absently, recalling the vicious sneer of Claudia Sinclair that day. "*Did you think we would ever permit Sinclair blood to align with yours when it is obvious to the entire* ton *that insanity swims in your veins?*"

"And yet, the younger one is essentially forbidden to marry without the consequence of losing her inheritance," Weatherstone mused. "That certainly makes your task easier."

Curious, Rafe pushed the old memories aside and focused on his friend. "How so?"

"Marry her off." Weatherstone straightened his cuffs and met his gaze. "Once she is married and the estate reverts to Lady Sinclair, you can continue with your contract. Of course, you would take your own solicitor with you, along with the remainder of the payment, settling the matter once and for all."

*Marry her off.* It seemed simple enough. After all, how hard could it be to find someone interested in marrying Hedley Sinclair? While she was no great beauty, her unique features had drawn his attention and held it. Her lips held a certain appeal, for example. And those eyes of hers seemed capable of ensnaring anyone who gazed too long. Well, perhaps not anyone. He'd managed to escape, hadn't he?

Surely someone interested in finding a bride could do worse than the resourceful Hedley Sinclair. All in all, it was a good plan. "I have until year's end to make it happen, at which point I will have the remainder of the money."

"Ah, the wager between Everhart, Montwood, and you." Weatherstone frowned. "You are counting monies you do not possess. That is never wise."

The morning after Rafe had made the drunken wager with his two housemates at Fallow Hall, he'd cringed at his own stupidity. He'd wagered against Montwood? The man had a tendency to win whenever he chose. On the bright side, however, Montwood was currently on a two-year losing streak. As for Everhart...

"I have already won." Drunken wager or not, Rafe was confident. Simply put, the last bachelor standing would win up to ten thousand pounds—five thousand pounds apiece—from the ones who were either married or betrothed in a year's time. "Everhart is now married—and in record time, the poor besotted fool." Rafe rubbed his hands together. He could feel the money already.

"Yes," Weatherstone said. "If neither you nor Montwood marry by year's end, then you will have to share the winnings."

Rafe laughed. "For my part, there is no *if* about it. I doubt that I will ever marry—by year's end or at any other time."

"Yet when the time has concluded, from what you said of your agreement with Lady Sinclair, five thousand pounds— though exorbitant—is only a portion of the sum required," Weatherstone added. In truth, he brought up a valid point. "Of course, if you succeeded in marrying off Montwood as well…then your wealth would double. You could make Greyson Park as grand as you choose."

Rafe nodded. That had occurred to him, too. Yet with the recent discovery of Hedley Sinclair in *his* house, his thoughts had been somewhat preoccupied. Now, all he needed was a way to rid himself of two problems. And Weatherstone had just offered the perfect solution.

If Montwood and Hedley married, then Rafe would have everything he ever wanted.

"You have quite the cunning mind, my friend," he said to Weatherstone, who answered with the lift of a brow. "Somewhat devious too. Did I detect a note of satisfaction in your voice at the idea of getting the better of Montwood?"

Weatherstone cleared his throat, his mouth in a firm, disapproving line. "He danced with Penelope during her debut season. She found him quite…*charming.*"

Rafe held his laugh in check this time. Montwood's predisposition to charm every woman he met had gained him many enemies among the gentlemen of their circle. Rafe wasn't the jealous sort. Then again, a man would have to entertain the notion of claiming a woman for his own in order for that to happen. And that would never happen. Not again.

Hedley hated greed.

She'd witnessed her mother's and her sister's greed all her life. They would take whatever they could, even lying in order to gain their treasures—from insignificant trinkets and baubles, to money and prestige.

That was the reason Hedley wanted to forget about Rafe Danvers and his threat to take Greyson Park away from her. She'd seen an all-too-familiar glint of determination in his gaze when he'd spoken of claiming it.

Yet a larger, more pressing worry settled in her breast as she scrubbed at the windows in the parlor. If Rafe Danvers had made a bargain with her mother for the sale of Greyson Park, who was to say that Hedley's inheritance was safe? Likely, her mother had entered into a contract, knowing that the property wasn't hers to sell, effectively stealing money from him. Therefore, he might have legal means to *remove* Hedley from her home.

She breathed hard against the glass. In all her life, she'd never possessed anything of her own. Now, even though it was so new, the thought of losing Greyson Park and returning to a life of locked attics and invisibility frightened her beyond imagining. While she may have learned to pick locks in order to escape—and to become invisible in order to roam about in a semblance of freedom—who was to say that would always be the case?

"I will not go back," she said to Boris, who'd wandered back over to Greyson Park a week ago and never left. He lounged in front of the fire in the parlor, with his chin resting on his paws. "If Rafe plans to run me out of the one thing that has ever been mine, then I must come up with a plan of my own."

Boris perked his ears but otherwise made no comment.

Hedley went back to rubbing the windowpanes in tiny circles and tried not to worry.

This week, she'd kept herself distracted with work. So far, she'd gone through the lower-level rooms, cleaning each in turn—removing the sheet coverings, dragging out rugs and the smaller chairs for airing. With the large pieces of upholstered furniture, she did her best with a beater. The tasks were tiring and time-consuming. So much so that she'd imagined Rafe Danvers would never have entered her thoughts.

She'd been wrong.

No matter how terribly their encounter had gone, she'd been left feeling the same way she had over six years ago when he'd spoken to her in the garden: visible. Being the object of his scrutiny was...indescribable. He'd made her heart beat faster, among other things. Things like, when she'd placed her arms behind her back and his perusal had shifted, she'd felt the tightening of her breasts. She'd wanted to press her hands over them to make it stop. But in his presence, she'd endured it instead.

She wondered—when Rafe returned from London with his news about Greyson Park—would he *notice* her again?

She should be more concerned about the news, of course. He was bound to be angry when faced with the truth of her inheritance. Even Mother had been angry, in her own coldly silent way. Although, Hedley had grown used to her scorn. What she didn't want was Rafe's.

"*Woof.*" Interrupting her worrisome musings, Boris rose to his feet, his head aimed toward the hall. In the same moment, the latch on the front door clicked, followed by the squeak of a hinge.

Hedley started. Had Rafe returned?

"Miss Sinclair?" the familiar voice asked. Familiar, but not Rafe's.

"*Woof! Woof! Woof!*" Boris went on full alert and moved to stand between her and the door to the parlor.

"Hush, Boris," she scolded firmly but with a gentle pat for his defense of her. For good measure, however, she bent and secured the beast to her side. "Mr. Tims. I am in the parlor with a friend from down the lane."

The older man peered around the corner, removing his bowler from his bald head. His thick, bushy gray eyebrows lifted in question. Uncannily, those brows resembled rolled clumps of dust, similar to what she'd found beneath the sofa. "Is that a dog or a horse?"

Boris growled.

"Mr. Tims is caretaker of Greyson Park." This explanation seemed to soothe the dog, even though she was certain he couldn't have understood her. Yet tilting his head, he gave her hand a lick. To Mr. Tims, she said, "He is a veritable beast but gentle. He has made a good companion this week."

Shoulders hunched, the caretaker shuffled into the room but kept a wary eye on Boris. "I imagine his companionship has nearly cleaned out your stores in the cellar. You've a soft heart, but you must think about your future here."

"I am," she said, attempting to reassure him. She wouldn't bother telling him that *all* she'd been able to think of was her future here at Greyson Park. Without a single farthing from her mother, Hedley didn't know how long the stores would last. And with spring's late arrival, she wasn't certain when she could begin to plant a vegetable garden. As for meat, Boris had already supplied her with two small but tasty pheasants.

Why spread her worry? Surely he had enough to think about with the rheumatism he often mentioned. "How was your trip to Grimsby?" she asked instead. "Are your grand-children much changed since you'd last seen them?"

While she'd never met Mr. Tims's family, hearing him speak of them with such affection had made her feel as if she knew them.

"Aye." He smiled, and those dusty eyebrows drew apart, the tail ends bracketing either side of his eyes. "Polly's growing into a beauty like her mother, and Walt—that scamp—is itching to climb aboard his father's fishing boat. Soon enough…too soon, he'll take his place beside his da."

For a moment, he simply stood there in the archway, his gaze far off to sea. Then, reaching inside a pocket flap on his trousers, he withdrew a red kerchief and blew his nose soundly.

Boris backed up a step, his ears perked. Hedley nearly laughed at the way the dog looked helplessly up at her. The honking geese at Sinclair House—the same ones that had supplied Mother and Ursa with pillow stuffing—didn't hold a candle to Mr. Tims.

"Eh. Maudlin thoughts are the curse of an old man," the caretaker grumbled, stowing his kerchief. "I came by to tell you that I have news."

"From Grimsby?"

"No. I stopped by Sinclair House before I arrived." He hesitated just long enough to fill her with dread. "Your sister and her husband have returned."

Distractedly, Hedley wondered if her eyes were as helpless-looking as Boris's had been a moment ago. She drew in a breath to help settle the jump in her nerves. "I'm certain Mother will be glad for the visit. Ursa and Mr. Cole must have left the colonies the moment word of Grandfather's death reached them." Or even before…Surely if one accounted for word to reach them and then time for their journey, it stood to reason that they'd set off before his death. Trembling now, she wondered at the reason.

Mr. Tims released a series of tsks as he shook his head. "I overheard them talking about your inheritance."

Suddenly, all the strength left Hedley's body. She sat down. On the floor. Next to Boris, who laid his head on her knee. "Why would Ursa be talking about Greyson Park?"

This place had never interested Ursa. She'd been only too happy to leave it behind and let it rot. While Hedley didn't know exactly how the property had been removed from her sister's dowry, she knew that Ursa's name no longer appeared on the deed to Greyson Park.

"From what I gather, that husband of your sister's, that *Mr. Cole*, knew a fellow whose family hailed from Lincolnshire." Mr. Tims's expression turned thoughtful. "Apparently, a few hundred years back or so, the family who used to own this land were goldsmiths. Over time, it was sold off in marriage, but the rumor of treasure here in this very house lingers."

"Treasure? Here?" Impossible. She shook her head, even as the weight of foreboding settled over her.

A raspy cough escaped him as he shook his head. "When I heard it, I nearly gave myself away by laughing. To think that Greyson Park, under my own care these past few years, is full of treasure."

Over the years, this estate had been under the care of many men who'd been discarded by the Sinclair family. Mr. Tims had worked as the family gardener since shortly after Hedley was born. He used to live in a cottage near Sinclair House and had worked from dawn to dusk each day because Hedley's mother refused to hire additional laborers. Then, when age diminished his ability to maintain the land to Mother's satisfaction, she'd sent him here to live in the old gatehouse.

The gatehouse at Greyson Park served the purpose of an almshouse, leaving the main house essentially untended. Even Mr. Tims had admitted that his rheumatism forced him to avoid the stairs.

Accounting for all of that, it was *possible* that a treasure could exist, and it had been left under the noses of all who'd been assigned to oversee Greyson Park.

Sickening dread churned within Hedley. Ursa would have come to the same conclusion. If she'd traveled all the way from the former colonies in search of treasure at Greyson Park, nothing would stop her from getting everything she wanted.

Yet Ursa hadn't wanted Greyson Park before...No, it had been Rafe Danvers. Peculiarly, he still wanted it, even in its current state. Which raised the question—had Rafe known about this supposed treasure all along?

# CHAPTER FOUR

Later that afternoon, Rafe stood inside Hawthorne Manor near London and handed his brother-in-law a scotch.

Oliver Goswick, Viscount Rathburn, didn't even see him. He was too busy pressing his ear to the door, eyes wide in something akin to terror. "Did you hear that? I think Emma called for me."

They had always been the best of friends, even before the tragic fire that had claimed Rathburn's father and brought him into the bosom of the Danvers clan. Now, since Rathburn's marriage to Rafe's sister last spring, they were true brothers.

"Drink," Rafe said, pushing the glass into Rathburn's hand. His own was unsteady, but he kept that fact hidden by staying in motion.

Rafe's little sister was upstairs, giving birth to her first child. When he'd heard her cry out an hour ago, the instinct to protect her from harm had had him mounting the stairs in tandem with Rathburn...

Until the fierce Dowager Duchess of Heathcoat had stopped them both at the top. "Come one step closer," she'd warned, "and I'll throttle you both with my cane."

Rathbun had stood tall against his grandmother, but his voice was weak. "She needs me."

The dowager's glower had softened and she'd laid a hand over Rathbun's arm. "Emma is strong. Be brave for her."

Then, for good measure, the old dragon had ordered the head butler to lock them in the study.

Now, here they were—Rathbun, Weatherstone, Rafe, and his father—trapped in the study together.

Cuthbert Danvers crossed the room and clutched both Rafe and Rathbun by the shoulders. Above a vibrant paisley cravat, he offered a grin, an unlit pipe clenched between his teeth. "These things take time, boys. Why, I remember, that Celestine spent the better part of two days in her chamber for you, Rafe. Longest hours of my life. But worth it." He patted Rafe's cheek.

"I destroyed *six* ledgers the day Penelope had our son," Ethan Weatherstone said from behind them. Rising from the chair near the hearth, he smiled as if pleased by the memory. For a man who preferred order in his life above all things, this was a startling confession. "Nearly tore the door from the hinges to get to her"—he adjusted his cravat—"but I imagine that's to be expected."

The image of Weatherstone turning into a man possessed caused Rafe to grin. Their acquaintance had begun in school when a bullying prefect had taunted Weatherstone about his perfectly numbered columns in his perfectly ordered ledgers.

Both Rafe and Rathburn had come to Weatherstone's defense, and ever since they'd remained close. Weatherstone had also stood by the Danverses during their disgrace. That loyalty meant the world to Rafe.

"I tore a canvas to shreds with my bare hands, waiting for Emma to be born," Cuthbert Danvers admitted, as if this were the perfect opportunity to confess to madness. Then he turned to Rathburn. "Oliver, your father took a sledgehammer to an old Crofter's cottage and brought it to the ground the day you were born. He would have been so proud to stand here with you today."

Rathburn clutched his shoulder and nodded. "I—"

The shrill sound of a baby's cry interrupted him. Turning toward the door, he pushed the untouched glass of scotch back at Rafe, barely giving him the chance to grab it. Then, like a man possessed, he rammed his shoulder through the seam in the doors, splintering the wood where the lock once held.

Rafe stared after his friend as he ran up the stairs.

It took a moment to realize that his father was gripping Rafe by the arm, holding him back. "She's Oliver's responsibility now," his father said quietly.

Rafe knew that, of course. He'd known for quite some time that Rathburn was the best of men. Like Weatherstone, the entire Goswick family had stood beside the Danverses when they'd been cut off from society. Only the best man would have done for his sister.

"You've always been our family's steadfast shield," his father quipped, ruffling his hair. "It would do my heart good to see you with a family of your own."

The words were like a vinegary dose of reality. He swallowed down the pungent brew, reminded of how close he'd once been. Until Ursa Sinclair, and her whole family, had played him for a fool.

"Not until Greyson Park is mine." And likely not even then. The entire ordeal had soured him on the idea of marriage.

His father withdrew the pipe from his teeth and pointed at him with it. "That house has been out of our family for over a hundred years, sold off in a marriage bargain. These things happen."

But Greyson Park was more than just a house. The *treasure* it held could restore the Danvers name in society. Not that the *ton* mattered to Rafe, but he was still looking to protect his family. He wanted the best for them. Emma had a perfect life with Rathburn. Now, his parents were long overdue for theirs.

"Dear me!" a feminine voice exclaimed. "Did Rathburn break through the door?"

Looking out into the hall and up to the top of the stairs, Rafe saw two of Emma's closest friends—Merribeth and Delaney—begin their descent.

"Aye. He did," Rafe said.

Merribeth arched a dark eyebrow and shook her head. "Then I am glad I told Simon to spend the day at Tattersall's. I wouldn't want him to get any ideas," she said with one hand on the rail and the other over her gently rounded belly.

"And I am glad Griffin is with him," Delaney added, glowing brightly beneath a fall of auburn hair. "That way we can simply tell our husbands how patient Rathburn was and to live by his example." Both women laughed as they crossed the hall to the study.

"How is Emma?" Rafe was still tempted to mount the stairs.

Merribeth beamed. "She is positively resplendent."

"But tired," Delaney said, looking first to Rafe's father and then to him. "And your grandson—and your nephew—has all ten of his fingers and ten of his toes."

"And a healthy set of lungs," Merribeth added.

"Grandson," Cuthbert Danvers said, clutching Rafe's shoulder again and giving it a squeeze.

"Nephew," Rafe breathed. A mixture of familial pride and something he would almost describe as a bittersweet yearning filled him. But the latter was more likely the effects of fine scotch on an empty stomach.

"Penelope should be down directly," Delaney said to Weatherstone. She walked into the room and sat in one of the wing-backed chairs. "She wanted to retrieve your son from the nursery."

Merribeth sat across from her and sighed. "In the meantime, the new grandmothers *and* great-grandmother are cooing over the baby while Rathburn and Emma have a moment alone together."

"A son. That reminds me," Weatherstone said, withdrawing a small ledger from inside his coat. "Danvers, I believe you and I have won the wager. Both Croft and Knightswold claimed the child would be a girl."

"You wagered on your own sister's child?" Merribeth gasped.

Rafe looked to Weatherstone, wondering if he was missing the significance. His friend closed the ledger and tucked it away with a shrug. What else was a man to do when presented with fifty-fifty chance of winning?

"Men will wager on absolutely anything," Delaney said, as Penelope Weatherstone sauntered to the study, bouncing a handsome lad on her hip. A maidservant followed with a tray of tea.

While the women were distracted with pouring, and Weatherstone with his wife and son, Rafe's father shook his head and poked him with the tip of his pipe. "I've recently heard of another wager, though I *sincerely* hope I've been misinformed."

It was foolish to believe the wager between Everhart, Montwood, and himself would remain a secret. Rafe and his father stepped into the hall for a more private conversation. The last thing he wanted to do was cast a pall over their merry party. "In my own defense, I know I cannot lose."

"I'm certain that not even Weatherstone could calculate how many times men have turned that phrase…"

Making an attempt at levity, Rafe offered, "Some of them were bound to be right."

"Not many, I'd gather." There was an unmistakable edge to his father's voice. "I assume that this is a continuation of your quest for Greyson Park?"

"I made an offer, and it was accepted." There was no point in denying it. "The only problem is that, apparently, when I paid a good-faith sum and signed a contract, I was not aware that the estate had been settled upon a *different* Sinclair as an inheritance."

"A different Sinclair?"

Rafe was still disgusted with himself for being so blinded by victory. After so many years of waiting, why hadn't he taken the necessary precautions of having his own solicitor oversee the contract? "The younger daughter inherited the property."

"I wasn't aware there was *another* daughter." His father looked wary, as if the possibility of having two women like Ursa Sinclair on this earth was two too many. And he would be right.

"Neither was I. Although, I had met her on a prior occasion," Rafe added, the memory sparking anew.

Hedley's hair had been braided that day, in a thick golden plait that nearly reached the fingertips she'd kept clasped behind her back. With her green shawl and brown dress, she'd nearly blended in to the garden shrubs and trees around her. But when she'd turned at the sound of his voice and that startled gaze had alighted on him, he'd realized his mistake—she hadn't blended in at all.

For a moment, he'd thought he'd snared a wood sprite, and all from a single comment about her shawl. Then, hearing Ursa, he'd turned away. And when he'd looked back, the sprite had disappeared.

He'd convinced himself that she hadn't been real after all. Then, upon seeing her again, he realized that she had been—and still was—all too real. And regrettably, another Sinclair.

"It had never occurred to me," he continued, "that the young woman I'd noticed in the garden was the Sinclairs' other daughter."

His father tapped the tip of the pipe against the side of his mouth. "The sisters hold no similarities?"

Rafe shook his head. "Neither in appearance nor in design. If you can believe it, Hedley wears rags. Whereas her sister had never worn the same gown twice."

"Hedley?" His father lifted his brows. "You don't refer to her as *Miss Sinclair?*"

"Surely you can understand that using that particular address would sour my stomach." Rafe didn't bother to explain it further. Calling Hedley by her Christian name was nothing more than a way of separating the two sisters in his mind. Not that he needed to separate them. Or that he spent time—not too much, at any rate—thinking about the differences between them. It was just a matter of convenience. Nothing more. The reason his thoughts kept drifting to Hedley was purely because of recent developments, he was sure.

"Opposites, you say?" His father turned his head toward the sound of a soft cry up the stairs.

Rafe followed his gaze and listened with an absent ear, his thoughts far away in Lincolnshire. "Quite. Hedley has pale features and an artless way about her, whereas her sister is both dark in her looks and in her demeanor." He found the contrast in Hedley refreshing.

Even when she'd attempted to lie about having an ailing grandmother and four elder brothers, her cheeks had turned pink, betraying her. Ursa, on the other hand, had been able to lie directly to his face for weeks without batting an eye.

"If the girl is pale, perhaps she is sickly. That could explain why no one has heard of her."

Rafe dismissed that with a wry laugh. An instant image of her bending at the waist with her dress dampened against her legs flashed in his mind. "No. There must be another reason because the young woman I met was quite hale. Her unspoiled complexion is more like…Devonshire cream or the moon when it crests the treeline."

Except for when she blushed. And then her cheeks became tinged with the most extraordinary hue. He wondered if he could re-create that particular shade of pink in his glasswork.

"Are her eyes not that unmistakable obsidian like the Sinclairs?"

"No." There was no trace of the Sinclairs in *her* eyes. For that, he was grateful because he couldn't seem to erase them from his mind. Whenever he closed his eyes... "They are blue."

"Bah. That is no answer to me. *Blue* is the same as saying that rain appears wet." His father always appreciated exactitude when it came to color.

"Very well. They are blue, like cornflower petals beneath a veil of fog. Wide and guileless..."

His father cleared his throat in some manner of approval. "And what do you plan to do about Greyson Park once you return to Fallow Hall?"

Rafe shrugged. "A stipulation of her inheritance states that she will lose Greyson Park if she marries. If you take my wager with Everhart and Montwood into account, it's in my best interest to marry her off to Montwood, who is the only remaining bachelor."

First, he would need to learn if she displayed a prowess for flirting in order to lure his friend. Then, perhaps, he would purchase a new shawl for her. Something that would set an enticing frame around her features.

"Aside from you," his father corrected, pulling Rafe away from a silent attempt to define the exact shade of pink on her cheeks. "You are *also* a bachelor."

He'd heard this before. "Yes, but I am a more permanent type of bachelor, Father. Surely you'd never expect me to marry."

"I seem to recall a young boy saying something rashly similar about mounting a horse again after he'd broken his arm in a fall."

Rafe scoffed. "I was eight years old at the time."

"Ah, yes." He lifted his pipe. "But you were ten before you'd ever set your feet into the stirrups. Such a stubborn child. Over these past years, I've often wondered if you were more concerned about wounding your person...or your pride."

Hedley dragged the heavy Turkish carpet up the stairs and paused to catch her breath. "Almost...there..." she panted, wiping the beads of perspiration from her brow.

Then, she made the mistake of looking over her shoulder.

The majority of the carpet was still rolled in a log, taking up half the staircase. She issued a sound of disgust. This work was beyond exhausting. Yet she refused to stop. This was her home. She wasn't going to sit around and wait for Ursa to arrive and threaten to take possession of Greyson Park. Hedley was prepared to fight for it.

At least, she *hoped* she was prepared. Battling her sister had always been next to impossible.

Ursa had learned the power of manipulation early on in her life. Not only that, but the family greed had the strongest hold on her. It was no secret why Hedley had never received clothes of her own. Ursa had blackmailed Mother with threats of revealing Hedley's *ailment* to society, as well as the common suspicion that she was not a true Sinclair.

Wanting no reminder of Hedley's existence to disrupt her position in society, Mother had submitted to Ursa's demands time and time again, until there had been no further need for blackmail. Until it had become common practice to pretend Hedley didn't exist. And soon enough, people simply forgot that she did.

Even the servants had grown used to looking through her.

"But that is over," Hedley reminded herself. Grandfather had given her a home of her very own. Still, she wondered why. Now that he was gone, however, she would never know. Looking around at the slanted doorways and cracked walls, she smiled, regardless of the reason. Hers. This was all hers.

At least, for now. Until Ursa…

Before she could finish the thought, Hedley heard the unmistakable jangle of rigging. Her ears were always tuned to the sound of a horse and carriage. And each time she heard it, she relived part of her worst nightmare.

It took a moment before she could draw a breath. She told herself that it was merely Mr. Tims returning from the market. Then, however, she remembered that the caretaker's rheumatism had a "fierce hold" on him today. Which meant that he would remain in his cottage for the day.

Perhaps it was Rafe Danvers, dropping by to *notice* her again. Yet that wish was altogether foolish and abruptly crushed the moment she heard Ursa's unmistakable laugh.

A shock of panic froze Hedley to the spot. Earlier, she'd left the front door open to air the house. The last thing she wanted was for Ursa to see that as an invitation.

Another sharp peal of laughter broke through, sending Hedley into motion.

Scrambling down the stairs, half straddling the rolled carpet, she tried not to lose her footing. Her stockings snagged too many times to count. The hem of her dress ripped…again. And now, a hunk of tattered muslin drooped between her feet, tripping her as she rushed across the foyer and over the threshold. She slammed the door closed behind her.

At the end of the path, Ursa's head quirked toward the sound. Her dark eyes narrowed. Slipping a hand into the crook of her husband's arm, they continued forward with the appearance of having come all this way for a stroll.

Nathan Cole was a handsome, robust sort of man, broad shouldered and barrel-chested, with wavy light brown hair and a square jaw. He'd made a fortune in fur trading. Ursa could have done no better, especially when her husband's calf-eyed gaze made him appear as though he worshipped the ground she walked upon.

Beside him, Ursa was as beautiful as ever. Dark, lustrous hair. Dark, exotic features. *Dark, greedy soul.*

Beneath a smart burgundy hat, which matched her velvet pelisse, Ursa's expression turned mocking with the purse of her lips. "Surely this *creature* before me couldn't be Hedley."

"None other," Hedley replied, hating that her voice quavered. If she had learned anything from her sister, it was that a hint of cowardice only whetted Ursa's appetite. Therefore, Hedley stood her ground, hoping to hide the fact that her legs were trembling. The tremors were so violent that she feared the narrow stone landing beneath her feet would begin to crack.

"Mother said you'd turned quite *cowish* while I was away. Of course, I didn't believe her. Until now. What have you been eating—aside from *everything*?"

Hedley drew in a breath. Her ill-fitting stays and dress cinched around her breasts like barrel straps. "It's *always* a pleasure to see you, Ursa, and you, Mr. Cole."

"Miss Sinclair," Mr. Cole said with a pasted smile, enunciating the *r* at the end of her name in a way no native Brit would.

"Dear, dear simpleton"—Ursa trilled another high laugh—"you should curtsy before us. Mr. Cole is fourth in line for a baronetcy."

The first time they'd met, six years ago, Mr. Cole had been *seventh* in line. Hedley couldn't help but wonder if her sister had since killed off the other three. In fact, Hedley could almost hear Ursa laughing over the dead bodies as she crossed their names off a list. *"Only three more to go, darling,"* she'd likely say while blowing a kiss to Mr. Cole.

Hedley did not curtsy. Even though she wasn't at all certain about the rules of society, she instinctively knew that Ursa did not deserve one. Not only that, but she didn't trust her legs not to buckle beneath her. "If you came all this way for a visit—"

"Not far at all," Ursa interrupted. "You see, we decided to stay with Aunt Corliss. Her home is not four miles away. It is such an easy distance, in fact, that we may drop by whenever we choose."

Hedley's stomach churned. "Greyson Park is in no state for company. It had been abandoned and untended for too long."

"Hmm…yes. And doesn't that make one wonder why Grandfather would choose such a place for you?" Ursa's mocking gaze swept over the façade. "Truly, this is not an improvement over the attics at Sinclair House. You should return home, where you belong, and leave this hovel to rot. Wouldn't you agree, Mr. Cole?"

Nathan Cole cast an appraising—and far less condemning—gaze over the structure. "Greyson Park is not as fine as Sinclair House. Although if we were to find that it is still part of your dowry, then we could tear this down and build a hunting box."

Tear down Greyson Park! A new shock of terror gripped Hedley's lungs in a vise. She staggered back a step until she was pressed against the door. Even though she was outside, she felt like a cornered stable cat. It took a good deal of effort not to bare her teeth. "Ursa never wanted Greyson Park."

Mr. Cole did not respond. Her sister's lips slowly spread into a smile. "I want it now. That is all that matters."

"All that matters is my name on the deed," Hedley replied.

Her sister's eyes glinted in the sunlight. "I thought perhaps you would be smart enough by now to realize how pointless it is to fight against me. But I see nothing has changed." She clucked her tongue. "Part of me is glad, you know. I so enjoy teaching you your place."

"My place is here."

Ursa looked up at her husband and batted her eyes. "Darling, doesn't she sound just like that parrot we saw on our travels—the one that kept repeating the same inane phrase over and over again?"

"Yes," he answered with a pitying glance at Hedley. In that moment, she realized that Mr. Cole *believed* she was the family lunatic, one who did not know her own mind. "I believe the bird's owner kept it locked in a cage all its life for its own protection."

*Locked away*…Hedley swallowed. Her throat had gone impossibly dry. She was unable to say anything before Ursa and Mr. Cole turned and walked the path toward their carriage.

Leaning against the door for support, Hedley realized she couldn't fight them alone. She needed help.

Unfortunately, the only person who valued Greyson Park as much she did was Rafe Danvers. But if she asked for his assistance, she might end up losing her home anyway.

## CHAPTER FIVE

The sky darkened ominously as Hedley approached Fallow Hall the following morning. She didn't want to enlist Rafe Danvers's assistance, but Ursa had left her little choice.

Hedley didn't believe there was treasure at Greyson Park. She'd searched every room she could. There were a number of them, however, with the doorframes tilted in such a way that wedged the doors in their jambs. No amount of budging had worked so far.

She'd like nothing more than to open every door, just to prove to Ursa that there was no treasure. Yet even Hedley knew that if Ursa was determined to find treasure at Greyson Park, seeing empty, treasure-less rooms would not deter her. Not at all. Because then, Ursa would simply tear it down. She would stop at nothing.

As if sensing her thoughts, Boris offered a supportive *woof* beside her.

She wished he'd been around yesterday. Although he'd likely gone into hiding the moment he'd heard Ursa's piercing laugh. Now, pausing in front of the wide oaken door, Hedley scratched Boris behind the ears.

A large iron knocker in the shape of a ring of twisted rope hung from the center of the black door. It almost resembled a noose. Her throat seemed to tighten as she reached for it. Could she really go through with this?

Before she found her answer, Boris yawped.

In the next instant, the door opened as if under his command. A stately, somber-faced man, dressed in black finery and a pristine white cravat, answered the door. In such attire, she knew he couldn't be the butler. The butler at Sinclair House—in fact, all the servants—dressed in green livery and appeared as if they all belonged to a traveling carnival.

Therefore, this man must be one of the other gentlemen living here. "Yes, miss?"

Hedley glanced down to her shoes. Though soiled from the wet path, the red color offered a sense of assurance. After yesterday's reminder of how little she knew about the proper rules of society, she did what she imagined anyone in her position would do. She curtsied.

It wasn't until her knees were bent, with one leg positioned behind the other, that she realized she didn't know how *long* to hold a curtsy. Just in case, she remained that way while she spoke. "Miss Hedley Sinclair of Greyson Park to see Mr. Danvers."

The man's thin gray eyebrow twitched. "Right this way, miss, if you please."

"Thank you." Assuming it was safe to rise, she did so. Boris traipsed in ahead of her, while the nice gentleman stepped aside and even held the door for her.

Gray stone walls rose up to a lofty arched ceiling. Above her, an immense chandelier hung suspended from a black chain with myriad branches shooting off from the center like a dark spider web. The front hall opened up like the chapel at Sinclair House. Only the chapel was far more ornate—with plaster moldings, gilded mosaics on every wall, and harp-playing cherubs overhead—to the point of being suffocating. She found the dark, masculine simplicity of this hall appealing.

The gentleman escorted her inside. She wanted to ask his name but to inquire seemed to go against what Rafe had said about proper introductions.

"Please wait here in the drawing room, Miss Sinclair," the man said and summarily disappeared.

A wide expanse of windows took up the far wall, revealing a view of the darkening sky. The rolling green landscape gradually blended into the budding treeline that separated Fallow Hall and Greyson Park.

From this vantage point, her home looked like a quaint cottage with tiny curls of smoke rising from the kitchen chimney. In truth, the manor was much larger than even she warranted, and it had turned out to be quite a bit to manage for one person. With seven rooms on the ground floor and eight bedrooms upstairs—not to mention the cellar, the cook's chamber, and the butler's pantry—she still hadn't cleaned it all. As for the attic, she was determined *never* to step foot in there.

Distracted by her thoughts, she turned away from the window and sat down on the midnight blue sofa. Opposite her stood an immense glass-fronted armoire. Inside, an assortment of colorful vases, crosscut stemware, and bowls that resembled flowers captured the meager light from the window, transforming the cabinet into a wondrous display of color.

Captivated and unable to sit still, she crossed the room for a closer look. She didn't dare open the cabinet doors. Instead, she simply looked her fill, gazing from one shelf to the next.

"Mr. Danvers for Miss Hedley Sinclair of Greyson Park," the gentleman announced from the door, inclining his head.

Hedley quickly curtsied again and rose just in time to watch Rafe Danvers stroll into the room. Instantly, her heart squished in that *pwum-pum-pum* sensation. His hair fell in rakish waves over his forehead, and his darkly rich brown eyes were lit with a devilish gleam that made her stomach bobble.

"Why are you curtsying to Valentine?" he asked, his mouth curling into a smirk. "While I'm certain it's high time someone paid him respect, I do not believe he expects the guests to address him as if he were lord of the manor."

Hedley felt her cheeks grow warm. So then, he was the butler after all? But with his impeccable dress and manners she...

She looked down at her worn clothes, to the frayed hem of yet another dress that was beyond mending. It had once been a cheerful buttercup yellow but was now the color of a dying leaf from an overwatered plant. Soon enough, this garment would meet a similar fate.

She hoped that Valentine had simply recognized her as a recluse with no social graces, instead of someone who intended to mock him. "Please forgive me. I meant no offense."

"None taken, miss," he replied with the same stoicism as before. Then, without another word, he turned and left her alone with Rafe.

Clearly, she didn't belong here. She knew nothing of this world, other than how to blend in with the shadows and slip through doorways unseen. She'd never paid attention to what mattered, to social customs, or even manners of address. Now, she was surprised that Valentine had let her inside at all. It made her wonder at the state of Fallow Hall's *other* visitors.

"To what do I owe the pleasure of your company so early in the morning?" Rafe asked, drawing her attention.

She glanced to the small rosewood clock on the mantel and noted that it was nearly nine. The servants would have been up for hours by now. Although at Sinclair House, her mother and sister had usually slept past noon. Was that the proper way of things? "Is it too early to pay a call?"

Rafe moved deeper into the room, fishing out the cuffs of his shirt sleeves from beneath his fitted gray coat. The open front exposed a cerulean waistcoat with brass buttons over his lean torso. His breeches, a shade lighter than his coat, were tucked into a pair of glossy Hessians.

Then, before she had the chance to truly appreciate the flex of his muscles as he walked, he stopped in front of the cabinet and faced her. His amused countenance made it clear that he noticed her perusal.

Her cheeks grew warmer.

Even though the door of the parlor remained open, she suddenly felt as if the room were shrinking. As she'd foolishly hoped only a day ago, Rafe was indeed noticing her. From the top of her head—no doubt noting her hair's dampness because she'd walked in the drizzle without a bonnet—to the fringed knot of her shawl over her breasts, and then all the way down to the tips of her shoes.

His gaze made an equally thorough assessment on the way up. "Yes, it is too early to pay a call."

"It won't happen again." She would have to learn these things gradually, she supposed. It would help if she would stop ogling Rafe Danvers as if he were leg of mutton on a table set for her dining pleasure. At the wayward thought, she bit her upper lip and turned back to the cabinet of glass. "This is quite a lovely collection."

"And that was a clumsy change of topic," he said, moving beside her. "A young woman in society usually flirts when given the opportunity."

How was she supposed to flirt when she could barely think? He stood close enough that she could feel the alluring heat rising from his body. She drew in a breath in an effort to think of a response. When she did, however, her nostrils filled with a pleasant scent that only made her want to draw in another breath. It was *his* fragrance. From their previous encounter, she recognized the woodsy essence and a trace of sweet smoke.

Hedley caught herself rocking onto the balls of her feet to get closer but then quickly fell back onto her heels. She swallowed, her throat suddenly dry. "I am not in society. Nor am I likely to be. Therefore, I have no reason to flirt."

"You don't need a reason." He leaned in, his voice low. The angular cut of his side whiskers seemed to direct her gaze toward his mouth. "Flirting is a skill. You use it to get what you want."

Hedley forgot why she'd come here…*to get what you want*…

The more she stared at Rafe's mouth, the heavier her eyelids seemed to weigh. Why was she suddenly so tired? Perhaps it *was* too early to pay a call. Or perhaps it was because he stood so close that his warmth blanketed her. It would only take a single step to rest her head against his shoulder. "Like a type of currency used in society?"

"An astute observation." He grinned.

She was definitely out of her element. The least she could do was *try* to keep her wits about her. "Then, I should assume that you want something from me."

He moved closer, but she dared not imagine that he was under the same trance. No, he was far too skilled in the ways of society for that.

Even so, the curve of his knuckles brushed her cheek. "What shade of pink do you suppose this is?"

"And that was a terrible change of topic." Believing that he was speaking of one of the colored glass vases in the cabinet, she looked them over. She found deep red, the color of merlot; a blue vase, bright and clear as a summer sky; and daffodil yellow, among other hues. "Besides, I see no pink."

"No, this color. Here." His thumb caressed her cheek, his fingers settling beneath her jaw.

Was it possible for a man to have eyelashes that looked as if they were smudged with soot, all soft and curled up at the ends? It didn't seem possible to her. Yet that's exactly what she saw as he studied her. Knowing that her skin had betrayed her thoughts in a blush should make her want to shy away. Yet she'd gone too long without being noticed to feel an ounce of shame. Instead, she reveled in the attentiveness of his gaze, the nearness and warmth of his body, and the contact of his flesh on hers—even if it was a false show for him.

While not entirely certain that he expected her to answer, she indulged him. "Some roses are pink."

"True." He tilted her chin. Four thin, horizontal lines appeared above the bridge of his nose as if he truly were studying her. "Though when I think of rosy pink, it is darker, redder than this."

She tasted his breath on her lips. Other than their clumsy spill on the ice, this was the closest she'd ever been to a man. Heat poured from his body, sweeping over her, compelling her to draw nearer to the source. She couldn't help it.

"Berries are sometimes pink," she whispered, wondering if he could feel her breath as well.

He licked his lips. "Only *unripe* berries are pink, and you are a most decidedly ripe fruit, sweeting."

The tone of his voice changed ever so slightly. The silky timbre turned deeper, indulgent, like slipping into a pair of warm velvet slippers.

She wanted to sink into that sound. "Pink carnations."

"Yes. That's it." His hand slipped away. "A carnation pink blush, and berry-stained lips."

Missing the contact, her chin tilted of its own accord. His gaze slowly dipped to her mouth. Whatever this game was, she wanted it to continue. "Is this a lesson in flirting, or is the color of actual importance?"

Abruptly, he turned from her and headed toward a tasseled bell pull on the far wall. It was almost as if he suddenly wanted to put as much distance between them as possible.

She had her answer. He was only flirting in order to gain something. The only thing she possessed that Rafe Danvers wanted, however, was not for sale. No matter how tempting the currency, she would not give him Greyson Park.

*W*as this a lesson in flirting? If so, then he was the pupil.

Rafe held fast to this spot on the carpet, tempted to wrap the bell-pull strap around his wrist to keep him from standing too close to Hedley again. Yet even a distance apart from her, his blood pulsed hot and heavy in his veins.

Apparently, the long journey from London had left him addle-brained. He'd only planned to test her ability to tempt Montwood. He needed to discover if Hedley knew anything about flirting or teasing, enough to ignite Montwood's interest. Unfortunately, what Rafe had discovered when he'd held her face and stood recklessly close was that she knew nothing of artifice. Her responses were too open and unguarded. *Far too beguiling.* He'd never witnessed such a curious mixture of desire and innocence before.

It was more alluring than he wanted to admit.

Clearly, he never should have driven so far without a rest. He'd changed horses at Stampton, but nothing more. And all so that he could be reassured by the sight of Greyson Park from this very window.

Standing here in this room, however, he had to wonder why his gaze had not strayed to the window. Not once.

He needed to end their encounter quickly and before he was tempted by another Sinclair.

"And why wouldn't the exact shade be important? I come from a family of artists, after all." He tugged the bell pull again for good measure. "And if they were to ask me to describe the wicked Sinclair woman who holds Greyson Park hostage, I would have to be precise."

"It must be thrilling to come from such a family." She turned toward the window and clasped her hands. "The freedom. The acceptance."

Rafe was about to respond to her overly romantic ideals of artists, when Valentine appeared in the doorway.

"Sir?"

"I left a parcel in my chamber," Rafe said. "Would you be so good as to send a footman to retrieve it?"

The butler bowed and summarily left them alone again. Valentine's presence added to the reminder of how removed from society this young woman was. She hadn't even known how to address a butler. A swift rise of irritation flooded him when he thought of how she'd been kept a secret. He had to wonder why.

Turning his back on the door, Rafe crossed the room to her. This time, however, he kept his distance. He'd learned his lesson.

"You have it wrong about freedom and acceptance for artists. Not only that, but there was a time when I would have preferred an invisible family."

She shook her head. "You shouldn't wish that upon anyone."

Her expression was so tortured that he had an overwhelming urge to put his hands to her face and blot away those furrowed lines on her brow with his lips

But he didn't. Even so, he found himself drawing nearer.

"Not everyone casts such a pleasing light over artists. In fact, many in society—including those in your family—see artists as a disgrace."

Her eyes widened. "I don't understand."

Had she not even heard the reason for Ursa's abandonment? He was beginning to wonder if Hedley wasn't simply kept a secret from society, but if her own family hadn't separated themselves from her as well.

"As a member of the peerage," he said, pushing those thoughts aside for the moment, "my father's portrait skills were in high demand among his set. One day, however, it became known that he wasn't solely painting the *ton's* elite but their servants as well. These were not flattering portraits either, but displayed the grittier side of those fine houses."

As if she were an expert on the matter, she pursed her lips. "And they were ashamed of what they saw."

He admired her quick understanding but then wondered…Was shame the reason that her family kept her dressed in rags? He wanted to solve the mystery more than he cared to admit.

"Because of one portrait in particular, he was cast out of society—along with my family."

"And Ursa did not stand by your side," she said, matter-of-factly.

Rafe gave Hedley credit for her skills of observation. For someone who had been virtually invisible during his visits to Sinclair House, this surprised him. Yet he reasoned that someone who was kept hidden would have learned to be watchful.

Still, the idea disturbed him. "Your sister loathed me and my family, only I'd been too besotted to realize in time." And blind to Ursa's true nature—the avarice that ruled her every action.

"I apologize for my family's behavior toward you." That open cornflower blue gaze revealed her sincerity.

No. He did not want her taking responsibility for what her family had done. That would be too convenient for them. "That does me no good, because until very recently, I did not know you existed. It will take me some time before I am able to harbor enough ill will toward you," he teased. "As long as you hold Greyson Park, however, we are off to a good start."

It pleased him when her eyes narrowed. He would rather have her annoyed with him than tilting those lips at such a tempting angle. Strangely, he wasn't certain he would be able to resist if she renewed her unspoken invitation for a kiss.

"Since we are already speaking of unpleasantness," Hedley began, "I will state the purpose of my visit here."

He didn't like the sound of that. And liked it even less when she didn't immediately continue. Instead, Hedley adjusted the threadbare shawl around her shoulders. Her gloves were worse than before. Now, an entire finger was exposed, the rip too frayed to allow mending.

She drew in a breath and met his gaze. "I have recently learned—through Mr. Tims—that my family believes Greyson Park houses a treasure."

Rafe went utterly still at this announcement.

She hesitated, as if waiting for him to absorb this first bit before she went on to explain the history of the manor and the belief that the goldsmith had left something behind.

"I know the story," he said, clenching his teeth so hard he expected his jaw to shatter.

"Is that your reason for wanting it?"

He sidestepped the question. "To imagine that the estate hosts a treasure of gold is ludicrous."

It held a different sort of treasure, though nothing that the Sinclairs would deem of worth. It was his family's legacy—historically significant art, fashioned by his ancestor hundreds of years ago.

She nodded. "That is exactly what Mr. Tims and I believe. Unfortunately, my sister is not likely to be swayed from her quest."

"Your sister." Rafe swallowed down a sudden rise of bile up the back of his throat. "What does she have to do with this?"

Hedley turned toward the window. The curling tracks of rain on the glass cast blurred shadows on her face. "Ursa has returned. She came to Greyson Park yesterday."

He raked a hand through his hair and began to pace the room. "She must have had this notion for some time, then. Time enough to book passage from the American colonies."

"Had she known I was to inherit Greyson Park, she would have come sooner," she said with quiet resolve. "I'm certain Ursa will attempt to find a way to nullify my inheritance and revert it back to being part of her dowry, as it was previously."

Rage tore through him. The only reason Greyson Park had ever been part of Ursa's dowry was because he had bargained for it! Or *begged*, more like. The Sinclair family had humbled him on too many occasions.

After Ursa had sailed off with her new husband, Rafe remembered the relief he'd felt that the manor had been removed from her dowry. Neither Greyson Park nor Rafe had been prestigious enough for her. Which had suited him and his purpose in the end.

And now, she wanted to take it back? He wouldn't allow it!

Pivoting on his heel, he stared at Hedley's silhouette. During all this, it had not escaped his notice that everyone—including him—was trying to take Greyson Park away from her. A fact which must be weighing on her mind. After all, she'd come here to tell him of Ursa's plans. "Why come all this way to tell *me*?"

"I would like your help," she said without facing him. "I know my sister. She will stop at nothing to find the treasure. Greyson Park is already in disrepair. I cannot imagine that destroying a wall to enter a room would be beneath them. She has already said as much."

It seemed that the Sinclairs were put upon this earth to destroy everything. "And you believe *I* could stop them?"

"I thought you knew more about the manor. Perhaps you even acquired the original drawings during your betrothal. They weren't among Grandfather's papers." She turned her head. Her beseeching gaze compelled him to listen, despite the unpleasant reminder. "There are many doors that will not open. Neither Mr. Tims nor I have the strength. If I could simply show them that there is nothing hidden, no secret rooms, then they might leave Greyson Park alone."

"And what happens if *you* find a treasure?"

She shook her head. "I have no interest in it. All I want is to live at Greyson Park in peace. I don't want to see my home destroyed because of their greed."

*Damn it all*, he believed her—an entirely foolish inclination. Hadn't he been burned by the Sinclair women enough in this life to ever trust one of them again? And yet, guilt niggled at the corners of his conscience. While Hedley might want to live at Greyson Park in peace, he couldn't let that happen. Just as he was about to remind her of that, a footman appeared in the doorway, holding a paper-wrapped parcel tied with string.

"Thank you, John," Rafe said, grateful for the distraction. Crossing the room once more, he took the hefty package in both hands. "That will be all."

Inside, there was new cornflower blue muslin dress, a worsted-weight petticoat, two chemises, a short corset, several pairs of wool stockings, kid gloves and silk gloves, and a pink paisley shawl. He'd purchased far more than he'd intended, yet each item was chosen for the specific purpose of luring Montwood. Lucky for Rafe, his friend had always been drawn to damsels in distress. That blue gown was sure to bring Montwood's focus to those haunting eyes.

Rafe set the bundle down on a round mahogany table on the opposite side of the room. He crinkled the thick brown paper with the quick press of his hand. "This is for you."

He'd intended to deliver it to her at Greyson Park, but he was beginning to suspect that being alone with her, far removed from either servants or societal rules, might not be the most prudent choice.

Hedley turned from the window, her inquisitive gaze drawing together as tightly as the parcel strings. "For me?"

He shrugged as if it was a matter of happenstance. In truth, he'd spent the better part of a week in shops searching for just the right items. The only thing he hadn't found was a pair of red shoes. She seemed fond of the color.

"It is just the gesture of a gentleman, wishing to make reparations for our previous encounter." Yet while he told himself the purchase was solely part of his plan to draw Montwood closer to marriage and losing the wager, even Rafe knew it was somewhat odd to have gone to such lengths for the precise color of shawl. "Although I do not imagine you would care to open it in my presence. Something tells me that your carnation pink blush would return."

"Reparations for what?" she asked, genuinely baffled.

"I noticed that my clumsiness ruined the clothes you wore," he lied smoothly. "Not to mention what Boris did to your shawl."

Confusion knitted her wispy brows. Her mouth opened. Closed. Then opened again. "Is this common practice in society?"

"Of course." He fought the urge to cross his fingers behind his back as if he were a child. "Otherwise, I would not have given it a second thought."

"Oh." She inched forward, wary and wide-eyed. "Then thank you. However, I must say that it is unexpected and unnecessary."

He pursed his lips and lowered his chin. "I do hope you will not insult my honor by refusing it."

She swallowed. "It would not be my intention to insult you."

"Then you must accept."

"Again, I thank you." She drew in a breath, her expression weighted as if he'd told her to drink poison or else he'd stab her with a knife. "Will you aid me with Greyson Park as well?"

He considered it for a moment. "As long as you understand that I will do everything within my power to severe its link to the Sinclair family in the end."

His declaration must have snapped her out of her shock because that dimpled chin flashed up at him.

It was clear by her huff of indignation that asking for his assistance had taken a great deal of effort. "Let us fight one battle at a time, shall we?"

He nodded in agreement but couldn't resist teasing her once more. "Then all that is left is to see you to your temporary home. I'll order a carriage."

Instantly, Hedley went deathly pale. "I'll walk."

"It is raining. The distance is nearly two miles," he argued. "Therefore, I must insist."

"I would rather risk death than enter a carriage again. One would be akin to the other," she said, her voice hollow, as if she truly feared death by carriage. There was no accounting for it. And her reaction both puzzled and concerned him.

Without another word, she rushed out of the room.

Running the risk of being another specter on her heels, he followed.

# CHAPTER SIX

"I do not need an escort," Hedley said as she marched down the path away from Fallow Hall.

Rafe paid no attention. Instead, he lifted an umbrella over her head and kept pace beside her. "Then you force my hand as a gentleman."

Was this truly how men in society behaved—unneeded escorts and clothing reparations? Since she had nothing to compare it against, she was forced to take him at his word. Besides, part of her was curious about what the parcel held.

Unfortunately, in her momentary distress after he'd offered the carriage, she'd left it behind. For now, she didn't mention it, because she knew he would ask why she'd left in such haste.

Thankfully, he didn't press her. He kept silent, other than a low, musical whistle that blended perfectly with the rain. The sound was so lovely, in fact, that if she'd known how to whistle, she would have joined him. Then, when they reached a turn in the lane, he settled his hand into the curve of her lower back, as if it were the most natural thing for a gentleman to do.

For Hedley, however, it was…distracting. She tried to recall her reason for not wanting his escort.

An enthralling woodsy fragrance rose from him. It was like breathing in the air from the deepest, darkest part of the forest. The faintest hint of smoke blended with it, as if a welcoming cottage waited nearby. Several times, she'd had to stop herself from turning her head in his direction to inhale deeply. Combined with the sweet scent of rain in the air, her ability to resist that temptation waned even more.

By the time they reached Greyson Park, the rain had stopped. The clouds overhead resembled a sumptuous gray fur, the lane spotted with dark, silky puddles. Under normal circumstances, Hedley would never have imagined that a puddle looked silky, yet after walking two miles pressed against Rafe's side beneath a shared umbrella, the world seemed more decadent. And all of her senses were attuned to it.

Outside her door, Rafe removed his hand from her lower back—slowly, as if he were reluctant to end their contact. Then, he placed the umbrella on the ground, propping it against the stone casing. It was as if he planned to stay.

Somehow, she sensed that wasn't a good idea. "You should take the umbrella with you on your return to Fallow Hall."

"I will." He nudged the door open. Since the house was uneven in many places, the door swung wide, revealing the snug foyer that hosted no more than a bench along the far wall. "But first, I should like to ensure that Greyson Park is secure and…that you have a fire in your parlor."

An innocent request, she told herself. Yet, when he spoke in that same velvety timbre she remembered from the drawing room of Fallow Hall a short while ago, it didn't *sound* innocent.

Her stomach bobbled once more. "I can tend my own fire."

"*Mmm...*" A slow, devilish grin curved his lips. "I should like to see that."

Hedley blushed without knowing the reason. "While I realize that I know little of societal rules, I must wonder if it is appropriate for you to accompany me inside."

"I have been inside before. Alone with you." That tone was warm enough without any fire nearby. "Did you at any time feel as though I would make advances?"

"Of course not. I was more concerned for the advances you would make on Greyson Park."

His dark eyes glittered with amusement, as if he held a secret he was unwilling to share. "Yet you have asked for my assistance."

The only reason he'd even remained in her company was because she was the key to getting what he wanted, she reminded herself. "And you have promised to take it from me."

"But not today." Extending his arm, he gestured over the threshold. "Today, I merely want to be warm before I return to Fallow Hall."

As if to mock his statement, the air inside the house was equally as bracing as outside. He turned to close the door behind them. Yet before he could, the unmistakable jangle of a horse and carriage approaching caused a dire coldness to seep into her.

"It could only be Ursa. She and her husband are staying with our mother's aunt," Hedley whispered, a shiver rushing down her limbs. "Perhaps you should leave by way of the kitchen."

His gaze turned fierce, his mouth set in a firm line. "Ashamed to be seen with me, Miss Sinclair?"

The irritation brewing just beneath the surface of his eyes and tight smile took her aback. Instantly, it was obvious that he saw her as an extension of her family. The same people who'd taken part in his family's public disgrace. "I did not think you would want to see her. That is all."

And if he knew everything about Hedley, he most certainly wouldn't want to be seen with *her*.

"Very true, indeed." He closed the door, sealing them inside before looking past her and up the stairs. "Come. The only true way to know what your sister plans to do is to make certain she believes she is alone."

Hedley had learned as much by being invisible most of her life. People tended to reveal much more of their character when they thought no one was looking. "Very well, then. If you want to become invisible, then I am the one to show you how."

"I'm under your command," he said with a grin.

Then, he nullified his subservience by taking her hand and rushing up the stairs. All the way up, she couldn't catch her breath, but she wasn't certain it was from the quick pace. Surely a simple touch shouldn't affect her so. He didn't appear winded. Therefore, she warned herself to stop being foolish.

The upstairs was situated with bedchambers along the outer walls and a servant's passageway in the middle. Keeping her at his side, Rafe tried the first bedchamber door. It wouldn't budge.

"Locked?"

She shook her head and pointed with her free hand to the tilted doorframe. "Wedged, but that isn't where we're going. Come with me."

He frowned but followed her toward the servants' passageway.

Below them, the front door opened. Ursa's falsely sweet voice called out. "Hedley? Oh, Hedleeeeey?"

Both Hedley and Rafe froze for an instant.

"My dearest simpleton…are you here?"

Embarrassed by the address, Hedley felt her skin grow prickly. Raft cast a hard glance down the stairs as his hand tightened around hers. An inexplicable thrill shot up her arm and made her heart beat in that odd squishy rhythm. Apparently, her heart was just as silly as the rest of her.

"Hedley, it's proper to greet your visitors at the door and *not* make them hunt for you," Ursa said, her tone turning waspish and more familiar.

"Do you think she's not here?" Mr. Cole asked, making his presence known.

A muscle above Rafe's jaw twitched. Hedley couldn't help but wonder if he was jealous of the man who had wooed Ursa. She hoped not. She hoped that after six years, he wasn't still pining for her sister. Yet admittedly, she knew too little about the man beside her to understand him fully. Or to know his real reason for wanting Greyson Park.

But there was no time for these musings. It wouldn't take Ursa long before she decided to snoop through the entire house.

At the first creak of a foot upon the bottom tread, Hedley pulled Rafe across the hall and into the servants' passageway. It was a narrow doorway and painted in pale green to blend in with the wall. Like the others, the frame was tilted. When she tried to close the door, the top of it caught on the jamb, leaving a gap.

"Here. Let me," Rafe whispered.

Without thinking, Hedley covered his mouth with her hand. Then, they both went still. Through the hole in her glove, she felt the firm, velvety texture of his lips. Exhaling through his nostrils, Rafe's warm breath caressed her exposed flesh. She hadn't noticed how dark and secluded it was here in the servants' passage until now. Her intention merely had been to remind him that they were trying to be invisible, but suddenly, all she could think about was how close they stood.

Rafe could have brushed her hand aside. But he did not. Instead, he settled his hands at her waist. Unexpectedly, he turned her so that she was behind the door, the wall at her back.

"Perhaps she's locked herself in the attic for a sense of home." From somewhere near the end of the hall, Ursa laughed.

Hedley hated that sound. The times she'd spent locked in the attic were not a laughing matter. And now, Rafe knew…

Yet he held her gaze without shrinking away or giving her a look of pity. Instead, he remained steady, fierce.

"Though, knowing her," Ursa continued, "she's likely wandering about in this horrid weather. I am glad you rescued me from this damp, dreary place, Mr. Cole."

The irritation Hedley normally would have felt at the sound of her sister's taunting, went unheeded. She lowered her fingers, and now Rafe's breath brushed her lips.

"I would give you the moon, if it had a price," Ursa's husband drawled as the couple approached.

Rafe ignored Cole's syrupy phrase and focused on Hedley. The telltale tensing of her body when Ursa spoke revealed a great deal. He thought he'd known the scope of Ursa's cruel nature, yet he never thought her capable of locking her sister in an attic. Then again, likely her mother had managed the affairs of the house—which meant that he'd been justified in hating them all this time. He was just getting acquainted with Hedley, but he knew enough to realize that she never deserved such treatment. If he'd have known when he saw her in the garden years ago, he would have done something for her. *What* exactly, he didn't know. Perhaps he could have removed her from the ones who'd kept her locked away.

Yet he could not travel back in time to save that wood sprite he'd glimpsed years ago.

Frustrated by the futility of such thoughts, his hands tightened on her waist. Although *why* he'd settled his hands there in the first place was a mystery he could not explain. Now that he had her positioned behind the door and out of sight, he could easily remove them. And yet…he didn't.

The reason was likely that the slender firmness of her waist surprised him, almost as much as the flare of her hips enticed him. Her form, while looking soft and supple—and yes, it was that too—was remarkably toned. From the purposeful stride of her steps along the lane from Fallow Hall earlier, he'd garnered that she did a great deal of walking.

His hand at the small of her back had seemed natural at the time. Or more so, an indefinable impulse, much like the way he'd taken her hand before mounting the stairs. He couldn't seem to stop touching her.

Leaning in to whisper, his cheek brushed hers. "We must stand close so we are both behind the door. For the purpose of concealment."

A plausible excuse. Even he almost believed it.

"Of course," she said on a breath, the warmth of it caressing his flesh. Her hands gripped his biceps, and with each quick intake of air, her breasts pressed invitingly against him. "For the purpose of invisibility."

His heart pounded like a hammer, boring through his ribcage. He pulled her closer, unconsciously aligning her hips with his. Or perhaps it wasn't entirely *unconscious*. His body seemed to know exactly where to fit against hers.

"Then it is a good thing for you, Mr. Cole, that the moon does not have a price, for I would want it." Ursa cackled, her voice trailing away as if they'd taken another branch off the hall. "For now, I will gladly take the treasure hidden here at Greyson Park."

"Should we wait until your sister returns?" Cole asked, his voice also carrying off in a different direction.

"No. Try this door," Ursa said. A distant knock followed. "Besides, what better time will we have than right now, when she isn't here?"

Rafe turned his head. His body, however, refused to budge. Why was it proving a challenge to take a single step back? He held his breath, trying hard not to—well, not to be so *hard*.

"I don't know how meticulous your sister intends to be. With her poking around upstairs, we are essentially trapped." As he spoke, his mouth drifted closer to Hedley's until he found himself speaking each word against her lips. "We might have to endure this…proximity for a while."

"I don't mind." She shook her head. Her lips grazed ever so slightly across his.

The next thing he knew, his mouth was on hers. Those full, berry-stained lips parted on a gasp. *Damn*. He couldn't resist a moment longer.

Here, she was all soft and supple. And sweet. She tasted like a confection and like…

Before he could finish his discovery, she broke from the kiss. In the meager light, he saw her eyes narrow.

"You kissed me," she hissed.

Not the reaction he'd expected.

Not when she'd given every indication of wanting to be kissed. Then again, what in the hell was *he* doing kissing a Sinclair in the first place?

"You stole my first kiss, when it was mine to give."

*Her first kiss?* Shock jolted through him. *Surely not.*

How many years had it been since his first kiss? He could scarcely remember, though the girl had worn pigtails, and he likely hadn't been far removed from leading strings. What he did remember was that he'd liked kissing girls. That first kiss had started him off on a very pleasurable journey. And not once had he been accused of thievery. Seduction? Yes. Stealing like a common pickpocket? Never. "What is your age?"

"Not that it matters"—she lifted that pert chin—"but I am three and twenty."

He let that answer settle in, only to discover that he wanted to push it aside. Something wasn't right.

"I'd hardly call it stolen," he argued. "With the way you were beseeching me with those wanton gazes, you were going to give me that kiss anyway."

"*Wanton.*" She huffed. "You don't know that."

But he did.

A woman with lips like hers deserved long, thorough kisses. He found his hands still holding firm to her hips, keeping her close. Through the threadbare layers of muslin, he could almost get a sense of her flesh beneath his grasp. Soft, warm, yielding…*Her first kiss—*

"Did you hear something?" Ursa's voice cut through Rafe's thoughts. She was right outside the servants' passageway. Out of instinct, he crowded closer to Hedley, wanting to shield her.

"I could have sworn I heard a voice."

Hedley's grip tightened on Rafe's arms. Silently, he wedged his leg and boot against the door. Should either of the trespassers attempt to enter, they would assume it was stuck like the others.

"Mice, no doubt," Cole murmured.

Ursa sighed. "I don't know why I am surprised by this disappointment. Most of the doors are sealed."

"We will return better prepared. I'm certain your aunt's servants will assist. Though I cannot guarantee the doors we open will ever close again once I am finished," Cole said. "My darling, I promise you will have your treasure."

Apparently, he was as much of a besotted fool as Rafe had once been.

"I couldn't care a fig for the state of Greyson Park once we leave," Ursa added. "I like your notion of tearing it down and building a hunting box here."

*Tear down Greyson Park?* No. Rafe wouldn't allow it. Where did Ursa expect her sister to live? He felt a growl brewing deep down.

Distracting him, Hedley's hands lifted from his arms and settled on either side of his face. She shook her head as if in warning. And then, as if out of alternatives, after rolling those blue eyes, she rose up on her toes and fitted her delectable lips to his once more.

His entire body turned molten on contact. Such a chaste, closed-mouth kiss shouldn't have this effect on him, he knew. But it did.

Reaching up, he tilted her chin and deepened the kiss, seeking more of that confection. She was delicious. Indescribable.

"We'll hire a crew in London and draw up plans for the best hunting box in Lincolnshire, my dear," Cole promised, his voice receding down the stairs along with their footsteps.

Rafe stopped caring about the intruders the instant Hedley's tongue slid tentatively against his. *Damn.* Desire rushed through him, hot and heavy. His shaft throbbed.

Unable to resist, he plundered the depths of her mouth. She rewarded him with a luscious *mewl* of pleasure. He gorged himself on it. Pulling her hips closer, he rocked against her. Her body molded to him as if they were two halves of the same cast. If a prison existed for stealing kisses, then this one would surely have him facing the gallows.

But wait, wasn't she the one who'd kissed him?

He felt the brush of her fingers in his hair, just above the line of his cravat. Somewhere, far away, he heard the sound of a door closing. Still, neither of them pulled apart.

He moved his foot away from the door and stepped forward, pressing Hedley against the wall. Subtly, her hips shifted against his. A low, breathy moan escaped her. A quiet, delectable sound. He wanted to devour it. They were alone now. He *could* devour it.

*Her first kiss.*

His thoughts turned primitive. *Kiss. Mine. Want…*

Yet…*she is innocent*, he reminded himself. Hedley knew nothing about flirting, or pleasure, or about the natural progression of kisses like this.

He could easily show her. Too easily. Never in his life had he been so tempted to take a virgin to bed. And not just any virgin but a Sinclair.

*A Sinclair.*

Rafe pulled away. For good measure, he dropped his hands and staggered apart from her until his back was against the opposite wall in the corridor. His lungs burned with each rapid breath he drew.

*A Sinclair.*

"Did you"—Hedley took a breath—"kiss my sister like *that?*"

Kiss Ursa? He almost laughed. More than six years ago, that thought had been the focus of each day and every frustrated evening. However, since his father had received the cut direct shortly after their betrothal, she'd rarely deigned to accompany him in public. While he had managed to lure

Ursa away from prying eyes on a few occasions, she'd been quite stealthy at avoiding his attempts. At the time, he'd thought she was simply shy and innocent. She'd refused him coyly but always with enough heat in her gaze to keep him hoping. To keep him chasing after her. All along, she'd only been toying with him. Ashamed of him.

"No. I never kissed your sister."

Hedley sagged against the wall in a way that tempted him to return to her. "If you had, she would have married you. I'm certain."

Rafe stared at the guileless creature across from him, his thoughts turning in so many directions that his head ached. He wanted Greyson Park. He wanted to win the wager. He wanted the legacy that belonged to his family.

And with the sweet taste of her on his lips, *he wanted* . . .

"Lesson learned," he said, extending his hand for hers. When she slipped the fingers of her tattered gloves into his palms, he was reminded again of the parcel at Fallow Hall. Not trusting himself to return with it later and not linger, he decided in that moment that he would send a footman with it.

Drawing her out into the hall, he noted the plumpness of her lips and the becoming shade of pink on her cheeks. She knew little of society and far too little of the ways of men. "This was a lesson to you as well. You should never entertain a gentleman without a proper chaperone."

She sputtered as he tugged her down the stairs beside him. "As you'll recall, I mentioned that very thing to you earlier."

True. Although at the time, he'd never intended to kiss her in a servants' passage. Now that he had, he wasn't certain if he could ever trust himself alone with her again.

"You shouldn't have listened to me, and now you know why." *Odd.* He'd kissed scores of women in his life, but none had ever made him forget himself the way she had. He shook the queer notion away as they reached the base of the stairs. "I'm not certain I should have agreed to assist you after all."

She jerked her hand from his. Those large cornflower blue eyes stared at him in a mixture of pique and confusion. "Are you saying you'll not return to help me save Greyson Park, and all because *you* kissed me?"

"No." He drew in a deep breath and released it slowly. "It's because *you* kissed *me.*"

She scoffed at that, her temper rising with her color. "I am hardly to blame. You are a veritable devil. If it wasn't for your stolen kiss, none of the rest would have followed."

Of the two of them, she was a far better thief, because she'd managed to steal his sanity as well. And if there was a devil among them, it was also she. After all, who better than a devil to know precisely how to tempt him to continue a discourse that would *inevitably* lead to more kissing?

Before he could confess that the true blame was hers—in the flavor of her mouth, the shape of her body, and in the soft sounds from her throat—he bowed to her.

"Good day to you, Miss"—but *Sinclair* soured the sweet taste lingering on his tongue, so instead he addressed her as—"Hedley."

She gritted her teeth and walked past him to open the door. "Don't forget your umbrella, *Mister* Danvers."

"If you want me to reconsider, then I suggest you call me *Rafe.*" He brushed by her. Outside, he reached for his umbrella, only to find it gone. Automatically, he looked over his shoulder to the road where Mr. and *Mrs.* Nathan Cole had gone. Hadn't Ursa already taken enough from him?

"It will only get worse," Hedley warned. "She'll continue to take what she wants until Greyson Park is no more. That is why I need your assistance."

It was the perfect reminder that the Sinclair women were brought up to take what they wanted. "And you?" He faced her. "What will you take in the end?"

She set her hands on her hips and cocked her head. "Only what's mine. Nothing more."

While she might believe herself, he did not. In fact, he suspected that she was already taking even more than she knew.

## CHAPTER SEVEN

Hedley found treasure at Greyson Park.

Or perhaps it was more correct to say that the treasure had been among the meager belongings she'd brought with her from Sinclair House. Either way, it was a treasure in the sense that it would help her purchase food to replenish the pantry and seeds to begin a garden.

Standing in the village shop, Lynch & Twyck, she brushed her hand over the beautiful perfume cask that had once belonged to her grandmother. An inlay of gold and mother-of-pearl accented the intricate rosewood grain.

"Two shillings," the portly Mr. Lynch said with a sniff.

Two shillings wouldn't buy much. Hedley had to make sound decisions. She was on her own, after all. Foolishly, she'd hoped her mother would relent and offer her an allowance, but she'd refused to help in any way. Even Mr. Tims had confessed that he hadn't received a salary since her grandfather died. Apparently, that had been the reason the caretaker had gone to Sinclair House on the day that he'd overheard the conversation about the treasure.

"A crown." She pointed to the lovely detail work. "This is gold."

To her, the cask was worth much more. It was a keepsake. Even though she'd never known her grandmother, Hedley had often found herself imagining that Grandmother never would have permitted Hedley's imprisonment in the attic.

Mr. Lynch opened the lid of the cask and waved his hands over the six slender bottles within. "Tell me this: what use are these bottles with no stoppers?"

There once had been stoppers, made of silver and adorned with a swirling S on each top. Then Mother had discovered the cask in Hedley's attic room and sold each one.

"You could offer the lot as an assortment of small vases," Hedley suggested. It was the first idea that popped into her head, but the more she thought about it, the more she liked it. "A single bloom per vase for…six days of the week. You could adorn each vase with a different colored ribbon."

"Did I hear a mention of vases?" This question came from a woman who'd been admiring a display of combs. Several locks of dark blonde hair escaped from beneath a blue bonnet as she moved toward the clerk's counter. Stopping beside Hedley, she smiled in such an amiable manner that it almost felt as if they were friends. "I am forever in want of them. Right now, Fallow Hall has an inordinately high number of lilies of the valley."

"Fallow Hall?" Hedley started. "I live at Greyson Park."

Recognition shone in the woman's lively brown eyes. "Ah, then you must be the infamous Miss Sinclair who inherited the property."

"I am she." *Infamous*. Hedley might be able to guess who would cast her in such a light. So then, was this woman some-one close to Rafe? Without reason, Hedley's stomach began to churn and twist into knots.

"My name is Calliope *Croft*—oops—I mean, *Ludlow*," the woman said with a laugh. "You see, I'm newly married and still not used to the name."

And suddenly, those knots loosened. She exhaled a breath. "Hedley Sinclair."

"Miss Sinclair." Mr. Lynch cleared his throat. "Since there appears to be *some* interest in your stopper-less bottles, I will increase my offer to two shillings and sixpence."

"Only *half* a crown?" Calliope asked, pursing her lips. "Surely, that price is for the vases alone. Why, the cask is worth its own price. Just look at that detail. Did you say gold *and* mother-of-pearl, Miss Sinclair?"

"Um…yes." Hedley was too stunned by her newly intro-duced neighbor's support to speak. This had never happened before. In her of years living at Sinclair House, no one had ever stood up in *her* favor. "Quite."

Mr. Lynch squinted at Calliope and then at Hedley, as if he suspected them of trying to cheat him. "A crown for the box, stopper-less bottles, *and*…the shawl."

Hedley drew back, laying a protective hand over the pin that held the two ends of the shawl together. Rafe had given this to her. Even though it had meant nothing more than rec-ompense for him, this shawl, and the other items, were the first new clothes she'd ever received. "The shawl is not for sale."

The clerk's mouth twisted with regret. "Half a crown for the box and bottles. That is all I can spare."

It was better than leaving empty-handed.

Reluctantly, Hedley nodded. She cast one final look at the perfume cask and took the coin from the clerk. Beside her, Calliope was silent as they left the shop.

Together, they stood outside in the narrow alleyway that served as the village market. Shop fronts displayed their wares from boxed windows with freshly whitewashed trim. Men, women, and children alike crowded the serpentine cobblestone path. Spring had arrived, and everyone, it seemed, had decided to venture out of doors.

Calliope shook her head and frowned. "I don't understand it. My sister-in-law has a knack for bargaining, where in most instances, the shopkeepers end up *giving* her things. Obviously, I have been a poor student. I was certain Mr. Lynch would give the crown you were after."

Hedley offered a genuine smile to her neighbor. "I thought you did splendidly. And I cannot thank you enough for your efforts."

Still, without many items to sell, Hedley wondered how she was going to live. She would have to find work. Unfortunately, she didn't have enough education to be a governess or even a laundress. She could sew quite well. However, she'd been informed on a previous jaunt to the village that nearly every local girl could sew. The dress shop wanted only an experienced *modiste*. What was she to do?

If circumstances didn't change in her favor soon, she would end up starving to death in Greyson Park. In the end, it might have been better if she'd stayed invisible.

At the depressing thought, Hedley automatically looked down at her shoes. Still red. Not invisible. Good.

"You're very kind to say it," Calliope said, her expression remaining piqued. Then suddenly, it transformed into one of pure radiance as her gaze shifted over Hedley's shoulder.

"Here is my bride, at last," a man said as he approached the two of them. He was an uncommonly handsome man with pale blond hair and blue-green eyes that never left Calliope's face. With a broad grin, he slipped an arm around her waist and pulled her close. "I can't tell you how many times I returned to the bookstore in search of you. And then I remembered how you told me that you needed a comb, after I so carelessly broke one last evening—"

"Everhart," Calliope interrupted, rosy color rising to her cheeks. "It is inappropriate to speak of such things or hold me so close while I am meeting our new neighbor."

Though Calliope scolded her husband, she did nothing to dissuade him. In fact, she leaned into him. Hedley had witnessed this type of response from a few of the servants at Sinclair House. To her, it was indicative of a close personal relationship. She'd often wondered if it was a conscious reaction or something that a person was unaware of doing. Yet after kissing Rafe, she realized that the reaction was beyond a person's control.

"Neighbor, hmm?" Calliope's husband grinned at Hedley. "Are you the young woman living at Greyson Park?"

Calliope spoke for her. "My love, this is Miss Hedley Sinclair. And Miss Sinclair, this is my husband Gabriel Ludlow, Viscount Everhart."

He inclined his head. "Miss Sinclair, a pleasure."

A viscount? Hedley fell into a panicked curtsy. Was she supposed to kiss his hand or something? "It is an honor, sir—my lord—Your Grace."

The viscount chuckled. "*Everhart* will do."

She looked to Calliope, embarrassed that all this time she'd been talking to her without knowing. "And that makes you—"

"A friend," Calliope answered, placing a hand on her shoulder. "Someone to talk to over tea, perhaps. There is a lovely shop on the corner. Mrs. Dudley bakes the most scrumptious scones and biscuits."

"Why not invite Miss Sinclair to Fallow Hall instead?" Everhart asked, directing the question both to his wife and then to Hedley. "We could all travel together. I'm certain Danvers is nearly finished sifting through washing soda by now."

When he nodded in the direction of the far corner of the market, Hedley's gaze followed. There stood Rafe Danvers, wearing a burgundy coat and buff breeches and looking every bit the dashing rake.

Yet he wasn't alone. A woman with inky black hair stood with him. Hedley recognized her as the laundress, the widow Richardson. The widow laughed and brushed her hand over his shoulder in a familiar gesture, as if the two were well acquainted. *Very* well acquainted, indeed.

Hedley's stomach churned anew, twisting end over end. The surface of her skin pricked with heat. And for a moment, she envisioned herself marching down the alleyway and jerking the widow Richardson away from Rafe.

The thought stunned her. She'd never done anything remotely like that in her life. But this rise of...*annoyance* was foreign to her, and she couldn't get the idea out of her head.

Then, as if he felt her gaze, Rafe glanced to where she stood. For an instant, she saw recognition flash in the depths of his dark irises. Something else flared to life as well. She would have sworn that his gaze had dipped to her shawl, but he looked away too quickly for her to be certain. So quickly, it was as if he hadn't seen her at all.

Hedley pulled her gaze away and fought the urge to glance down to her shoes to ensure she wasn't invisible. She even managed a smile for her new friend. "Thank you for the kind offer for tea, but I have business I must attend before returning home."

Calliope cast a quick glance down the alleyway, her eyes bright. "Might I call on you for a visit?"

Hedley felt a rush of excitement at the idea of having her first guest at Greyson Park. Well…if she didn't include Rafe's two visits. And those hadn't truly been visits; they'd been…*more*. She broke away from the memory with the sudden sting of heat to her cheeks. "I would be honored." Inclining her head in the same way Everhart had, she added, "It was a pleasure to meet you both."

Then, before she was tempted to let her gaze stray to the far corner of the market, she quickly headed off in the opposite direction.

Rafe tugged at his cravat. The early spring sun was brighter than he realized. A flood of heat coated his skin, as if he stood before a furnace instead of before the widow Richardson. Yet he was almost certain that it was not his companion who'd put him in this state, but more so the glimpse of a young woman wearing a pink paisley shawl.

Wasn't it bad enough that she'd haunted his dreams for the past few days? Must she also tempt him in the light of day?

The very fact that he'd seen her the moment before he was prepared to make plans for a tryst with the widow irritated him. He needed a release from the state Hedley and her damnable kiss had put him in.

"I've missed you." The widow trailed her fingertips along the outer edge of his sleeve.

Rafe refocused his attention on the woman before him. Her features were lovely—slanted dark brows, seductive eyes, and a mouth experienced in pleasure. Yet for the first time, he felt no automatic stirring within. "Business in London kept me away for too long."

"Usually, when you return, I'll see you the same evening," she crooned, wetting her lips. "This time, I learned from one of the maids at Fallow Hall that you've been back for a few days."

A prickle of irritation tightened his grin. Knowing that she spoke of him behind his back was too reminiscent of the way the *ton* had whispered about his family. "Gossip rarely leads to good."

The widow knew enough about his family's disgrace to know how much he despised the practice. Though, for a laundress, she had made an effort to curb her tongue. At least, around him.

She dismissed his comment with a flick of her wrist as she moved her hand to the buttons of his waistcoat. "I was worried that I'd have to find a new lover. Mr. Abbot has spoken of his interest."

The village butcher? If this was her attempt at trying to make him jealous, she would have to try harder. By the size of the man's belly, he would not be able to pleasure her in all the ways that Rafe had.

Not surprisingly, the comment didn't bother Rafe in the least. He'd never been the jealous sort. Not even when Ursa had left him. Her betrayal had bothered him far more than her marrying another man.

"Perhaps you shouldn't be too hasty to discount him." Rafe tipped his hat. "For now, I bid you good day."

The widow took hold of his sleeve. "I didn't mean it. I just wanted to make you realize that other men find me desirable as well. And you shouldn't discount *me*."

"You are right. I shouldn't have." But the truth was, he had. In fact, in the recent weeks, he'd barely given her a passing thought. There was someone else occupying his mind—though not in the same way. Not entirely. Hedley's presence in his mind was like a fire that slowly consumed him. And the only way to save himself was to set his plans firmly in motion. She would marry Montwood. She would leave Greyson Park and take those tempting lips and beguiling eyes with her.

Removing the widow's hand from his sleeve, he lifted it to his mouth for a kiss. "You deserve a man who isn't distracted by business matters."

With that, he turned and left, leaving their arrangement an open-ended conversation for another time. Down the way, he met up with Everhart, who was now standing alone outside the shop window to Gravett's Emporium.

"One day, you'll have to show me how you make these wonders, Danvers." Everhart pointed with the tip of his walking stick to the crosscut carafe and matching goblets that Rafe had delivered a mere hour ago.

"You know I never let anyone watch me work," Rafe said. For him, working with glass was a way to pour himself into each piece. It was almost a religious experience that filled an empty place inside of him.

Even so, he managed to separate his attachment to some of his art and sell them off. Yet there were a few pieces with which he couldn't part. Somewhere inside his mind, he planned on leaving a legacy. The notion had become more prevalent in his mind after he'd held his new nephew in his arms.

Everhart turned. "Calliope loves the vase you gave us for a wedding gift, but now I must warn you that she has asked for several small vases as well."

"I doubt I could create enough vases to sustain our strange abundance of lilies of the valley," Rafe said with a laugh. "If she manages to purchase more of those biscuits from Mrs. Dudley, however, I might be persuaded to try."

"That is precisely what she thought. Calliope is in the shop this very moment, collecting pastries in order to persuade you," Everhart answered. "It's a pity that you just missed our new neighbor. Apparently, Miss Hedley Sinclair of Greyson Park just sold a cask of small bottles at Lynch & Twyck, which is the very reason my wife is determined to have a collection of bud vases."

Rafe abruptly became aware of a slow, radiating heat at the mention of their neighbor. At the same time, his sweet tooth—and tongue—felt an inexplicable pang of longing for a specific confection. "Why doesn't your new bride simply purchase the ones that gave her the notion?"

Everhart grinned, his gaze veering across the way toward the teashop window. "She was rather embarrassed at a failed attempt to bargain with Mr. Lynch. Nevertheless, she is determined."

"And now you are determined, as well." Rafe didn't bother hiding his amusement. Of the three of them who'd declared never to marry, Everhart had fallen within the first month after their wager. The poor fool.

*Yet he was a poor fool who had a beautiful woman in his bed every night…*

The wayward thought took him off guard. Rafe quickly shook it off. He could easily have any number of beautiful women in his bed. Settling on only one wasn't necessarily appealing. Or at least, it shouldn't be…

"I would consider it a favor," Everhart said, drawing Rafe away from the disturbing direction of his thoughts.

"A favor?" Rafe almost laughed. The look in Everhart's face stated clearly that he wouldn't take *no* for an answer.

Rafe hesitated before responding. Since the wager was a constant presence in the forefront of his mind, the opportunity of using any possible advantage against Montwood was too appealing to pass up. "Then in repayment, perhaps you could assist me in a certain matter."

Everhart lifted his brows. "I can only assume you're speaking about the wager. I was wondering when you would approach me."

Did that mean Montwood already *had* or *had not*? "The stipulations of our wager dictate that if you remain the sole loser, you will have to pay out ten thousand pounds. However, if you could convince Montwood to marry, then your debt would be reduced by half."

"And if you both marry, then I will have no debt at all."

Now, Rafe did laugh and clapped Everhart on the shoulder. "You're deluding yourself, my friend. Is that what happens to married men? Their minds slowly turn to mush? Or quickly, in your case…"

"Be careful, Danvers. For one day, you may very well dine on those words." Everhart smirked. "My only hope for you is that they are sweet."

*Sweet.* A slow shiver cascaded over Rafe's tongue, sliding down his throat and through his torso and limbs. It lingered, and for a moment, he could almost taste Hedley's kiss once more.

"I have no appetite for marriage, but perhaps with your assistance, Montwood will."

Everhart offered an absent shrug as he began to walk across the way. "Valentine informed me that you met with our new neighbor the other day. He also mentioned how it wasn't your first meeting with Miss Sinclair."

"And how would Valentine know that?"

"He said that not only did you need no introduction to our guest but that you had a parcel for her, as if…" Everhart glanced over his shoulder, eyebrows arched. "As if you'd been anticipating seeing her *again*."

Rafe tried not to let his friend's smugness needle him into offering a reaction. "I had merely been interested in discovering who was trespassing in Greyson Park."

"*Hmm*… And the parcel?"

Rafe narrowed his eyes. "I recall, not so long ago, an instance where you accused me of fishing for information regarding your interest in Calliope. Of course, in that circumstance, I happened to be correct. You, however, have no bait on your hook and a hole in your net."

"Are you sure about that?"

"Irrefutably."

"Then it is strange, indeed," Everhart mused, his gaze bright with speculation. "I received a letter from our friend, Weatherstone. He referenced how he'd spent an afternoon with you, visiting no fewer than *seven* shops, where you were determined to find a shawl in a particular shade of pink."

Rafe scoffed. It couldn't have been seven shops. "Nonsense. Weatherstone was…was exaggerating."

"Ah, yes. Our friend, who keeps a ledger with him at all times and values the precision of numbers, *clearly* embellished this one time."

Everhart was right. Weatherstone had never been one to overstate. *Seven* shops?

As if he noticed precisely how disturbed Rafe was by the realization, Everhart grinned and sketched a bow. "Now, who is the fisherman, Danvers?"

## CHAPTER EIGHT

Over the years, Hedley had learned to avoid horses and coffins—or *carriages*, rather. Although one was the same as the other, in her opinion.

Since an encounter was one of the hazards of traveling into the village, however, she'd carefully planned to skirt through narrow side streets to avoid traffic altogether. Unfortunately, at the final turn on her path, she found the avenue blocked by a wayward flock of sheep. Distracted by his conversation with a rosy-cheeked girl, the shepherd seemed in no hurry to move them along.

As a whole, the village was built in a somewhat twisted fashion. Therefore, the prospect of going back the way she came would only put her on the path of the main road or return her to the market. If she chose to forge ahead through the sheep, she would soil her shoes irreparably.

Hedley drew in a deep breath, deciding what to do. She would chance walking a short distance on the main road until she reached the rolling and somewhat rocky hills that would lead her to Greyson Park.

Keeping her gaze down, she reached the main road. She hurried along, hoping to avoid the thing she dreaded most. Yet that was not to be. In the next instant, she heard the harsh clink and jangle of a carriage coming up behind her. Hedley's skin grew clammy and icy cold. Beside her, the wheels slowed, keeping pace with the quick steps of her red shoes, the spokes turning in a deadly spiral. She turned her head, blocking the carriage from her peripheral vision. Each breath she took felt as if hundreds of barbed icicles lined the inside of her lungs.

She could never forget the last day she'd been inside a carriage or the nightmare that had followed. Even now, she could hear the high laughter that had swiftly turned to screams. She could still smell the pungent scent of terror combined with fetid offal. Could still taste the harsh, metallic flavor of the blood that had coated every inch of her.

Shaking, Hedley turned her back on the road and stopped walking.

Unfortunately, the carriage stopped as well.

"A nice day for a walk, to be sure," a stranger said from behind her. "But a far fairer prospect from the carriage."

She opened her mouth to respond, but no sound emerged. Then, after clearing her throat, she tried again. "Thank you. No," she rasped.

"Come now, pet. Where do you live? It cannot be far. After all, not many a young miss walks along the road alone. Not for long."

Shards of alarm broke through her frozen terror. Yet instead of it spurring her into motion, it only compounded her inability to move. Her mouth was dry. Her tongue thick.

She couldn't swallow. And when she breathed she could only smell the horse...and that reminded her of the blood.

*Move, Hedley. Lift your feet. Stop your shaking. Leave at once*, she silently pleaded. Her head was filled with those screams again. And her heart pounded in a terrible cadence that sounded like the rush of horses hooves.

She was frozen. *Useless.* "*Afraid of her own shadow*," as her mother had said to the servants before the lock in the attic door had clicked into place.

*Please, Hedley*, she urged again. Only the voice in her mind didn't sound like her own anymore. Shockingly enough, it sounded like Rafe's.

"What have you done?" that voice shouted.

*She*, however, couldn't answer.

The voice of the stranger in the carriage came instead. "Nothing more than ask if she'd like a ride home. Didn't say much else. Girl just sort of stood there, all-trembling and such, and for no reason at all."

"Hedley?"

*Hedley, say something.*

"Leave here. Your manner of assistance is not required." The voice that sounded like Rafe's growled. "And if you should ever approach her again, I'll mount your head on my wall."

"You can have that one. A right solid loon is what she is."

*A right solid loon.* Yes, she was that, wasn't she?

But gradually, she heard the sounds of the carriage drift away. Breathing became easier. She felt warmth on her shoulders and then hot tears streaming down her cheeks.

"Can you hear me, sweeting?"

*Sweeting*...Rafe had called her that, she thought as her mind slowly started to thaw. "Rafe?"

He released a lengthy exhale. "Aye. It is."

She blinked several times until his face came into focus. When she saw his brows knitted in worry and his eyes squinted with apprehension, a wave of dread and nausea turned in her stomach. She'd never wanted to be invisible more than she did in this moment.

When Rafe had spotted the pink paisley shawl, along with the stopped carriage, he'd known instantly that something was wrong. Even from a distance, he could see Hedley shaking. Spurring Frit to a full gallop, he'd stopped amidst a cloud of dust and leapt to the ground.

The driver had been up to no good—that much was certain. However, Rafe's instincts told him that it wasn't only the driver who'd frightened her. And Hedley was clearly terrified.

Her skin was paler than usual, her lips white with fear, and her eyes even more haunted. As if she were living a nightmare that very moment. It took an eternity before she finally responded to him. He felt aged in a matter of moments.

"Rafe," she said again. Although, it still sounded hoarse, like his name was being dragged out of her lungs.

He'd never felt such relief. He wanted to pull her to him and embrace her, right here on the side of the road. Instead, he settled for chafing her arms up and down, warming her until the color returned to her face. "Why did you not ride with Everhart and Calliope? They told me they'd met you."

"I do not ride in"—she swallowed—"carriages."

She trembled from head to foot. Even the fringes of her shawl were quivering. Puzzled, he studied her. Had it been some sort of fit? If so, how often did these occur? Seeing her this way, he was more concerned than wary. In fact, knowing that she was suffering made him feel completely helpless.

"Then allow me to see you home. We could ride together. I'm sure Frit wouldn't mind," he said, trying to keep his tone light.

"*R-ride?*" She turned just enough to see the swish of Frit's tail before she snapped around again. Tears began to gather along the rims of her eyes. "*Please. S-send it away…*"

Rafe didn't hesitate.

"Home, Frit," he commanded and accompanied it with the whistled melody he'd used to train him. Another melody would bring him back. And yet another would entreat him to bend a foreleg toward the ground, as if he were bowing. All these tricks had been designed for the purpose of either hunting or gaining a young woman's favor.

Strangely, Rafe was standing with the one woman who likely wouldn't appreciate any of it.

As the sound of Frit's plodding disappeared, Hedley's shoulders began to relax beneath his hands. Her lashes were damp and clumped together in brown spikes that resembled thorns around her cornflower eyes. He had a peculiar compulsion to tilt her face up and press his lips there.

Instead, he withdrew a handkerchief and dried her eyes. "What happened, sweeting? Was it the driver? If it was, I will run him through this very instant, and you will never need worry about him again." The tender vehemence in his tone, and resolve to do exactly as he promised, surprised him.

Some of the color returned to her face, but her lips were still pale, unripe berries. She lifted that unforgiving chin as if in challenge—and likely not knowing how that one action tempted him beyond reason to place a kiss right on that dimple. "You witnessed my madness."

At the mention, Rafe heard Weatherstone's voice in his head. *Many hide their less sound-minded family members from society out of disgrace. Some even lock them away.* A sickening feeling filled him. "What we overheard from your sister about being locked..."

He couldn't even say the words. The idea appalled him.

Hedley looked down, as if she were ashamed. "That is why you'll never find me venturing into the attic at Greyson Park."

Knowing that his family's legacy in the attic was safe *should* have filled him with relief. Yet all he felt was anger—no, rage—for what she'd suffered.

"And you may run off to London and inform my family's solicitor what you witnessed and try to use it to gain Greyson Park," she continued, "but he already knows. In fact, I imagine the only reason my mother allowed me to inherit was because she believes I could never survive living there."

"She is your mother. Surely..." But even as he started to form the words that might provide a semblance of comfort to Hedley, he refused to lie. Claudia Sinclair was not prone to bouts of tenderness. She was shrewd, calculating, and cold. And she'd hidden the existence of her daughter from society.

"Since you've met her, you must know that I am neither exaggerating nor suffering from hysterical delusions. At least, not right now."

What he'd witnessed wasn't hysteria. It had been pure terror.

Rafe stared at her for a moment, filled with an overwhelming urge to…*protect* her. It was the only way to describe this inexplicable reaction she kindled inside him. Typically, this basic response was something reserved for his closest friends and family.

Feeling it with such intensity now honestly frightened him.

He let his fingers skim down her arm and took her hand. "Come. I'll escort you to Greyson Park."

"I do not expect it of you. The road only lasts a little while longer." But she curled her fingers around his palm nonetheless.

They walked for some time in silence, simply holding hands. She wasn't wearing gloves—neither the new ones he'd purchased for her nor her old ones—and he had removed his when he'd dismounted Frit. More than anything, he wanted to keep her close, skin to skin. Yet this purely chaste contact would be viewed as scandalous. Unfortunately, the sound of another carriage off in the distance reminded him of that and of her innocence. This simple, albeit public, gesture could condemn her in the eyes of society.

Reluctantly, after a few more steps, he released her. "Forgive me. I am not being much of a friend to you at the moment. Your reputation would be in tatters if anyone saw me holding your hand. The gesture suggests an intimacy between us."

Which wasn't entirely untrue, he thought.

"You're saying that if we are caught holding hands in public, society will imagine that we've"—she paused long enough to cast him an impish grin—"*kissed in private?*"

Damned if he didn't feel challenged by that grin. But no, he told himself. She was someone he needed to protect. *Like a close friend or family*, he reminded. *A young woman whose reputation would be ruined if I gave into impulse…again.*

"That happened once and will not be repeated." He shook his head to make sure both of them fully understood.

"Of course not." She turned her gaze toward the curve at the end of the road. "I am a Sinclair *and* the woman standing in the way of your possession of Greyson Park, after all."

The sound of that carriage drew closer, though remained beyond their sight, hidden in the copse of trees a short distance away. Rafe saw Hedley stiffen and glance over her shoulder toward the sound.

"I've known many people who've developed a fear of horses after a fall, myself included," he said, wondering if that was the root behind hers.

"While I imagine it was simple for you to overcome *your* fear, I did not fall from a horse. So that ability is something I lack."

"I don't believe that for an instant. You are fully capable. You have your wits about you—"

"At the moment," she interrupted and glanced once more to the path behind them. "But I know very well that whatever sense or *wit* I might have will abandon me once that carriage comes close. My body will seize, and I will have no control. I will become a prisoner inside my body, as if someone had locked the door to my mind."

Stunned by her words, Rafe reacted by taking her hand once more. There was only one thing he could do to protect her. He began walking faster, keeping her beside him. Hedley matched him, stride for stride.

They stepped off the curve of the road to a small gully. Just beyond it stood a grassy hill dotted with white boulders shaped like tombstones jutting up from the ground. He glanced over his shoulder, seeing the carriage on the road. "Pick up your skirts," he urged with a squeeze of her hand.

She let out a startled laugh but gripped a handful of skirt all the same. "They will call us *both* mad."

"Let them." If he could help outrun her fear and never witness her terror again, then he would keep running until they reached Greyson Park.

Once they gained the other side of the hill and the road had disappeared from view, she stopped, effectively stopping him too. Her cheeks were bright pink, and her lips were ripe once again. Just as they should be.

"Madness suits you," she said, smiling.

He raked a hand through his unruly curls, pleased by the comment. Considering the way his family was viewed by the *ton*, or even his history with the Sinclairs, he shouldn't be grinning. But he was. "Does it?"

Hedley nodded and then looked away quickly, her expression somber.

She slipped her hand from his and moved toward a pair of boulders to lean against one. "There were five of us girls in the carriage that day. All the village children were given the chance to take a tour around the maypole festival."

Rafe felt his grin fade and knew that she was going to tell him about her fear. He didn't stop her or make any response. He merely leaned back against the boulder beside hers.

"Henrietta was my dearest friend. We often played together, both of us wanting an escape—her from the strictures of the vicar and his wife who'd taken her in as orphan, and me from Ursa." Hedley drew in a breath before she continued. "The night of the festival, Henrietta feared that the vicar wouldn't approve of the celebration. I begged her to go anyway. Then, soon enough we were waving from the windows with streamers dangling from our hands. We felt like princesses."

Rolling her head to the side, she looked at him. A ghost of a smile flitted across her lips, but then her cornflower blue eyes clouded over. "I'm not certain what happened next. The driver shouted. The horse let out a cry. Suddenly, we tipped. Three of the girls were thrown from the carriage. Henrietta and I were on the side that crashed to the ground. Everything went silent for a moment. Still and suspended, the same way the morning sounds after a heavy snowfall. The groaning of the carriage, the shouts from the driver, the horse…all fell eerily silent."

She took another breath, and Rafe realized that he was holding his. He could see the events in her haunted eyes and pale face once more.

"I won't describe the rest," she whispered. "I'm certain you already know what sounds breached the silence."

Screams, he thought. Dozens of screams—from the people witnessing the horror, to the girls within it. Hedley's screams. And he imagined that was one of the things that had been locked inside her when he'd found her beside that carriage earlier.

"Did all five of the girls survive?" he asked, but his voice was edged with trepidation. He wasn't sure he wanted to know the answer.

"Not Henrietta." Hedley drew in a staggered breath and looked away. "I remember how her eyes were open so wide, I thought she was looking at me for help. I reached for her hand, to pull her to safety, but I couldn't hold on. It was too slippery. When her arm dropped, it fell against the door as if it were boneless. It wasn't until I looked—I *truly* looked—that I saw…" Hedley swallowed and tears began to stream down her face. "Henrietta was on the outside, between the carriage and ground. Crushed. And her hands were slippery because she was covered in blood. I was covered in her blood too."

He was silent for a long while. At some point during this, he'd taken her hand in his again. He wasn't sure if it was to provide himself comfort or her. But he liked knowing she was here beside him, and he refused to look any deeper than that.

## CHAPTER NINE

**H**edley awoke the following morning feeling lightheaded and somewhat dizzy. It took a moment to orient herself before she padded across her bedchamber to the washstand in the corner. By rote, she lifted the chipped brown pitcher, poured cold water into the rutted basin, and began to wash her face.

That was when she noticed that her eyes were tender and slightly swollen. But that puffy flesh beneath her fingers made her smile at the memory of what caused it.

Yesterday, for the first time in her life, she'd told someone about the accident. And afterward, Rafe had turned to her, tucked her head beneath his chin, and simply held her as she'd cried.

Just thinking about it made the slushy *pwum-pum-pum* beat of her heart return.

They hadn't spoken much after that. But he'd walked her to Greyson Park and made sure she had enough firewood before he'd set off for Fallow Hall.

He'd told her that he was her friend. She hadn't had a friend since Henrietta, and so Hedley decided she liked having Rafe as hers. Very much, indeed.

Of course, he still wanted to take Greyson Park from her. Yet that didn't really bother her right now.

Gradually, the sense of dizziness faded as she donned her clothes for the day. She still hadn't worn the lovely blue dress that Rafe had purchased. In fact, she hadn't intended to wear any of the clothing in the parcel because her days centered on cleaning. The clothes were so beautiful that she didn't want to ruin them. She would never forgive herself for snagging that fine, colorful muslin.

Yet when it had come time to dress for the market yesterday, she'd given in and worn the new shawl. Today, she couldn't help but wonder what the pale pink chemise would feel like against her skin. The new stays didn't have a single bone exposed. And the petticoat was so white and lovely...

*No*, she thought. She would not wear a pristine petticoat when she had to sweep out the cellar today. For that matter, she wouldn't risk sullying the new chemise or stays either. "One day, when I've got nothing better to do than sit around all day, then Rafe's clothes will be the perfect things to wear."

That day was not today, however. She slipped into a threadbare cream-colored dress that had once had beautiful green piping around the neck, the cap sleeves, and the hem, along with a sash to match. And since the sash had long since shredded into bits, Hedley made her own sash out of strips of cloth she'd kept from other dresses that had degraded too much over the years. And as always, she slipped into her red shoes.

After spending hours in the cellar, Hedley was not only exhausted but thirsty. Unfortunately, her tea tin was empty. Not a single leaf remained. She'd found a few dried herbs, but that was all.

Undeterred, she filled the kettle. She'd simply drink a cup of hot rosemary water in the parlor. By the time she started a fresh fire in the kitchen stove, she heard a knock on the door. Not having heard a carriage and knowing that Ursa wouldn't bother to knock, Hedley eagerly answered it.

There to greet her was none other than Calliope Ludlow, Viscountess Everhart.

"Hullo," Calliope said, her face aglow with cheer beneath a straw bonnet. She lifted up a basket. "A few odds and ends to bid you good welcome."

Grinning, Hedley didn't know what to think, but she couldn't have been more pleased. Her first guest! "Please, come inside. Your visit is just the thing to brighten my day, but *oh*—I must look like a chimney sweep. I hope you can forgive my appearance." Feeling self-conscious, Hedley began to brush her hands over her dress to clear away the errant smudges and sticky cobwebs.

Calliope gently stayed her hand. "Nonsense. I came to see you, not your clothes. And I hope the items in this basket will offer the perfect distraction."

Grateful beyond words, Hedley took the basket and led her neighbor into the parlor.

After washing the walls, floors, and windows, the parlor had become her favorite room. She'd freshened up the moldering sofa with new straw stuffing and upholstered it with the curtains from the far bedroom upstairs—the one with the broken window. She'd found two similarly sized end tables and placed them on either side of the sofa, along with a pair of stiff-backed chairs, sitting at an angle for ease of conversation.

"It's lovely," Calliope said as she glanced around the room, never once mentioning the hole in the ceiling. "So cheerful. You can tell a great deal about a woman by the state of her parlor."

This intrigued Hedley. She suddenly wanted to know about the parlor in Fallow Hall and even the ones in London, especially since she would never go there to see any for herself.

"You can?" she asked, placing the basket on the low table in front of the sofa.

"Oh, yes. My mother's parlor, for example, is full of bright colors and plump pillows, rather like her disposition and her person." Calliope laughed and sat down on the sofa. As if perfectly at home, she untied her bonnet and lifted it away, setting it down beside her. "My sister-in-law—the one I mentioned to you yesterday—enjoys shopping a great deal. The parlor's appearance changes each time I visit."

"And yours?" Hedley sat across from her. She'd never felt so at ease as she did now. Certainly not in her mother's company or Ursa's. She'd always had to prepare herself for the next insult or threat to lock her out of sight.

Calliope pressed her index finger to the end table and grinned. "You will find a book, or two, on each table."

"And flowers."

"Most definitely flowers," Calliope said with a laugh. "Which is why I've asked Rafe to make me a set of small vases, so that I can put flowers all throughout the manor."

At this, Hedley quirked her head to the side. "Rafe makes vases?"

And in that same moment, it hit her. The glass front cabinet in the drawing room at Fallow Hall. *Of course!* All those lovely creations. They were Rafe's. She should have known the moment he'd told her about the artists in his family. Now, she was eager to see him again in order to ask about his craft.

Yet if she were honest with herself, the impulse to see him didn't begin with this discovery. She'd carried it with her all day long.

"Vases, bowls, decanters, stemware…" Calliope allowed her list to trail on as she sat forward and focused on the basket. After a moment, she reached inside and withdrew a small wooden chest with the word *Oolong* painted in gold. "What do you think of continuing our conversation over a cup of tea?"

"I already have the kettle on."

"Splendid!"

While the tea brewed, Calliope told her of spending time in the kitchen in their house in London and how her family's cook, Mrs. Shortingham, made *"the best gingerbread in the entire world."* Hedley didn't believe she'd ever eaten gingerbread, but it sounded quite delicious.

Gradually, the conversation drifted back to parlors, and Hedley learned about Calliope's other friends and even the Dowager Duchess of Heathcoat. It was amazing to Hedley, to sit and talk with someone related to a dowager duchess—and even a duke, for that matter. Yet during the entirety of their discourse, Calliope never once made her feel as if she were backward for the questions she asked.

After Calliope had fashioned a tray with cups, saucers, spoons, serviettes, and an assortment of empty dishes—whose purpose was still unknown to Hedley—they were seated, once again, in the parlor.

"Do you mind if I pour?" Calliope asked.

"Um…no. Please do." Not only had Hedley's education lacked in societal behavior—how not to curtsy to the head butler, for instance—but she knew little of etiquette. She'd never attended a family meal. So what knowledge she possessed was from the years she'd spent dining in the nursery with the governess, before the accident.

Mimicking Calliope's actions, she gently laid a serviette over her lap.

"How do you take it?"

Hedley looked down to the liquid splashing into the cup and then up to Calliope, wondering what she meant. "The tea?" In receiving a nod, she wasn't sure what to tell her. Were there different ways?

"When I was putting this little basket together, I wasn't sure how you preferred your tea. I enjoy mint in mine, but not everyone is the same. Then, of course, as I was pondering this over, Danvers suggested I nip some sugar from the loaf."

Sugar in tea? She'd never heard of such decadence. Yet now that she looked at the basket, she saw a small brown sack, no bigger than a fist, marked SUGAR.

"Danvers takes sugar in his tea. But I brought mint and a lemon, just in case."

"I'll try it with sugar, I suppose," she said, and summarily watched a pair of scalloped tongs sink into the sugar and then open over her cup.

While Hedley stirred her tea, Calliope removed a tin from the basket and opened the lid. Then, gingerly, she reached inside and pulled out a small round biscuit. *A tin of biscuits!* What a luxury! It had been ages since she'd eaten a biscuit. After the accident, she wasn't permitted. A physician had recommended a diet of bread and broth. Over the years, her invisible self had maneuvered through the kitchen and secreted away breads, cheeses, and fruits. Yet never biscuits.

At present, her life was so altered that she hardly knew what she'd liked best. Unfortunately, just as she was trying to decide, she heard a carriage in the drive. Instant dread knotted her stomach. Her hand started to shake before she'd even taken her first sip of tea with sugar.

"Hedley, what's wrong?"

"My sister is here," she said, her voice hollow as she placed her teacup and saucer on the table. Slowly, as if someone else had control of her body, she stood and stared at the open parlor door.

She'd been having such lovely afternoon with her new friend and soon, she feared, she wouldn't have any friend at all.

Without a knock of warning, the front door opened.

"My dear simpleton…are you going to hide from me again? I've brought our mother for a special treat," Ursa chirruped. "She's visiting my aunt as well."

"You needn't speak to the girl," Mother said, her tone clipped. "She cannot understand you."

*The girl.* Ah yes, such a warm term of endearment. She'd ceased being *Hedley* to her mother within a year of the accident.

"I'm here, in the parlor." Her voice cracked ever so slightly when she saw Calliope's look of utter horror. Hedley looked away quickly.

"The parlor." Ursa laughed, emerging into the doorway. "Did you hear that Mother? She's actually named the rooms in this ruin. Oh, and she has a guest. Dear me, have I interrupted a tea party? How quaint. Don't be a dolt, if you can help it, sister, and introduce us."

Calliope folded her napkin and stood, turning to face them in a way that blocked her expression from Hedley. But it was all for the best. After all, she didn't want to see her neighbor's desire to bolt from the house and never return. So for now, Hedley pretended that they could still be friends.

"Calliope, this is my mother, Lady Claudia Sinclair, and my sister, Mrs. Nathan Cole." Hedley focused on the two pairs of black irises looking at her with disdain. At least, with this, she already knew to what to expect. "Mother, Ursa, this is my neighbor, the Viscountess Everhart."

At the mention of the title, both Mother and Ursa arched their brows and focused their attention on Calliope. Together, they inclined their heads and sank into graceful curtsies. Calliope did the same. Only with her, the courtesy seemed more natural and less of a production.

"How good of you to visit the infirmed at Greyson Park out of charity," Mother said, her lips spreading in something of a smile. At least, Hedley hoped it was a smile. It almost looked like a snarl.

"I too enjoy a bit of charity work," Ursa offered, fiddling with the ruffled cuff of her sleeve. Then she primped her hair in the manner she always did when she wanted to be admired. "Though I've always found it difficult to visit the infirmed without feeling as if I've degraded myself in some manner. Of course, she *is* my sister. So what can you do? We all have that one barmy relative."

"Contrary to what you might have assumed," Calliope said, her voice sweet but with an edge, "I am here visiting my friend. There is no charity here, other than what one friend provides another."

Hedley felt tears prick the backs of her eyes. *What a lovely thing to say*, she thought, and then conveyed that sentiment in her smile when Calliope turned to her.

"Then it is a tea party after all." Ursa didn't bat an eye but smiled more broadly. "The long drive has left me rather parched. Perhaps I could join you for a spell. Though we don't have long to dally."

Warning shot through Hedley as her sister sauntered around the sofa and walked directly to the low table. "I'm afraid I have no additional cups, Ursa."

Her sister feigned a cough into her glove. "Surely, you wouldn't deprive me from having a sip from your cup?"

Hedley didn't know what her sister planned to do, but she knew it wasn't good. Ursa would never drink from her cup. And yet, she reached for it, all the same. But then, just as Ursa was about to take a drink, her fingers opened and the cup started to fall.

It hit the basket, falling directly onto the open tin of biscuits and liquid splashed out, saturating the sack of sugar. Calliope gasped. Hedley merely stared at the disaster.

"Dear me," Ursa said, not bothering to hide her smile. "I do believe your cup was greasy. Quite slippery. Such a pity, though without a maid, it is no wonder. I should think it impossible to keep a house without servants. Wouldn't you agree, Lady Everhart? In fact, Mother and I are here to fetch her."

*Fetch her?* Imprison her was more like it. "I'm not going anywhere."

"You cannot possibly manage on your own," Ursa stated, matter-of-factly, before turning toward Calliope. "Lady Everhart, perhaps you could persuade her to end this delusion of hers, and return to the bosom of her family where someone with her...illness belongs."

Hedley interrupted before Calliope was obliged to respond. "Ursa, I hope that is not a tea stain on your lace."

"Where? Oh!" Her sister quickly examined her wrists. In seeing a slight discoloration, her histrionics began. "It will be ruined! I must have it cleaned immediately."

"Unfortunately, I have no maid to help you." Hedley said with a tsk. "In fact, I have nothing here for you at all."

"Come now, Ursa. We'll return to your aunt's," Mother said, already turning her back and heading into the foyer. "After your trip to London, we'll find a place to put the girl."

Then, without another word, they left.

"Good-bye, Mother. Ursa," Hedley said as the door closed a moment later.

She was too ashamed to look over at Calliope. Instead, she busied herself with cleaning up the mess on the table and within the basket. The small amount of tea in her cup seemed to have soaked everything.

In silence, Calliope bent down and used her serviette to wipe off the biscuit tin. Thankfully, the tea chest was still in the kitchen.

The entire basket had been such a lovely gift—no, it still was a lovely gift. And Hedley would never forget how wonderful it had been to see Calliope standing on her doorstep, eager to have a cup of tea with her. Eager to be her friend. It was heart-wrenching that their afternoon and their friendship had ended this way. But Hedley didn't blame Calliope for what was bound to happen.

"I apologize for what you witnessed and what happened to the lovely gift you brought," Hedley said, holding back tears.

Calliope balled up her serviette and threw it down. "I am positively appalled. Forgive me, but I can no longer hold my tongue."

Hedley cringed inwardly. She knew what was coming. Drawing in a deep breath, she lifted her head and met Calliope's gaze.

Calliope's lips were drawn tight. "I have never in my life spoken against another person's family, but your sister is…*horrible!* And your mother, to behave so coldly toward her *own* child"—she settled a hand over her middle as if in a gesture of protection—"is beyond my understanding. Hedley, you've no need to apologize. *I* am the one who should apologize to you. There was so much I wanted to say while they were here, but I was so stunned by their actions that I couldn't speak."

"You were going to—" Now, Hedley was speechless. Calliope was going to stand up for her?

"Absolutely," Calliope said with a firm nod. Her brown eyes were fierce with anger. "And if they walked through that door right now, I wouldn't hesitate. Not now, when all the perfect things *I'd wanted* to say have finally formed into coherent thoughts."

A watery laugh escaped Hedley. "That happens to me too. I always think of the perfect thing to say the moment the door closes."

Calliope laughed as well. "Between the two of us, we could manage a quite thorough set-down...albeit marginally delayed."

The more Hedley thought about the absurdity of laughing at this moment—especially after all that had happened—the more she laughed. And even more absurdly, Calliope joined her until they both had tears leaking from the corners of the eyes.

Grinning, Calliope used the corner of the serviette to dry her eyes and then placed it, gently this time, into the basket. "Let's take this disaster with us to Fallow Hall and see what can be made of it."

It was a lovely idea, but then Hedley looked down at the state of her clothes. Not only was her dress smudged, but now it was splattered with tea. "I'm not fit to be seen at the moment."

"Nonsense. We have clothes aplenty in the manor. Crates and crates." Calliope waved in a gesture of dismissal before she picked up the basket. "This time, I won't take no for an answer."

Hedley smiled.

# CHAPTER TEN

"I just knew we would find several evening gowns for you," Calliope said from her bedchamber while Hedley dressed behind a screen. Calliope's maid, Meg, had offered to help, but Hedley wasn't entirely comfortable with the idea.

Meg had discovered several costumes among the attic trunks that Calliope thought would fit Hedley's figure. But since Hedley had had ill-fitting garments to wear all her life, she hadn't allowed her hopes free rein. And slipping her arms into the cap sleeves of a peach-colored silk gown with a sheer white overdress, her doubts resurfaced.

"We are fortunate that they were packed so well. Only a few garments were moth eaten. Most of the lot is still lovely. And look," Meg said, draping a pair of elbow-length gloves over the top of the screen. "They are still white, for the most part."

"I've spent some time pilfering the crates," Calliope remarked. "Much was left in the attic when the current owner of this house took possession of Fallow Hall after he'd won it in a card game."

Pulling on the silk gloves, Hedley stalled halfway up her arm. "The gentlemen gambled for a house?"

"Men will wager on absolutely anything. In fact, the gentlemen here have—" Calliope didn't finish. Instead, she gasped when Hedley stepped out from behind the screen. Standing across the room, she'd been examining another gown, but it fell from her fingertips to the arm of a chair. "Oh, Hedley! You look divine. I had no idea you possessed such a tiny waist."

Meg ushered her to a full-length mirror, and Hedley stared blankly at her own reflection. It was her face, but the rest of the image looked nothing like her. Or perhaps *too* like her—when she wasn't wearing clothes at all. "I look naked."

"Isn't that a fine trick," Calliope cheered. "However did you fit all that bosom in the dress you wore today?"

And *all* of her bosom was well defined beneath the silk, square-cut bodice. "The dresses I have once belonged to Ursa. As you saw today, we do not have the same figure."

In the mirror, Calliope pursed her lips and sniffed. "Yes. She is very much like your mother. You must take after the women on your father's side."

"That's what I've heard." Hedley didn't elaborate or mention the rumors she'd heard throughout her life. Her new friend had already been subjected to enough of her family dealings for one day. "Are you certain the woman who left these clothes here won't be angry if I borrow this one for the night?"

"I am certain, though I hesitate to tell you the reason." Calliope leaned in to whisper. "It's quite scandalous."

"Tell me," Hedley whispered back, unable to suppress an errant thrill that shot through her. She hardly knew herself.

"According to my friend, Lady Knightswold, whose husband owns this house now, the previous owner was a notable member of Parliament. Rumor has it that his wife eloped with a French count and left all of her belongings here. The house was left empty for years before it was recklessly gambled away."

"So…I am wearing the clothes of a woman who had a scandalous love affair with a French count?"

Calliope nodded slowly. "I would completely understand if you would rather not…"

"No, I rather like the idea. Somehow, knowing the sordid history makes my skin tingle." Hedley laughed and Calliope joined her. Even Meg snickered.

"Oh, good, because it looks perfect on your figure." Calliope lifted a selection of combs, comparing each. "I must warn you, Hedley, this experience may change your life forever. Once a young woman finds a perfect dress…she always wants another."

Hedley could well imagine that being the truth. "Do you think I should try the blue one?"

"Well, it would certainly save me from having to coerce you."

Meg laughed. "If you were to debut wearing that gown, miss, you would be married by morning." Then, she addressed Calliope. "I'm sure many of the upstairs maids will wonder what Lord Lucan and Mr. Danvers will say."

"Hmm…" Calliope mused. "I find that gentlemen reveal more by what they do *not* say. Their actions usually speak for them."

Nervous at the turn of the conversation, Hedley raked her teeth over her top lip. "To say what, exactly?"

"Whether or not they are interested in pursuing you."

"Pursue...*me*?" The way that gentlemen callers had pursued Ursa? Surely not. It was one thing *not* to be invisible and quite another to be...pursuable. Hedley knew very well that she was not. "Oh, but I have no interest in marrying."

It was better to say it directly before anyone had aspirations.

"My darling friend," Calliope smiled broadly at Hedley's reflection. "Never say those words to a newlywed. It reeks of challenge."

Boris lifted his head from Rafe's knee and looked toward the open archway of the study.

By the sound of the familiar, methodical footsteps, Montwood had returned to Fallow Hall.

*At last*, Rafe thought, feeling a semblance of relief. After spending the day in his workshop, he'd been waiting for this opportunity. He needed to set his plan in motion before...Before he found himself distracted by Hedley Sinclair again.

Yesterday had altered him. He couldn't stop thinking about her account of the carriage accident. He could only imagine what it must have been like for a young girl to bear witness to such a tragic death. If Hedley's reactions to seeing a horse and carriage were so strong, even now, he could only imagine what they'd been like when she was a child.

And the Sinclairs had locked her away because of it. He didn't think it was possible to hate that family more, but he did. Strangely, he didn't see Hedley as an extension of her family.

Not any longer. In fact, he almost feared that he wouldn't be able to go through with his plan to take Greyson Park from her. Almost. Regaining control of Greyson Park was the only way to restore his family's legacy.

Even so, his plan had altered somewhat. Now, he was determined to make sure Montwood fell in love with Hedley and treated her in the manner she deserved.

Just then, the man in question strode in from the stables, handing off his hat and gloves to Valentine, who trailed him into the study. "Have any letters arrived for me?"

"None, my lord," Valentine said. "However, a messenger boy came by four days ago to inquire if you were in residence. I informed him that you were not."

Peculiarly, Montwood did not inquire further. Like any cardsharp worth his salt, his expression remained unchanged. "Very good, Valentine."

Summarily dismissed, the butler retreated. Montwood walked directly to the sideboard, poured a whiskey, drank it, and then poured another.

Sitting in the shadows of the study, Rafe cleared his throat to make his presence known.

"I know you are there, Danvers." Montwood tipped back the second glass and poured a third. "I've spent too much of my life in the dark not to be aware of those who linger in the shadows."

For a man who rarely spoke about his past, this uncharacteristic revelation surprised Rafe. But he knew better than to comment on it. "Did London treat you well?"

"I'm down 1,971 pounds and two shillings. I barely escaped having to put a bullet through a young buck's head because he'd foolishly challenged me to duel. And the stable master at Stampton's Inn refused to change my horse."

"Perhaps you shouldn't have slept with the man's wife." It was a guess, but Rafe knew it was either a case of a cuckolded man or one who'd lost a fortune gambling against him.

Montwood scoffed. "His *sister,* and she wasn't an innocent. Far from it. In fact, she might have even taught *me* things."

"Ah, yes, but you have that charming way about you that makes women fall in love with you." Rafe was counting on it.

Montwood turned and lifted his black eyebrows. His peculiar amber-colored eyes glinted with mischief. "And why, pray tell, are my romantic escapades suddenly under your quizzing glass?"

"Absent observation." Rafe shrugged.

Montwood's keen gaze sharpened. "I did hear mention of another matter while I was in town. There was a rumor flitting about, regarding the return of the infamous Ursa Sinclair—though she is Mrs. Nathan Cole now, isn't she?"

"I have heard the same rumor." Rafe admitted. He knew that the surest way to disguise a deception was to pepper in plenty of truth. "Apparently, she believes that a *treasure* was left behind at Greyson Park and desires to add it to her husband's fortune."

"Greedy lot, aren't they?" Montwood asked. "Say, does our dinner guest share the family trait?"

"Dinner guest?" Reflexively, Rafe's hand tightened around the glass. It suddenly felt hot, as if he'd just removed it from the furnace. *Hedley is here?* He should have realized that her presence was the reason for the restless feeling that had settled over him the moment he'd arrived.

"The kitchen maids were talking about our mysterious guest to a few of the groomsmen when I arrived," Montwood said offhandedly. "You can learn a plethora of information from overhearing a servant's conversation."

"And what else have you learned?" As if he didn't already suspect.

Montwood grinned, flashing a dimple. "That our dog spent a week with her. That she met with you in the drawing room. That she and Calliope have become fast friends. And, most important, that she inherited Greyson Park."

"*Amazing* what one gleans while eavesdropping." Rafe sneered as his friend chuckled. "And she quite adamantly refuses to sell."

"Can you blame her? From what I've heard, she was kept locked in the attic. I can tell you from experience that being locked in a room is not pleasant." Quite out of character, Montwood had revealed another peek into his past, though he did not elaborate. There was a dark edge that sometimes seeped through the cracks of the charming façade he'd adopted.

"You've *heard* a great deal about our neighbor." And most of it must have come from inquiries in London, because as far as Rafe knew, no one here, other than he, knew about her past. He realized that Montwood had likely wanted to test Rafe for how much *he* knew...and Rafe had fallen for the trap. Undeterred, he continued with his plan. "Do I detect a note of interest on your part?"

"I make it a point to learn all I can about my dining companions. One can never be too careful. Poison is a nasty way to go, after all." He swirled the liquid in his glass with an absent air. "Besides, I would have to be tempted beyond reason to woo an innocent. And I am never without reason."

Rafe knew better than to poke someone else's demon. So he eased off a bit. "I think she would make a good companion for Calliope. Hedley could live with them at Briar Heath when the repairs are finished."

Montwood's glass paused on the way to this mouth. "Such familiarity, *and* you are already planning her future."

"I simply abhor her surname," Rafe said, exhausted by the need to explain this. She wasn't one of the *Sinclairs*. They didn't deserve her. "As for her future, I care not, as long as she is absent from Greyson Park."

Montwood placed a hand to his chest. "You have heartily convinced me, good sir. Now I have no fear that you were attempting to put her in my path so that I would lose the wager."

*Damn.* His friend was too cunning by half. However, Rafe refused to give in. "We have already won—each of us earning five thousand pounds from Everhart's early ejection from our game."

"Ah, but five thousand pounds is not ten thousand pounds, is it? And I plan on winning it all, Danvers. I wouldn't have made the wager otherwise."

Rafe took the challenge and lifted his glass in a salute. "Then you shouldn't have wagered against me."

# CHAPTER ELEVEN

In the end, Hedley decided to wear the blue dress. She preferred not to be quite *so* visible for her very first dinner. The blue was a lovely satin accented with darker ribbons crisscrossed over the bodice, and a long skirt embroidered in silver thread. The best part was that it shimmered in the torchlight when she walked.

Instead of the tips of her red shoes peeking out from beneath her hem, white-beaded slippers caught her gaze, though they pinched ever so slightly. It served as a reminder that no matter how lovely her evening promised to be, she didn't really belong. The thought only amplified her nervousness and sent a fresh wave of icy dampness to her palms.

While she was glad to be here, this would be her first formal dinner. Before the accident, she'd dined in the nursery. She remembered how her nurse had constantly remarked on the number of rules to follow for a proper young lady. Yet Hedley had never finished those lessons. She only hoped that she wouldn't make a fool of herself.

"We should have a party here at Fallow Hall and invite all the neighbors. Since you never had a Season, we shall give you a party." Calliope linked arms with her as they walked down the long staircase.

Before Hedley could answer, a familiar gray beast bounded up the stairs, tongue lolling off to the side and tail wagging so wildly that he lost his balance and missed a step.

Hedley laughed, automatically reaching out to pet him but then hesitated when she saw her pristine white gloves. "Boris, I would pet you, but I am wearing borrowed gloves."

"*Woof!*"

"Not borrowed at all," Calliope said and reached out with her own elegantly adorned hand to scratch Boris behind the ears. "They are your gloves. In fact, all the clothes are yours."

"Oh, but I couldn't—"

"You'd prefer to pack them away in order to feed the moths and mice. Ah, you have a generous spirit, Miss Sinclair." Calliope laughed. "However, I would much rather give these clothes, and the others, a breath of life before they are moth-eaten and threadbare."

Hedley felt the flesh of her cheeks tighten from smiling so broadly. "Are you insisting?"

"I am."

"Very well, then." She was quite certain that her expression revealed that doing so was no hardship at all. Then, reaching out, she gave Boris a solid pat. "He's a good sort, isn't he?"

"Yes," Calliope answered. "Even if he cannot decide which name suits him."

Having his fill of affection, Boris turned around and bounded back down the stairs, tearing off through the hall. Hedley wondered why he seemed in such a hurry. "He has more than one?" Though, remembering back to her first encounter with Rafe at Greyson Park, she thought he had mentioned something similar.

Nearing the bottom of the stairs, Calliope nodded. "You have met the esteemed Boris Reginald James Brutus, also known as Duke. Danvers likes to call him Boris. Everhart and I call him Duke. Yet the truth is, our friend here has several names and does not come to any of them. Of course, you may choose whichever name suits you—although he seems to prefer that *you* call him Boris." Calliope's brows lifted in something of a secret smile but for reasons unknown to Hedley. "My aunt had called him a brute during her visit here and, I have recently learned, for good reason. Both her prized Pekingese are expecting a litter any day now. He was a very naughty matchmaker."

Naughty, indeed. "Matchmaker?"

"It's a bit of foolishness on my part," Calliope said with an absent wave of her hand. "But every time I turned around, he was always leading me to Everhart. That dog is *Cupid* on four legs. So if you truly do not want to marry, then be on your guard around that loveable beast."

Hedley laughed at the silliness. "I have been warned."

In the foyer, Valentine offered an elegant bow. "Good evening, my lady. Miss Sinclair."

"And to you, Valentine," Hedley said with a smile. His mouth twitched in something of a grin as they passed.

Together, Calliope and Hedley walked down a series of halls, admiring paintings and tapestries. Fallow Hall was a mixture of masculine and feminine, with little touches of freshly cut flowers here and there to soften the battle scenes on display.

"In typical English houses, we would all gather in the parlor or drawing room before dinner. Since this is Fallow Hall, however, we've taken to starting our evenings in the map room," Calliope offered, a rosy blush tinting her cheeks.

Hedley looked for the source of her friend's apparent warmth. When they reached a pair of French doors that led into a vast open chamber with Everhart waiting at the door, she understood Calliope's blush immediately. Heat and something akin to hunger fairly radiated from Everhart as he looked at his bride. Hedley looked away.

Within the room, a staircase curved to a loft above. The walls were covered with maps, and a cheery fire crackled in the hearth. By the time Hedley's gaze alighted on the other occupants of the room, she saw two of them seemingly arrested, glasses paused midway to their mouths. Boris stood between them, wagging his tail.

"Gentlemen, it is my pleasure to present to you the radiant Miss Hedley Sinclair." Calliope ushered her into the room. "Hedley, you know Everhart and Danvers, of course, but the other dashing gentleman before you is Lord Lucan Montwood."

The gentleman in question stepped forward and bowed. "Lucan Montwood, at your service, Miss Sinclair."

Uncertain of whether or not to curtsy, Hedley slid one foot behind the other and bent her knees. "My lord, a pleasure. And please call me Hedley."

As she rose, she looked to Rafe to see if he would mock her for doing the wrong thing. But he was still standing there with his glass suspended in his grasp.

"And you may call me whatever you like," Montwood replied with a grin as he looked from her to Rafe. Montwood chucked Rafe on the shoulder. "Danvers, where are your manners?"

Rafe blinked. Then he cleared his throat and lowered his glass. "Yes, of course. Might I introduce my friend Lord Lucan Montwood."

Calliope laughed and Everhart chuckled. Hedley saw a gleam brighten Montwood's gaze as he inclined his head once more. "At your service...*again*, Hedley."

Hedley recalled what her friend had told her earlier about gentlemen revealing more in their actions and in what they do *not* say. If that was true, then she'd managed to stun Rafe. His easy, devilish grin was absent. In fact, he was looking at her as if they were strangers.

Standing before him in all this finery, Hedley had stripped away the easy comfort between them. While the rest of the party might find it amusing, to her it was quite depressing.

Without saying a word to Rafe, she gave her attention to Montwood, who was now walking toward her.

He proffered his arm. "Might I be your escort this evening?"

"I would be delighted." And she hoped her smile was convincing.

Dinner was a grand affair. Hedley had never sat at such a fine table. At Sinclair House, she was usually given a tray of broth and a hunk of bread to eat by herself in the attic. Here, it was all elegance, with silverware that reflected the flame of each candle like mirrors, and crystal goblets that glistened, turning the lamplight into slashes of rainbows on the white tablecloth. Though the food was not better than the broth, or even the porridge, at Sinclair House, the setting and company made all the difference.

Surreptitiously, she kept her eye on Calliope, who sat at the end of the table, and mimicked everything she did. Everhart sat opposite his wife. Montwood sat at the corner, between Hedley and Calliope, and across the table, Rafe.

For reasons beyond her understanding, he'd turned surly. Each point of the conversation directed at his side of the table ended as quickly as it began. But she learned much from Everhart and Montwood, who effortlessly wove together new threads to the old in order to keep their dinner pleasant. All but one in the party made her feel as if she belonged here.

As dinner progressed, she began to wonder if Rafe regretted their familiarity. He would hardly look at her. Although when he did, his gaze turned fierce in a way that she hadn't witnessed before. He didn't eat much. More than anything, he pushed the food around on his plate. Not even the pudding pleased his palate. And when he looked across the table, his expression was accusatory, as if it were her fault.

His heated indictment, however, had the opposite effect he'd likely hoped for, she was sure. Because instead of losing her appetite, hers increased. She was ravenous. But the food did not satiate her. Instead, it left her feeling decidedly frustrated.

Not soon enough, the end of dinner came.

"Would you mind forgoing the usual custom of leaving the gentlemen alone with their port and cheroots, and instead gather in the music room?" Calliope asked as they stood beside the table.

"I would love to." Not only did Hedley want to put some distance between her and Rafe, but she was thrilled by the prospect of hearing music.

For years, Ursa had taken lessons from a piano master. Hedley, on the other hand, had become familiar with the perfect hiding places closest to the music room at Sinclair House. While Ursa's discordant playing had not been pleasant, the master had made such wondrous sounds that every note had seemed alive to Hedley. She'd always found herself humming the same tune for days.

Rafe cleared his throat and withdrew a slender silver case from his breast pocket. "I will join the party shortly. Montwood, I trust that you will see to our guest's enjoyment." His words came out short, clipped, as if under duress, leaving her to wonder why he didn't ask Calliope instead. After all, she seemed the more natural choice.

Montwood bowed. "It would be my pleasure."

Devoid of answer or explanation to Rafe's peculiar change in temperament, Hedley adjourned with the others.

Moments later, she found herself sitting next to Montwood at the piano, pleasantly distracted. The keys were so white and shiny below their black counterparts. She fought a terrible urge to remove her gloves and run her fingers over them. Instead, she contented herself with watching the effortless motions of Montwood's fingers.

It didn't even appear that he was touching the keys but, more so, gliding over them. Whenever he added a little trill that didn't seem like it belonged, she would look up at his face, and he would grin at her, flashing a dimple in his cheek.

She felt comfortable here, beside him. As comfortable as she was with Calliope. Hedley knew right away that Montwood was a kindred spirit. He didn't make her nervous or cause her heart to turn slushy. Instead, he possessed a pleasant, easy charm that she admired. Yet sometimes she noticed that a dark, haunted look would cross his gaze in an all-too-familiar way.

She'd seen a similar look in her own reflection.

"Have you played for many years?" she asked. He was just as good as the piano master had been, if not better.

"A few." For an instant, Montwood appeared as if that was all he would say on the matter. Then, he surprised Hedley by looking at her as if he too felt a connection. "One learns to do what one can in order to find acceptance. I play for my supper and for my friends."

"Then you are without a family as well?"

"Much in the same manner that you are." The music altered for a few beats, his focus on the lower notes even as he held her gaze. "Noble family lines tend to keep their secrets locked away."

A shiver of dread and commiseration slid down her spine and limbs. She had the urge to apologize for whatever trials he'd born but thought better of it. Such a conversation was better suited for another time. "Do you ever play for yourself?"

"Occasionally," he said, his amber eyes drifting down to the keys as the music brightened once again. "Though I have learned that most people prefer jovial tunes."

She understood. If she were able to play music, she wondered if the notes would be light and gay or dark and somber.

Yet, as she thought about it, she would prefer to leave the dark and somber parts of her life locked away. Even though Rafe likely didn't realize or...care, he'd helped her a great deal yesterday by simply listening to her and then holding her as she cried.

Perhaps she shouldn't think about that either. "You are very good with your hands."

"That's what all the ladies say." That dimple flashed once more.

Hedley blushed even before she understood his response.

Watching Hedley cozy up with Montwood on the piano bench, Rafe was suddenly reminded that nearly every man of Montwood's acquaintance wanted to kill him.

Although *why* the compulsion to wrap his hands around his friend's throat tore through him, he didn't know. Because he wasn't jealous. After all, his entire plan to secure Greyson Park and win the wager depended on Montwood's marrying Hedley. He *should* be cheering instead of clenching his fists.

Crossing the room, Rafe passed Everhart and Calliope as they danced the steps of a waltz in the snug space between the sofa and the back of the room. The lively music was for a cotillion, but they were so engrossed in each other, he doubted they realized.

Hedley glanced down at Montwood's hands and said something that Rafe could not hear. Then, shortly after Montwood's reply, carnation pink color flushed her cheeks.

Rafe's fists tightened until his fingertips ached from the pressure.

As if absently realizing there were other people in the room, both Montwood and Hedley looked in his direction.

"By your expression, that cheroot must have had a bitter taste, Danvers," Montwood said, striking an ominous chord on the piano that made Hedley smile as if she were privy to a joke.

Rafe fought the urge to glare at his amber-eyed friend. However, if the challenging grin he received in response was any indication, then he may not have succeeded. "You are mistaken. The cheroot was quite sweet." *Though not as sweet as a certain young woman's lips...*

Shifting his attention to Hedley, he saw her gaze dip to his mouth.

"I think I should like to try one," she said.

Montwood missed a note but recovered. Rafe missed a breath *and* a heartbeat. And he wasn't sure he *could* recover. Not at the thought of Hedley wrapping those berry-stained lips around the tip of a...cheroot.

Hedley's eyes widened. "*Oh dear.* Is it not an occupation for a lady?"

"It depends on the lady," Rafe said unable to shake free of the images sprouting in his mind. "Though many in society would frown upon it."

"Oh." She looked so disappointed that he was tempted to offer her one anyway. And teach her exactly how to hold it, light it, draw on it...

But then Montwood interrupted a perfectly good fantasy. "Why don't the two of you dance?"

"I'd much rather hear you play," Hedley said quickly.

Though thankful for the rescue, Rafe pressed his hand over his heart. "You wound me."

Montwood laughed. "Yes, my dear, you must allow Danvers to step on your feet *before* you refuse him."

She pursed her lips as if in thought. "I suppose I should have confessed that I do not know *how* to dance, rather than wound your ego."

"There is no shame in that. You are among friends," Montwood added, pouring on the charm. "And if the notion of dancing with Danvers lacks appeal, then I'd be more than happy to be your first partner."

Rafe growled at the thinly veiled innuendo.

Montwood would *never* dance with Hedley. Prepared to tell him just that, Rafe opened his mouth. But then he closed it again. This was what he *wanted*. Why did he need to keep reminding himself?

"I'd prefer not to dance at all, if you don't mind. I'm not graceful like Calliope." Hedley gazed at the couple with something akin to longing in her expression. "They move as one."

Relief washed over Rafe. While he knew he needed to encourage a romance between Montwood and Hedley, the idea of watching Montwood become the first to dance with her turned Rafe's stomach to stone—much like the undercooked potatoes in this evening's meal.

Just as he was about to lift his hand to discreetly press it against his gut, Boris appeared beside him and angled his head underneath that hand, begging for a scratch. Rafe complied, appreciating the distraction. But only for a moment, because then Boris ambled over to the piano bench and wedged his nose between Montwood and Hedley. If Rafe didn't know any better, he would swear that the dog was looking at him with expectation.

Hedley scratched Boris's head absently as she continued to study Montwood's fingers over the keys. Behind him, Everhart and Calliope had likely forgotten anyone else was in the room as their dance went on and on. And Rafe felt like an outcast.

He didn't like it.

Rafe turned to the window. As if Mother Nature mirrored the sentiment, a flash of lightning lit up the gray dusk. In the reflection of the glass, he saw Hedley stand, her expression wide with worry.

"It's later than I thought," she said. "I'd better return to Greyson Park before the storm arrives. Thank you all for your wonderful hospitality."

Montwood ceased playing instantly. "Nonsense. You must stay."

Calliope moved apart from Everhart. "We cannot let you risk your health in this weather. Surely the storm will be upon you too soon. Please stay. I've so enjoyed our time together and don't want it to end."

"*Woof*," Boris offered, earning another scratch behind the ears.

Hedley turned to Rafe, but he didn't say anything at all. If she decided to leave, he would insist on walking with her and seeing her safely inside. The temptation to linger, light a fire, and wait out the storm would likely develop into something far more scandalous.

Yet if she stayed, then she would be sleeping in a room beneath the same roof as he. The temptation to pad down the hall and rap on her door, solely to see to her comfort, would likely lead him down the same path of ruin.

There was no way he could win.

## Chapter Twelve

Hedley had never slept better in her life. For the first time in years, she had a feather pillow and mattress—both as soft as clouds—instead of rough, lumpy straw that made crunching sounds each time she shifted.

Heavy blue satin bedclothes trimmed in white fur had kept her warm all through the night. This morning before dawn, a maid had even entered her room to light a fire in the hearth and sweep out the old ash. Hedley had thanked her, which ended up startling the maid because, apparently, people usually slept while she went about her work.

Hedley felt safe here at Fallow Hall and comforted by the lack of groaning and creaking coming from the walls surrounding her. Sometimes, she feared that Greyson Park would collapse on her.

Calliope's chambermaid had found more clothes in the attic. Apparently, another crate hosted scores of day dresses, underclothes, shoes, and hatboxes. One of the dresses was a walking dress. Although more than a decade out of fashion, as Meg had told her, Hedley couldn't wait to see what it looked like.

Throwing back the covers, she raced across the room and washed. Donning this design of dress took her quite a bit longer than she imagined. In the end, however, she enjoyed the fit.

The bright plum-colored muslin hugged her torso in a way that might have been scandalous if not for the short velvet-trimmed jacket that hosted two rows of buttons. At her waist, the dress fell in thick pleats down to the floor. There was even a pair of half boots. Of course, these too pinched a bit, reminding her that these clothes weren't truly hers. But when she saw her reflection in the mirror, she didn't mind at all.

This was all such a wonderful dream that she never wanted to wake from it.

Outside her bedroom door, she was surprised to find Boris, sprawled out and looking like a spilled vat of lumpy gray gravy. Lifting his head, he yawned before assembling himself into a standing position.

"Were you my guardian last night?" She reached out to run a hand from the top of his head down the length of his spine, earning a tail wag. "I don't suppose anyone else is awake this morning."

Boris's tail wagged faster. He looked at her with his head tilted to one side. Then, as if he'd understood, he headed down the hall for a time before he looked back over his shoulder.

"Do you want me to follow you?"

She received a low *woof* in reply. So, with nothing better to do, she followed.

After a series of long halls adorned by polished tables topped with fresh flowers, beautiful landscape paintings on the walls, and even a statue or two, Boris suddenly stopped in front of a door.

Hedley knew enough from her tour of Fallow Hall to realize that this was a bedchamber door. "No, Boris, you shouldn't have brought me here," she scolded in a whisper.

But before she could lure him away, the dog lifted a massive paw and scratched the door.

Hedley reached down and took his paw in her hand. "I didn't expect you to wake someone."

Was she actually having a conversation with a dog? Perhaps she was mad after all. Yet just as she turned to slip away unnoticed, the door opened.

"Boris, is that—" Rafe Danvers appeared in the doorway, wearing nothing more than a pair of perfectly snug buff breeches. *Perfectly*...she swallowed...*snug*.

For an instant, they both simply stared at each other— lips parted, breathing halted, squishy *pwum-pum-pum* heartbeat. At least, on her part. She didn't know about Rafe, but he didn't appear to be breathing either.

Even though she knew it was rude to stand there, she couldn't move. Well, that wasn't entirely true. Her eyes moved. Several times, in fact. At first, it was nothing more than a glance. And then a more *lingering* perusal.

Rafe Danvers was magnificent.

"You have hair on your chest," she said, the words tumbling out unheeded. Short, dark curled hairs dusted the defined muscles of his chest and down the ridges of his abdomen, disappearing beneath the waist of his breeches. She wondered if the hair continued. Then, as her gaze slid down to the heavy fall of his breeches and past those thickly muscled thighs, she saw that the bottom half of his legs and even the tops of his feet were dusted with dark hair too.

Why the sight of it caused her stomach to dip and her body to heat, she wasn't certain. But she didn't mind at all.

Lifting her gaze, she took in the sight of his arms, the breadth of his shoulders, the tight cording of his neck, and prominence of his Adam's apple. Hedley knew, from this point forward, she would never be able to look at Rafe without imagining him just...like...this.

She let out a slow, appreciative breath. Her palms grew damp and suddenly, she wanted to unbutton her jacket in order to breathe easier.

The cording of Rafe's neck tightened as his Adam's apple shifted. "Have you come to my door to barter yourself for Greyson Park?"

The gruff sound of his voice cut through the thick fog in her mind. Yet his words didn't make sense.

"I already hold Greyson Park. It would make more sense for you to barter yourself." Suddenly, she realized what she'd said. With a start, her gaze flew to his. She covered her mouth with her hand. "I did not mean to suggest that...I don't even know why I'm here...Forgive me."

And then, Hedley was even more thankful for the extra fabric of the walking dress, because she picked up her skirts, turned, and ran.

A quarter hour later, Rafe found Hedley in the music room. Sitting at the piano bench, she stared blankly down at the keys. The image of her admiring every inch of his form was burned into his mind. He wondered if the image of his body was burned into hers.

He doubted he would ever forget the heat and hunger he'd witnessed in her eyes. They'd turned dark, like indigo cloth. In that moment, he would have willingly—foolishly—taken *her* over the promise of Greyson Park. Then he would have regretted it for the rest of his days.

Thankfully, she'd run away and saved them both.

"I am appalled by what I said to you," she whispered, apparently having noticed him after all.

He stepped into the room. "But not appalled by how you stood there, imagining me undressed?"

Her head snapped up as she glared at him. "You were already undressed."

"You didn't seem to mind."

Carnation pink flooded her cheeks and she pursed those lips. "I am unwilling to bargain for Greyson Park, no matter the currency."

"Pity." He grinned and let his gaze wander over her form—what little he could see of it from her position behind the piano.

She straightened and pressed a hand over the buttons of her jacket, as if to protect them from his perusal. "Do you expect recompense?"

"No," he said, though pure carnal desire made him amend his answer. "Not at the moment, at least."

Her eyes grew wider as he stepped closer. "I was not offering."

He sat beside her and put the topic aside for now. In order to keep his hands occupied, he played a simple tune that he'd first learned as a child. Or at least, it had been simple when he was a child. Now, his fingers trolled awkwardly over the keys, and he wished he hadn't played at all.

"As you can see, I do not have Montwood's innate ability to string notes together into a harmonious melody."

"He is rather skilled," she remarked.

Her blunt statement kindled a spark of jealousy within him. It was ludicrous to keep feeling this way when having her admire Montwood suited his own primary goal. "Perhaps you would care to try."

Her fingers floated reverently over the surface of the keys. "I wouldn't want to spoil it." She whispered the words so softly that he almost didn't hear them.

"Montwood bangs away on these keys day and night. I hardly think—" The rest of what he was going to say died abruptly when he saw her stark expression. She actually believed what she'd said. "You're serious? No. That is utter nonsense."

He shook his head and took hold of her hands. For an instant, he forgot his purpose. The feel of her bare flesh against his distracted him. Her skin was soft and cool but marked with tiny abrasions. He rubbed his thumb over the nearly healed scratch on her middle finger. Then tenderly, over another that marked her knuckles. Her palms began to heat as his fingertips caressed the barest of calluses. Placing her hands beneath his, he pressed down on the keys and made a harsh, discordant noise.

Hedley cringed.

"There. Nothing spoiled," he said, lifting away his hands.

Looking down, she touched the keys, but barely. Her slender fingers mostly hovered over the ivory. Her breasts rose and fell in quick shallow breaths, as if she felt like a thief, afraid of being caught. "You don't think he would mind?"

"Not at all." Rafe was arrested by the sight of her. Had he once regarded her face as odd? Impossible. Especially now, with her eyes so bright and eager that it made him ache. The air around her hummed, and those copper strands in her hair seemed to possess their own light. Her world was fresh and new, every moment a first step. A first glance. A first touch. A first *kiss*…

A heady, drunken feeling arose inside him, making him dizzy and begging to be part of each one of her firsts.

"All right then." She spread her fingers, each touching a different key. Starting with the little finger on her left hand, she pressed down, one note at a time. When she ended with the little finger on her right hand, she drew in a quick breath and faced him.

"That was…" Her smile seemed to make her words evaporate.

"Lovely," he supplied. "Now, try it again."

She did. And then she repeated the motion in the opposite direction. "Oh, listen. These were the notes his melody started with. Do you remember?" She played three notes, two from her left hand and one from her right.

Distracted, Rafe found himself nodding. *Were those the same notes?* "Surely you couldn't have remembered the first three notes after hearing the melody played only once."

"It went like this." She pressed her lips together and hummed a perfect representation of the cotillion that Montwood had played the night before.

The flesh of his brow furrowed. "How are you doing that?"

"I've always been fond of music." She smiled and found a fourth and fifth note among the keys. "I used to hide behind the tapestry that concealed the servants' hallway and listen to Ursa's piano tutor for hours."

*Ursa's piano tutor but not hers,* he thought. A familiar rush of anger aimed at Hedley's family filled him. She'd been kept a secret from the outside world and all because of a tragedy that had caused her to fear carriages. He could only imagine how accomplished she could have become with the right instruction. And yet…

If she'd had a different life, then he wouldn't have had the pleasure of seeing her in this beautiful, unguarded moment. His utter enjoyment of watching her clashed with his complete loathing for her family. The feelings within him were as harsh and discordant as that first press of the keys had been.

He felt a keen separation in his thoughts. There was Hedley. And then there was her family.

He didn't see her as the enemy, but she was still an obstacle in his path to getting what he wanted. He couldn't risk losing Greyson Park when he was so close to achieving his goal. "Montwood would be an excellent piano tutor for you." He bit back the bile that collected at the back of his throat.

"I wouldn't want to impose. People have taken too much from him already." She shook her head. Humming softly, she somehow managed to find the next note and then beamed. "I never knew it would be this easy."

"It isn't." He laughed, trying to ignore the fresh wave of jealousy that rushed through him when she'd come to Montwood's defense. Surely they couldn't have formed an attachment already. "Otherwise, I would be able to play. Instead, all I do is whistle."

Her attention on the piano ceased and she angled toward him, her knee brushing his. But she didn't seem to notice—or mind—because she didn't pull away. "I've heard you, and I've heard the servants whistle before, but I could never understand how it was done. Show me."

"Demanding bit of baggage," he teased, shaking his head. "It isn't something you learn from watching. It is something you learn from practicing."

She huffed. "I *have* practiced, but only air comes out, and I sound like a leaky window in a storm."

Because he saw how earnest she was, he tried not to laugh. He wasn't entirely successful. Holding up a finger, he said, "Now imagine this holds a candle flame you wish to blow out."

He realized in the next moment that this was a terrible idea.

She puckered those lips and blew on the tip of his finger. A swift jolt of arousal tore through him.

"Like that?"

*Yes. I like that very, very much.* He cleared his throat and shifted on the bench. His hand grazed one of the folds of her skirt, directly above her knee. He tried not to linger, but the contact made him abruptly aware of the soft muslin of her dress. He'd noticed earlier how it matched the color of her lips. Those temptingly sweet lips…

Hedley looked down at his hand and then met his gaze. "As you know, I've had no experience with societal rules. Right now, you have that same look about you that you had last night when I expressed a desire to try a cheroot. It makes me wonder if I'm doing something improper."

"You shouldn't sit so close to me," he warned, though still unable to draw his hand away.

She searched his gaze. "I sat this closely to Montwood last night, yet he did not rest his hand on my knee or look at me the way you are looking at me now."

Her unguarded honesty was going to kill him. It was only fair that he give her some of his own. "Because I'm a scoundrel, Hedley. I cannot be trusted to do the correct thing. Not where you're concerned."

"You are leaving proper conduct up to me?" She frowned. "Essentially, you're saying that I—or any young woman in society—is expected to draw back, even when everything inside of her is telling her not to. I don't understand. Why am I meant to ignore the fact that I like the feel of your hand on my knee?"

He cleared his throat and withdrew his errant hand. "I still plan to take Greyson Park."

"I still won't let you."

Neither of their threats came out with any vehemence. Instead, the words were hushed, like whispered vows.

"One battle at a time, sweeting." Rafe exhaled and gripped the side of the bench when he caught himself leaning toward her. This was killing him. "Now, place the tip of your tongue between your teeth, just behind your lips, and then try to blow out this candle."

Her sweet breath brushed over the tip of his finger once more, but no whistle came forth. Her brow furrowed in frustration. She raked her teeth over her top lip in a way that made him salivate. "I need to see you do it."

He'd like to tell her what *he* needed, but it was probably wiser to whistle instead. He decided on the cotillion, adding his own trilling notes. Again, he earned one of her radiant smiles, and it warmed him far more than it should have done.

"Ah, I see. You whistle like you kiss. Your lips form a pout while your tongue lies in wait. It's much easier to understand now." She studied his mouth. Her lids blinked drowsily. A soft blush colored her cheeks. "But perhaps, a young woman in society should not make such a reference."

"Perhaps not."

Hedley licked her lips. "Even though we are at war, do you think we could—"

A throat cleared in the doorway.

*Damn.* Now, those words were bound to haunt him for the remainder of the day. *"Do you think we could…"* continue the whistling lesson in your bedchamber? Study breathing techniques by removing all of our clothes? *Yes. We could. Absolutely. For hours.*

"Forgive me. Am I interrupting a lesson?"

With a low growl, Rafe looked over his shoulder to see Montwood lift his dark eyebrows in curiosity. Then, the blackguard strolled into the room, clearly glad to interrupt.

"Rafe was teaching me how to whistle," Hedley said as innocently as if she truly believed that was all he was doing.

By the skeptical quirk of his mouth, Montwood knew better. "I'll bet."

Rafe stood, stepping behind Hedley to the opposite side of the piano in order to hide the evidence of the aroused state she'd put him in.

*"Do you think we could…"*

Making an attempting of appearing unflustered, he gestured with a wave of his hand to the empty place on the bench beside her. "She'd never before played the piano until this morning and ended up revealing a natural affinity for music. Do you know that she hummed the music you played last night, note for note, after only hearing it once?"

Whatever mockery Montwood had planned for Rafe disappeared as his blatant interest alighted on Hedley. "This I would like to hear."

She pulled her upper lip between her teeth, not realizing what it did to Rafe. Then without waiting longer than a deep breath, she played those first notes again.

Montwood became enthralled by Hedley, quickly guiding her to the next notes.

Rafe could only stand there for so long, watching his friend's appreciation for Hedley grow. The satisfaction he'd anticipated was absent. In the end, however, he knew it would come to him.

As he left the room, Rafe reminded himself once again that this was what he wanted.

Hedley spent the next two hours beside Montwood, learning the piano. He never once laid his hand on her knee. Nor did she want him to. She didn't feel an overwhelming need to be as close as possible as she had with Rafe. Then again, she didn't feel uncomfortable near Montwood or repelled by him either. He emitted a pleasant sort of warmth but not one that she wanted to wrap around her. Yet she did feel as if they'd known each other for much longer than a single day.

"Your thoughts are no longer on the music," Montwood said, facing her. "Ruminating over Danvers?"

Her shoulders were starting to stiffen from the position she held, and she lowered her hands in her lap. "No, actually I was thinking about how strange it is to feel as if I already know you."

"I feel it, too. You're...*familiar* to me." He nodded sagely, continuing to play.

She attempted to mimic the quick work of his ring finger to the black key.

Noticing her struggle, he lifted his hand to the top of the piano and spread his fingers wide. Then, one by one, he lifted each finger. "This is a good exercise to practice wherever you are."

She pressed her hands to the top and mimicked him. Or tried to. She could barely lift her ring finger. Never before had she noticed how little strength that finger possessed. It was as if an unseen weight pressed down on it. Concentrating, she managed an almost imperceptible jump and found herself breathing heavily from the effort.

"Ah, there you are, Hedley," Calliope said from the doorway, arm in arm with her husband. The pair of them possessed a rosy glow and bright eyes, as if both were suffering the same affliction.

Hedley wondered if that was what love felt like—an illness that one doesn't mind catching. After all, both Calliope and Everhart appeared to endure it quite well. Thinking of Rafe, she wondered if the contagion was already inside her.

"Good morning. Montwood was just now teaching me the piano." She played a few notes of a melody that her tutor had deemed *rudimentary* but which she'd found rather charming.

Calliope gasped. "That is delightful. I didn't know you played."

"Neither did I." Hedley beamed with untapped pleasure.

"Our new friend had this locked inside, and all the while none of us even knew. Not even her." Montwood's expression darkened for a single instant before he masked it with a charming smile.

Quite abruptly, Hedley's borrowed boots gave her feet a little pinch. A reminder that she didn't truly fit in with her new friends. They'd all had full lives up until this point, while she was stumbling around like a newborn foal.

"I find that the later the talent is discovered and developed, the higher chance of success," Everhart said in the easy manner he possessed. There wasn't an ounce of pity in either his expression or his tone. And for that, Hedley was immensely grateful.

"And what latent talent have you discovered?" Montwood asked with a cheeky grin. "An affinity for making wagers and then losing them in record time?"

Everhart bit down on a smile, flashing his teeth.

"He has an affinity for being the best husband on earth," Calliope offered, a wealth of pride ringing in her tone. "Far better than you lot will ever be."

Montwood tsked as he lifted his hand, his index finger ticking back and forth like a metronome. "You cannot issue a new wager until the old one has concluded. And in a year's time, the only one you'll have to wager with will be Danvers, because I will be the sole winner."

"*Au contraire,* my friend," Everhart interrupted, gazing down adoringly at Calliope. "Thus far, I am the sole winner."

Calliope slipped her arms around Everhart's waist, lifting up on her toes to kiss his cheek. "Thank you, my love, for proving my point."

"What was the wager you won?" Hedley asked Everhart. Absently, she recalled Calliope mentioning something last evening about a wager between the gentlemen, but they were distracted before she could finish.

"It was a wager between three bachelors who'd vowed never to marry," Montwood answered instead. "And quite obviously, Everhart lost."

Calliope narrowed her eyes, but teasingly, at Montwood.

Hedley frowned, thinking about how this very house had changed hands. "I hope you are not saying that you forced a marriage upon Everhart and Calliope solely to win a wager."

"Sadly, I cannot take credit." Montwood dramatized a sigh. "The truth is, Everhart tightened his own noose willingly, and rather quickly, too."

"Which leaves only you and Danvers, pitted against one another," Everhart said with a grin.

Hedley looked from one man to the other, dread pressing on her as if she were beneath the piano instead of beside it.

"Everhart wants to ensure we are all married by year's end so he won't have to pay out ten thousand pounds," Montwood explained, studying her carefully, as if he was waiting for her understanding. "Of course, Danvers and I are plotting against each other as well, which will leave a single victor all the spoils."

Hedley caught on too quickly. "Pitted against each other. That means Rafe is attempting to marry you off..." *To me,* she thought but couldn't say the words aloud. A sharp stab of anger and hurt pierced her. She was being used.

"If it's any consolation, he has chosen his bait quite well," Montwood said, his voice quiet and sincere.

Hedley rose from the piano bench.

She met Calliope's distressed gaze. "I'm certain Montwood is wrong," her friend said. "I'm sorry Montwood, but I don't believe Danvers is capable of such a scheme. He wouldn't use Hedley that way."

Montwood didn't reply. Both he, and now Hedley, knew better.

"Mr. Danvers has already declared that he would do anything to secure Greyson Park," Hedley offered, her voice surprisingly calm. Especially when she felt capable of murder at the moment. "Where do you suppose I might find him?"

Rafe watched Frit roaming the meadow beyond the stable yard and felt a pang of envy. His horse had a simple existence. The stallion's day consisted of life's basic pleasures—food, a clean stall, exercise, and a rubdown. He wasn't forcing himself to stay out of doors in order for a ludicrous plot to form. He didn't have this raw, twisted knot in his stomach at the thought of Montwood and Hedley *together*. He wasn't plagued by jealousy. No, Frit was simply happy to nibble on new grass shoots.

Then again, if Frit's stall were next to a wide-eyed mare that had turned his world completely upside down, he wouldn't be out in the meadow, leaving Montwood's stallion, Quicksilver, alone with her.

Rafe blew out a frustrated breath. Marrying Hedley off to Montwood *was* the perfect plan. Wasn't it?

And Montwood already seemed taken with her, and she him.

*Damn it all.*

Rafe pushed away from the tree, whistled for Frit, and walked toward the stables, knowing his horse would follow.

Rounding the corner, he never expected to see Hedley coming straight for him. Instantly, he held out his hand. "Hedley, stop." It was a harsh command but one meant to protect her.

Looking over his shoulder and past a hedgerow, he saw Frit trotting across the meadow. Quickly, he whistled the halt command. However, since he'd never made such an order without being on Frit's back, he wasn't certain the horse would understand.

"You warned me time and again, Rafe Danvers." Paying no heed, Hedley strode forward, her hands balled into fists, her teeth clenched. "But I never once imagined that you would use *me* as the coin to purchase Greyson Park."

Rafe shook his head and extended his arms, palms facing her. "Now isn't the time for this—"

"If you want Montwood to marry in order for you to win your wager, then you will have to look for another convenient neighbor."

"Hedley, stop—"

"No. You will not stop me. I'm tired of being invisible. All my life I have been nothing." She stood toe-to-toe with him, hurt and anger flashing in her eyes. "Does my existence mean so little to you? In the end, when your plot doesn't work, will you try to lock me away as well?"

He recoiled. "You're comparing me to your family?"

"Right now there is little difference. You act as if I mean nothing to you."

"I have been honest—"

She scoffed and threw her hands in the air.

"All right, not *entirely* honest," he amended. "But I was up front about my pursuit of Greyson Park from the beginning."

Hedley opened her mouth to respond and then suddenly went silent. Her eyes rounded in terror. The color drained from her cheeks, and her lips parted.

Rafe reached for her automatically, taking her by the shoulders. "Look at me, Hedley." Then, when she didn't respond, he tried again. "Sweeting, look at me. Yes. That's right. Only me. Keep your eyes on mine. Good."

Beneath his hands, her body trembled. She emitted no heat, and she wasn't breathing.

"It's only Frit. You've met him before. You know he won't hurt you. He's trained by the sound of my whistle, remember?"

She kept her gaze locked on his, and it seemed to take an eternity for his words to filter through. But when they did, her head moved in an almost imperceptible nod.

"Take a breath, sweeting."

She did.

He took a breath too. "Good. You're doing splendidly. Now, lift your hands and place them on my chest. I'm going to pull you closer to warm you."

The rhythmic plod of Frit's slow gait came closer.

"Rafe…" she rasped.

"Just keep looking at me. I won't let anything happen." When he wasn't met with a look of reassurance, he thought of an idea. "I'll prove it. Frit knows a special trick. When I whistle, he'll kneel down on one foreleg and bow to you."

Without delay, he whistled. From the corner of his eye, he saw Frit's head dip and heard him whicker with pride. "See? He listens quite well."

For an instant, she nodded and started to relax. But then Frit stood and drew closer, nudging Rafe's shoulder.

"What is he doing? Why is he coming closer?"

Damn. Rafe had forgotten the apple. But his horse had not. "I have an apple in my pocket, and he knows he deserves a treat for listening to my commands. All I need to do is reach inside and—"

She shook her head. "Don't let go of me, Rafe."

"I won't." He pulled her closer. He would pull her inside of him and keep her safe for the rest of her days if he could. "If you reach into my pocket, you can simply drop it, and then Frit will roam over to the stables to find a drink of water."

Slowly, she lowered her hands from his chest and moved them down until she found the fruit in the pocket of his coat. Unfortunately, Frit had found it as well. Eager for his treat, he dipped his head to take it from her hand.

Hedley jerked her hand away, pulling it back within the protected space between them. The apple was still in her grasp.

Before Rafe could warn her that Frit was no fool when it came to apples, his horse lifted his head and pressed his nose to the top of Rafe's shoulder.

In an unexpected display of bravery, Hedley lifted her shaking hand. Eyes still locked on Rafe's, she stammered, "H-here i-i-is your-r-r apple."

Frit wasted no time and snatched it up. But before he left, he then pressed his nose against Hedley's hand and snuffed her affectionately.

She glanced down to her hand, eyes wide, as if to make sure it was still attached. As Rafe had promised, Frit wandered away in search of water. And Hedley relaxed beneath his hands.

"There now. You were absolutely marvelous." Rafe had never known such pride or relief. Wrapping his arms around her, he held her close and spun her in a circle. "You fed Frit an apple. Unbelievable! You know what this means, don't you. You did it, Hedley. You've met your fear head on."

"I fed a horse an apple," she said in apparent disbelief. Then, she blinked and her pupils widened. "I fed a horse an apple."

"I know," he said on a breath, so damn happy that he didn't know what to do with himself. So he spun her around once more. "You'll have a friend for life now. Frit gave you his approval."

"His nose was wet. He touched my hand with his nose." Gradually, her stunned expression transformed into a smile.

Rafe's heart pounded in a peculiar manner. It seemed to turn to jelly, all squishy and quivering. Words were lost on him as he stared down into her face. His reflection in her eyes was upside down. And that was exactly how he felt.

Hedley tilted her head, studying him closely. "Something is different in your gaze."

He stilled. "You are mistaken."

Her hands spread over his chest, no doubt detecting the odd cadence from within. She was too perceptive by half.

"You say there is nothing between us. Nothing more than Greyson Park. Not when you kissed me. Not when you held me. Not even now. Does this truly feel like nothing?"

"There is desire," he answered, giving her a portion of honesty. "I find you desirable. Your guilelessness is the most powerful aphrodisiac I've ever encountered. And what you feel for me is nothing more than the same. I am merely the first man you've responded to—there will be others. Someday, you may marry one of them."

Her soft laugh caressed his lips, tempting him. "I've spent all my life watching people from a distance, studying the language of their expressions and actions. There *is* something between us, Rafe, whether you admit it or not. I can feel it vibrating beneath your skin. I can see it in your gaze."

"Whatever we have is fleeting." And to cement the point, he dropped his arms from her and took a step back. Yet already he ached to hold her again. Even with this small separation, his skin, his muscles, and his bones all throbbed in near agony.

She drew in a deep breath and nodded. "Then I am glad. I would not want either of us to feel this way forever."

Then she turned on her heel and left.

# Chapter Thirteen

When Hedley returned to Greyson Park that afternoon, she soon learned that she wasn't the only one who'd suffered damage while she'd been away. Another large hunk of plaster had fallen from the hole in the parlor ceiling. And the broken window in the upstairs bedroom at the far corner had suffered another crack. Of course, the manor's damage had occurred during the storm last night. Hers had happened this morning and centered on her heart.

She knew very well that feeling the security of Rafe's arms around her had been instrumental in facing one of her fears. But what surprised her the most was how powerful she'd felt after surviving the encounter with his horse. She'd felt sure of herself. Confident. And unwilling to hold her tongue a moment longer.

Confessing to Rafe that she knew there was something between them had been exhilarating. Seeing his stark reaction, however, had compelled her not to tell him everything she felt.

Likely, he wouldn't appreciate hearing her admit to believing herself in love with him. Since she'd never been in love before, it was difficult to be certain. And yet, she *was* certain.

She loved Rafe. The feeling inside her was more than the peculiar slushy beats of her heart. More than how content she felt in his arms. More than the thrill of seeing him without his clothes…which was saying a great deal.

It was because he knew her secrets and darkest fears and had never once looked at her as if she were mad.

And now she knew that she wanted to live the rest of her life making sure all of his dreams came true…which brought her thoughts directly back to Greyson Park.

Looking around the parlor at the mess of horsehair plaster on the floor, she sighed. Why did Rafe want this house? He wanted it so badly, in fact, that he was willing to barter for it as if she were the coin and Montwood were the buyer. Now *that* she did not love about Rafe. Granted, he certainly was determined.

But so was she.

After changing back into her ill-fitting, threadbare clothes, she began to clean up the mess. Once she finished sweeping out the parlor and removing the shards of glass from the bedroom, she checked on Mr. Tims. His rheumatism had kept him abed for the past week. While she was in his cottage, she made him a pot of tea and swept his floors as well.

When she returned to Greyson Park, she was surprised to find Montwood waiting. He wore a gray frock coat trimmed in black and stood with his arms clasped behind his back, facing the front door. He must have heard her on the path, because he turned.

"Ah, there you are. And back to the old way of things, I see." Beneath his black hat, his dark brows lifted as his gaze looked over her clothes. "It is a rare woman, indeed, who would cast aside a new wardrobe for the old."

Grinning, she reached down and plucked at her skirt as she curtsied. "I hate to disappoint you, Montwood, but I am not as rare as you think. I would much prefer new clothes, but even more, I would not wish to ruin them as I cleaned."

"You are rarer than you think," he said with a bow and a charming smile. "In many ways."

Hedley eyed her new friend with speculation. "Surely you haven't come all this way to pay me a compliment."

"And clever too," he said, gesturing with his open hand to the unkempt lawn. "Would you care to walk with me? Since you have no chaperone, we'll keep to the open park between your fine house and Fallow Hall. We must be on constant guard of your reputation, you know."

She scoffed but walked beside him nonetheless. "Yes, the reputation of a madwoman is precious, indeed. Never mind the simple fact that I don't intend to marry."

"Not marry? And deprive a fortunate man years of wedded bliss?"

"So you *are* here solely to pay me compliments," she teased but then turned serious. There was no reason not to be forthcoming with Montwood. "The truth is, if I marry, I will lose Greyson Park, and it will revert back to my family."

He nodded, apparently not surprised. "And have you told Danvers this as well?"

"No, but I suspect he knows." Hedley sighed, the weight of disappointment and confusion pressing on her. "The suspicion began this morning, when I learned of your wager. Although knowing that he'd spent time in London and had contacted the solicitor to verify my claim of ownership, I should have presumed as much."

"He is quite determined to see us married." Montwood stopped and lifted her hand to his lips, his amber eyes shaded beneath the brim of his hat. "What do you say? Shall we run away together to spite him?"

Hedley didn't take him seriously. "You would lose a fortune."

He shrugged. "Fortunes come and go easily through these fingers. I would find a way to make another."

"Another flaw in your argument is the fact that Rafe would not be vexed in the least. In fact, he would be quite glad to gain ten thousand pounds and Greyson Park."

"For a time, perhaps. Men are notoriously slow at catching on to these things."

Sensing that Montwood's manipulations were not solely restricted to piano keys, she directed the conversation back to where they had begun. "Tell me the real reason you decided to visit me this afternoon."

Montwood laughed and resumed walking until they were directly in line with the break in the trees that revealed Fallow Hall in the distance.

"We are two halves of the same coin, Hedley. We both see things that others believe they've hidden. Your way is to confront, openly and honestly, while mine is...well, let's just say that I'm the side of the coin always facing down." But he made no apologies for his nature. "The truth is, I'm running away from Fallow Hall."

She laughed at his sincerity. "Why ever for?"

"Two plagues have descended on that house." He trembled mockingly. "And their names are Phoebe and Asteria Croft."

"Calliope's sisters? How lovely." Hedley smiled until she saw Montwood shake his head in earnest. "Why have you felt a need to escape them?"

"They believe themselves to be matchmakers when they actually are meddlesome tyrants—" He broke off and cleared his throat, likely because of Hedley's disapproving glower. "They will not rest until every gentleman they encounter is scrutinized, put on a list, and then summarily compared to a similar list of young women. Within five minutes of their arrival, they'd already chosen three potential brides for me."

Hedley looked through the trees once again and felt a twisted sort of dark pleasure fill her. "And do you think they are torturing Rafe this minute?"

"Undoubtedly."

She smiled. "Good."

R afe ducked out of the hall and into the map room the moment he glimpsed the sable coiffure of one of the Croft twins. Where there was one, there was bound to be the other. Thankfully, he didn't believe he'd been spotted.

"Quick, man! Up here!" Everhart leaned over the loft railing, holding a bottle of whiskey in one hand and two glasses in the other. "Lock the door."

"You're not supposed to run from your own relatives," Rafe chided when he reached the top of the circular staircase.

Beyond a short row of bookcases, Everhart stood beside the large map table, already pouring the amber liquid. "You can lecture me all you like once you've married your wife by special license—after being the one who'd not only broken her heart but caused her to swear off marriage for five years. I still believe her father plans to murder me in my sleep. The right cross on that man would astound you."

"Then I am grateful, for your sake, that they are only breaking their journey here for a single night." Rafe walked over, took his glass, and clinked it against Everhart's. "To family."

Everhart laughed wryly and tipped back the whiskey. "I'm still unsure if the darks looks from her father will lessen or worsen once we tell him about the baby. There is no disguising a premature birth, after all."

"Baby?" Rafe stared agape at his friend. "Calliope is…"

His friend nodded and a look of pride and tenderness showed in the smile that swept over his expression.

Rafe took the bottle and poured them both another drink. "To *your* family, Everhart."

The first of their set to have a child had been Weatherstone. Then Rafe's own sister, who'd married Everhart's cousin. And now Everhart. Soon everything would change, and when they gathered together, it would be to watch their children play in the garden.

Well…*their* children. *Not mine and none with cornflower blue eyes and hair threaded with copper,* Rafe reminded himself, unsure why that thought had found its way into his head. Or why, for an instant, he'd imagined such a child among the frolicking brood.

He downed the second glass, hoping it would help to cool the burning anxiety he'd been carrying with him most of the day. Ever since his encounter with Hedley this morning. "Where do you suppose Montwood is off to?"

"Valentine informed me that our friend headed off in the direction of Greyson Park some time ago." A muscle in Everhart's jaw twitched. It was his *tell*—and a sign that he was holding something back.

Did that mean Montwood had expressed an interest in Hedley?

"Alone?" Rafe asked over the rim of his glass.

"I believe so. Why? Wasn't it your intention to prod him into a match with Miss Sinclair?"

"Of course." Losing his thirst, he lowered the glass. "You're saying that as if I'm bothered by it, when—I assure you—the opposite is true. I couldn't be more delighted. I just don't want Montwood to need a special license."

Everhart laughed heartily. "You do realize you're saying that about our wagering-cardsharp of a friend, right?"

"Are you saying he's not to be trusted?"

"Aren't you counting on it? How else do you plan to win?"

## CHAPTER FOURTEEN

Rafe spotted Montwood ahead of him on the lane between Fallow Hall and Greyson Park. Hedley was nowhere in sight. Surely she would have accompanied him on the return to the manor in order to dine with them this evening. Unless the blackguard walking this way had upset her or made advances—

He hastened his steps, stopping just short of a physical collision. "You have spent the afternoon with our neighbor. Alone."

"If you are worried about her reputation, I made sure to contain our visit to the park, well within sight of the caretaker's cottage." Montwood grinned, his amber eyes glinting beneath the brim of his hat. "You wanted me to court her, didn't you?"

Rafe shifted, moving his neck in a way to break the tightness that began at his fists and moved up his arms to his shoulders. "You may court whomever you please. I was merely inquiring as a measure of protection. She is, after all, without family."

"That speaks less of protection and more of staking your claim, Danvers."

*She* is *mine!* A fierce voice inside of him shouted those words again and again, though Rafe didn't know what had come over him. "Nothing of the sort."

Montwood arched a dubious brow. "I am glad. I think when the year is up and the wager is won, I will court her. I am eager to engage in the...*wooing* of Hedley Sinclair."

Rafe wasn't entirely certain how it happened, but one minute he was talking to Montwood, and the next, his friend was flat on his arse with his hat in his lap. And the pain in his own knuckles didn't bother him a bit.

Hedley looked around the room that she had cleaned only hours before. Now, it was littered with baskets, flower petals, stems, teacups, and small plates of gingerbread crumbs. And she couldn't have been happier with any other mess.

Calliope settled into the corner of the sofa on the cushion beside her. "I hope you don't mind that we've taken over your parlor like a group of marauders. I have no idea how my mother remained sane with all of us beneath the same roof."

Before Hedley could answer, Tess chimed in. "My sisters tend to be quite overwhelming." Even at thirteen years old, the youngest of Calliope's sisters was a true beauty with wavy, bright golden locks. Sitting on the edge of the rug with her legs tucked beneath her, she contentedly fashioned a tiara of purple flowers as if she hadn't a care in the world.

"You are simply too young to understand how important our jobs are," Phoebe, the eldest of the sable-haired twins, said from one of the stiff-backed chairs, before reaching over to tug on one of Tess's curls. The instant she received a squinty-eyed glare from her younger sister, she grinned, and her brown eyes glinted with mischief.

Asteria, the twin with blue eyes, nodded as she sipped the last of her tea. "Think of it this way, Tess—if there weren't matchmakers like us, then society would fall into ruins. Men cannot be trusted to choose wisely and therefore must be guided to the perfect matrimonial candidates."

"Quite," Phoebe agreed. Then, sitting up straighter, she aimed that glinting gaze at Hedley. "Which brings to mind our need to catalog your interests."

Asteria sat forward and placed her cup on the low table, all of her considerable attention now on Hedley. "Yes, we must know who is best suited for you."

This visit was by far the most pleasant exchange between siblings Hedley had ever experienced. They filled the room with effervescence and warmth. And yet, they were also a lot to take on all at once.

"I can assure you, dear sisters," Calliope intervened, "that our new friend already knows her own mind. Perhaps you should concentrate on sorting out the men on your list."

Phoebe tapped her finger against the side of her mouth. "Hmm…yes, but the only unmarried men in Lincolnshire we know—"

"Are the gentlemen at Fallow Hall," Asteria finished for her. The twins exchanged a look. Their dark, wispy brows rose in unison. Then, they leaned in closer and began to chatter.

Calliope laughed to Hedley. "Do not worry. They are leaving at first light."

"Even at the risk of becoming a victim of their plot, I am already sad that they will be leaving so soon," Hedley admitted.

Her life with Ursa had had no joy in it. There'd been only cruelty. And until now, Hedley had never witnessed what a family could be like. Nevertheless, she'd always hoped it would be just like this. By Calliope's tender expression and the hand that reached over and squeezed her own, Hedley knew she understood.

"If it's any consolation—although I do not know how it could be," Calliope said in a teasing tone, "they will break their journey once more on the way back from Brannaleigh Hall. This is the first trip in many years that Father has made to Scotland, and it is important for him to rest each night. Both he and Mother were already sound asleep before we left Fallow Hall. I doubt they will rouse for dinner."

"Will you be coming to dinner, Hedley?" Phoebe asked.

"Not this evening." Hedley looked from one twin to the other, with both looking back as if their heads were brewing with plans. She nearly shuddered at the level of determination they possessed. She was tired of matchmaking, however, and especially tired of being someone's plot.

The giddiness she'd felt yesterday while in Rafe's arms, after having confronted one of her fears, had faded as the truth settled in. Rafe was certain there was nothing more than desire between them. While she refuted it on her own behalf, she knew very well that she couldn't force Rafe to feel differently.

Drawing in a breath, she looked to the twins and decided that an immediate redirection was in order. "I should like to hear all about what it is like to have a Season. How many gentlemen are pursuing each of you?"

Calliope gave her a nod and grin as if to say, "*Well done.*"

The eldest twin sobered and clasped her hands in her lap. "We have had little success with true candidates."

"There was one," Asteria added, casting a sly sideways glance at her sister. "If you include your persistent suitor, Phoebe."

"Lord *Nobody* is far too old. At least two years older than our brother." Phoebe tsked and shook her head. "And no manners to speak of. He soiled my best gloves."

Asteria leaned forward. "Then, instead of flowers, he sent her *gloves* the next day."

Hedley didn't understand why the twins appeared scandalized. "That was kind of him to offer reparation."

"No. No." Phoebe's spine went rigid. "A woman dare not accept such a gift at the risk of openly accepting a gentleman's pursuit."

"And once she does," Asteria added, "he will cease wooing her at all, believing that the game is done."

Calliope clucked her tongue. "Love and marriage are not games."

"There are rules one must follow in courtship, aren't there?" Phoebe asked.

Asteria nodded with a scholarly expression. "And then each player must move of his or her own accord."

"That does sound like a game," Tess remarked, situating her flower tiara on her head.

Calliope let out a breath and offered a helpless shrug. "I suppose you are right."

Hedley observed this exchange with fascination. Then, taking the gentlemen's wager into account as well, she was beginning to see things in a new light. This visit was turning into a study of society. Not to mention, helpful insight.

By accepting that parcel from Rafe, early on, she'd granted him the control of the game that he'd decided to play, and summarily used her as a pawn. His rules. His game. And she was left wondering what to do next.

But now, it was time to introduce a few of her own rules.

Tess stood and brushed out her skirts. "Is it true that there is a treasure here at Greyson Park?"

Hedley smiled at her new friends. "Yes. Right here. The parlor hosts the greatest treasure of all."

## CHAPTER FIFTEEN

The following morning, Hedley walked to Fallow Hall. Loping along the path toward her was Boris. He eagerly greeted her with a *woof* and a vigorous tail wag. Adjusting the parcel in her grasp, she gave him a good scratch behind his ears.

The charmer looked up at her with soulful eyes and his tongue lolling, in apparent bliss. "All right, you sly matchmaker," she said. "If Calliope is right, then you'll take me directly to either Lucan or Rafe. It doesn't matter which, as long as I can return this parcel. So lead on."

Boris licked the side of her hand before turning off the footpath. With one more *woof*, he looked back over his shoulder.

Since the day was bright and green, with new shoots of grass and small flowers sprouting up everywhere, and she had no pressing matters, she followed. Today, she treated herself to wearing one of the dresses that Calliope had sent over yesterday afternoon. The pale pink muslin was light and airy but not threadbare. The tapered style, however, did not allow for longer strides but demure steps instead. Therefore, she'd altered the hem, adding extra piping in vertical segments to accommodate her customary gait.

Along the walk, white- and pink-blossomed trees dotted the line at the edge of the wood that bordered the two estates. Boris's ambling took them past Fallow Hall and then the stable yard.

A narrow path through a blooming orchard kept her too near the fence for her liking. Even though the wooden fence looked to be in good order, she wasn't certain if it was high enough. She would feel much better if it was built with stone and was as tall as a castle's keep. Beside her, she heard the unmistakable hollow thumps of a horse's canter. Clutching her parcel, she kept her gaze straight ahead and continued to follow Boris. Yet even then, she was fully aware of the dark shadow that appeared in her peripheral vision and the slowed hoofbeats on the paddock.

Her pulse quickened. She could feel the horse drawing near to the edge of the fence. On the other side of her, low branches kept her from skirting farther away. She walked faster. The horse matched her pace. When she slowed, peculiarly the horse slowed too.

Shaking her head, an incredulous laugh escaped her. "Is that you, Frit?"

A low whicker was the response.

Rafe had warned her that she'd made a friend for life after feeding Frit that apple. Did she dare turn and face the animal?

She stopped and held her breath. After a moment's deliberation, she turned.

Indeed, it was Frit. He lifted his head in a way that caused his dark forelock to brush against the white speckled blaze over his nose. She hadn't taken any time before to acknowledge that he was actually a very pretty horse. If one were inclined to like such beasts. She still wasn't sure.

"I don't have an apple," she told him, wondering if that was the reason behind his interest.

He whickered again and tossed his mane with a flick of his head. His round, dark eyes stayed with her, as if he was waiting for something.

"I don't know how to whistle either." Though she gave it another go for good measure. Nope. Nothing but air. Then, with a speculative glance at her companion, she decided to hum the tune that Rafe had whistled the other day.

To her surprise, Frit bent one foreleg and bowed to her.

Enchanted, Hedley smiled. And before she even knew what she was doing, she stepped to the fence and lifted her hand. In the next instant, his nose was nestled up against it.

A moment of shocked stillness followed. And then, dumbfounded and amazed, she stroked him. His coat was smooth and soft beneath her fingers. She couldn't believe what she was doing. Not only that, but she wasn't shaking the slightest bit.

"Do you want to know a secret?"

Frit snuffed her with his nostrils in response, his long eyelashes drifting down.

"Out of all the horses in the entire world, I like you best."

Soon after, she was on her way again, Boris ahead of her. He'd stopped at the stable yard too, and she wondered if he'd been just as surprised by her actions as she was. She couldn't wait to tell Rafe. But wait…wasn't she irritated with him?

*That's right. I am,* she thought, suddenly remembering her purpose for coming all this way. After all, she couldn't let Rafe continue to believe she had no say in her own fate.

Gradually the path opened into a clearing. A stone hut stood in the center, smoke billowing from the chimney.

Her steps slowed. Was this a crofter's cottage? She certainly didn't want to disturb the caretaker of the estate. Perhaps she should have been more specific in her instructions.

Boris turned around and sat, staring at her. Then, in the next instant, he tilted his head back and released a howl, loud enough to startle flocks of birds from their nests.

"I never let anyone watch me work and that includes you, Boris," Rafe's voice called from inside the cottage.

Boris looked at her, and she could have sworn that the flesh above his left eye arched as if in answer to her challenge.

Hedley walked over to the rough-hewed door and gave it solid knock. "I'm not here to bother you. I'm just leaving a parcel behind. Forget I was ever here."

By the time she turned around and took two steps away from cottage, the door opened behind her, banging against the stone façade. She resisted the urge to stop and turn around but kept walking. A clean break. It was better this way.

"Hedley?"

She lifted a hand. "I didn't see a thing. Your secret work is safe."

"Hedley," Rafe growled. "Come back here."

Then again, perhaps she should say a few words to let him know why she planned to sever contact. Yet as she turned around, all thought fled.

Rafe stood in the doorway of the cottage with his shirt sleeves rolled up to expose the darker skin of his forearms. He wore a heavy black apron tied at his narrow waist that fell to the tops of his scarred boots. He looked so delicious, her teeth ached.

One of those boots nudged the parcel she'd left on the ground. "What is this?"

"That"—she pointed—"is *nothing*. The same nothing that is between us." At least for him. And soon enough for her. She hoped.

He crossed those swarthy arms and narrowed his eyes. "You cannot return my reparation."

"I've recently learned that accepting such a gift, whatever the intention, is quite scandalous in society." In addition, she refused to allow him to think that he could purchase her cooperation in his scheme to get Montwood to marry her.

"We are not in *society*. We are…" His words trailed off, his mouth open as if the answer eluded him.

"Outside?"

His glower turned serious. "Did Montwood tell you to return the clothes?"

Now, *she* glowered and crossed her arms. "Do you think so little of me as to assume that I cannot make my own decisions?"

He exhaled audibly, his nostrils flaring. "Come inside." When she merely stood her ground, he amended the command with "please."

Prepared to speak her mind and end her involvement in his scheme, she walked past him. Her will wavered slightly as he shifted his stance, and her sleeve brushed his. Beneath his woodsy, smoky scent, a stronger essence clung to him. It was earthy and...*male*. And it stirred something within her that was quite the opposite of anger.

*Desire*. And more.

Rafe stared down at their almost-touching arms for a few breaths before he withdrew a step. "I need to keep working or I will fracture." Spoken under his breath, the words came out as little more than a growl.

She wasn't sure if she was meant to hear them. Nevertheless, she responded. "I did not intend to disturb or hinder your work."

He released a wry laugh as he pulled on a pair of heavy-looking black gloves but made no other comment. Apparently, he wasn't too disturbed by her presence, because he began to move around the cottage. Which was less of a cottage and more of a sweltering hearth room. The hearth in question was a glowing furnace with a hole cut in the center of a pair of doors. Built into the brick beside it stood an oven, with a hefty stack of wood on the floor. A single stool and three tables of different heights and sizes were the only pieces of furniture. The tables were mostly laid bare aside from a few odd-looking tools and charred squares of cloth. Nearest the furnace, a narrow trough of dark water shimmered, reflecting a glow that resembled liquid copper.

She kept close enough to the door for a reprieve from the heat, yet leaned forward for a good vantage point to see what Rafe's work entailed.

Lifting a long piece of pipe up from the table, Rafe proceeded to push one end through the small round hole in the doors of the furnace. Something about the act caused her stomach to bobble. So she pressed a hand to her middle.

As she watched, the firelight caressed his profile, bathing him in golden light. Above the cuff of his gloves and below his rolled-up shirt sleeves, the muscles of his forearms flexed and bunched in a sinuous dance. Unable to help herself, she imagined him working in nothing more than snug-fitting breeches. Naturally, her gaze dipped lower to the firm flesh of his buttocks and thighs, well-defined beneath a buttery-colored cloth.

Hedley swallowed and felt her hand tighten over her middle, wrinkling the pale pink muslin she wore.

In that moment, she knew this wasn't going to be easy.

But it had to be done. "I came by to tell you that I refuse to be a party to your scheme. If I choose to allow anyone to court me, it will not be because of a wager. More specifically, you cannot purchase my acquiescence."

Rafe's profile hardened, his mouth pressed in a firm line. "Did Montwood kiss you?"

She started. "Wha—"

"I will kill him," he growled, withdrawing the pipe from the furnace. On the end was a sort of misshapen ball of mush. Moving quickly—angrily, it seemed—he laid the middle of the pipe over the narrow table and began to roll it from side to side. Then, as if he'd developed a rhythm he liked, he bent at the waist and fitted his mouth to the opposite end of the pipe.

Hedley's knees went weak. A trickle of perspiration slid down her temple. She pressed her fingers to her lips. No wonder he didn't allow anyone to watch him work. It was far too erotic. And, she imagined, *scandalous*. She didn't need to be part of society in order to know that what she was feeling right now could not possibly be acceptable.

It took her a moment to recover. "If kissing is suddenly a killing offense, then you and I are slated for the gallows as well."

She probably shouldn't have enjoyed the dark look he sent her as he stood. Or the way that it caused her to notice the heat dampening her flesh. She had no desire to fan herself. Instead, she wanted to be closer to the source.

Without a word, Rafe turned and pushed the end of his pipe back into the furnace. His arms flexed, pulling his shirt tight across his shoulders.

"Then of course," she added, her throat dry, "Greyson Park—your apparent reason for living—would suffer because of it."

"It is not my reason for living. Greyson Park holds my legacy." He withdrew the pipe again and went to a different table. This time, he rolled the hot, glowing end into what looked like a littered mess of glass shards, before returning once again to the furnace. "And you did not answer my question."

He still had Montwood on his mind. Did he have any idea how absurd it was to think that Montwood would have kissed her? Or that she would have permitted him?

"Fine. I will answer your question as soon as you explain how your legacy ended up in my house."

He adjusted his grip on the pipe, keeping his gaze toward the hole in the furnace door. "The property once belonged to my family. During the reign of Henry III, one of my ancestors was commissioned to be part of the rebuilding of the abbey and subsequently the king's chamber, which later became known as the Painted Chamber. Later on, a fire destroyed part of the chamber. Certain works of art were damaged, some restored, and some…removed for safe keeping."

As his words slowly sank in, she watched him maneuver back to the first table. His back to her, he picked up a tool here and there, moving fluidly, going about his work as if she wasn't in the room.

"Are you saying that…Greyson Park actually does hold a treasure?"

He shook his head. "Only to antiquarians."

"And to the descendants of the artist." She suddenly felt as if she were looking directly into the furnace. "*That* is what you meant by your legacy. I can only imagine how such an important artifact would also restore your father's name. Now, I understand why you would do anything for Greyson Park."

She truly did. Although she was not quick to forgive him. "You could have saved yourself a great deal of silliness and scheming if you'd told me from the beginning. Surely it doesn't matter who owns the property. Your family would get credit."

"In this particular case, it will not work that way. Lord Fitzherbert is the head of the Society. His wife was the one who gave my father the cut direct, casting him out of the *ton*'s good graces. The Royal Antiquarian Society has refused my claim on the grounds of my lack of ownership. They've gone so far as to label me a trespasser on the property of the family who publicly humiliated me."

She heard what sounded like a sudden break of glass and gasped. In the seconds that followed, she worried that he'd done all that work for naught. And that her presence here had caused him to ruin a piece of art.

Yet when he faced her, he held a small bottle in his hand, with swirls of blue intermingled with the clear glass. Then, watching her closely, he set it down on the largest table in front of her.

"It's lovely," she said, thoroughly amazed. "Calliope will be pleased. It is exactly the size of those bottles from my grandmother's cask. How did you get it to be so perfectly formed? And blue, as well."

"Practice," he said with a cocky shrug of shoulder, but his expression was not as aloof. He seemed to study her for a moment before he gestured to the table littered with shards of glass. Reaching out, he scooped up a handful and sifted it though his fingers. "And the color comes from these pieces of *frit*."

Ah, so that was where his horse came by his peculiar name. She was learning so much about Rafe. It made it even more difficult to remember that—for him—she was only a means to an end.

Before she could forget again, she took a step back until she could feel the breeze coming through the door. "I will write this Lord Fitzherbert and explain how my family never knew of this artifact, and that—through marriage many years ago—the estate changed hands without anyone the wiser. That way—"

"It won't work," he interrupted with a solemn shake of his head.

"You sir, are no optimist." Of course it would work. She owned Greyson Park and would be seen as an authority on the property.

"When I spoke of my discovery to Lord Fitzherbert, he made it clear that he wouldn't validate any finding of mine unless the 'journey' of the artifact was documented by a member of the Society. Besides, I cannot remove the *treasure* without damaging it. I've already tried." He removed his gloves and raked a hand through his hair. "And last, they would need to validate your ownership. From there, they would inquire about the young Sinclair woman who had never been presented in society—whose name is not listed in *Debrett's*—and then discover the stipulations of your inheritance."

Oh. Perhaps it wasn't as simple as she thought. "And it would only be a matter of time before they assumed that reason for my absence in society is because I am considered...the family lunatic."

"If it's any consolation, I've never believed it for an instant."

"I know." She offered a wan smile. "I appreciate that you did not judge me on circumstance. Now, if only I could find a member of your Society who would do the same. But perhaps the only way would be to meet one of them in person and prove that I am of sound mind."

Rafe stepped forward and took her hand. "They are in London, Hedley. They have refused my numerous invitations to travel here."

Thus the reasons he'd schemed to get her to marry Montwood.

She wasn't about to give up Greyson Park and return to a locked attic room. There was, however, one thing she could do. Hedley squeezed his hand in return and then slipped free. She'd made up her mind.

"I will go to London and speak to them myself," she said. It was the only way. Then, feeling suddenly lightheaded, she placed her hand on the doorframe. "First, I'd like you to help me face my fear of carriages."

His presence had helped her with her first encounter with Frit, after all. Now—especially after what had happened moments ago—she was much surer of herself. Facing one fear had given her confidence. She was ready to face the rest.

"No. Absolutely not. I will not allow you to put yourself through an ordeal," Rafe said, adamant.

Hiding her disappointment, she turned to the door but hesitated. "This fear has plagued me for most of my life. I plan my days around avoidance so that I will not be caught in that icy grip—that prison that has crippled me and made me an outcast." She glanced over her shoulder once more before leaving. "Don't you see? Until recently, I never imagined I would have the strength to face it. If I don't…then it will be an ongoing ordeal."

And just like that, her mind was made up.

# CHAPTER SIXTEEN

If Rafe wouldn't help her, then Hedley would do it on her own. The carriage house at Greyson Park had intimidated her long enough. Each time she had to bring wood in for the fire, it was there, taunting her with nightmarish memories. She wanted to banish those for good.

A shiver assaulted her as she gained the path between the two estates, making her misstep.

Trailing her all the while, Rafe suddenly reached out and steadied her by taking her arm. "You are not going to do this for me, Hedley. There is another way."

"What way?" she challenged, already knowing the answer. Slipping her arm free of him, she continued her hike. Greyson Park lay just ahead, through the copse of trees.

"Once the wager is won, I will…" His words trailed off into the void of alternative ideas between them. He released an oath under his breath. "I will think of something."

Hedley ducked beneath a low budding branch. Unfortunately, part of it caught in her hair. Her pins came loose.

When she straightened, the thick plait fell, the length of it resting down the center of her back, all the way to her hips.

*Lucifer's talons!* She grumbled as she pulled a twig free of a tangle. "No. It is up to me. Unless I marry Montwood, there is no other way. And you and I both know that he would wait until he'd won the wager first. And I doubt you want to wait another year. Besides, I would prefer to go to my potential future husband as a complete person, not one who freezes in terror every time a horse and carriage is near."

Rafe growled and brushed her hands aside, assisting her. "Why do you insist on mentioning Montwood in that context?"

"I don't believe I'm *insisting*. Merely remarking. You were, after all, the one who put the idea into my head." It served him right to believe that she was in earnest. "You never once encouraged my association with anyone other than Montwood. You could have chosen a local merchant instead. Although, I admit, I certainly wasn't entranced by Mr. Lynch the way you were by the laundress."

When the gentle movements of his fingers stopped, she turned.

Holding the weight of her braid in his grasp, Rafe grinned at her and gave her a playful tug that drew her closer to him. "You're jealous."

The heat of a blush rose to her cheeks. She hoped that beneath the shadowed canopy of branches that he wouldn't notice. "Only as jealous as you are of Montwood—which is to say not one whit."

His devilish grin spread as he toyed with her braid, brushing the end over the pad of his thumb. "You have a great deal of hair."

"Which is the reason I keep it pinned. It tends to get in the way. Now, I'd like to find my pins before I can face this next task." Of course, she knew that pinning her hair up again wouldn't erase her fear, but it was a way of giving her another moment before forging ahead.

Slowly, Rafe shook his head. "I like it this way."

She swallowed and felt her stomach dip low. It settled deep down inside her and made her aware of every inch of space between them. With a single step, her body would touch his. She knew what it felt like to have nothing but layers of clothes between them, and she yearned to be that close again. Yet an even stronger yearning pulsed within her to have nothing between them. Not clothing. Not doubt. Not Greyson Park.

She let out a breath and silently told her stomach to return to its proper place.

Most likely, Rafe was stalling as well, solely as a means of helping her avoid what she must do. Or…he simply didn't want to help her at all.

She took a step back and watched her braid slide through his palm. "I can do this on my own. It was thoughtless of me to ask you when you have so much at stake as well."

"I don't want to see you hurt," he said with quiet sincerity.

Hedley looked down to see his hand open. Most of her pins lay across his palm. Taking that as his readiness to leave her, she took them. "Thank you."

Turning away, she walked across the courtyard toward the carriage house. To keep her mind occupied, she busied herself with pinning her plait in place.

"Hedley, stop."

She saw him stride up beside her, but she was almost to the door. And if she stopped now, she might never return. "I need to do this, Rafe. I need to stop the fear from controlling my life. I want to live free of this burden. I will do it alone and—"

"No. You've done enough on your own." He stepped in front of her and placed his hands on her shoulders. "I want you to lean on me. I want to give you my strength."

Those words went directly to her heart. She was powerless against them and against the overwhelming surge of love that filled her. "My hands are shaking."

He reached down and settled her hands against this chest. Since he'd only donned a coat while leaving the cottage, she could feel the warmth of his body through the linen of his shirt. "Just keep your hands on me. Keep your gaze on mine, like before with Frit. Don't look away."

"I won't," she promised. She suddenly felt that she could face anything.

Rafe opened the door. The hinges groaned with the movement, like a bellowed warning. Dank, musty air escaped on a cold breeze. Hedley shivered. She knew there was a carriage inside because she'd seen it before. At the time, all she could do was stand in the doorway and experience the terror she'd felt as a child, unable to look away for what had seemed like an eternity.

Now, it was different. She wasn't facing this alone.

"We can turn back any time…"

She was already shaking her head before he finished. "I'm ready to conquer this." Surprisingly, her voice didn't quaver. Rafe had helped her discover her inner strength.

Then carefully, as if she were one of his delicate glass creations, he guided her through the door, backing her into the carriage house.

"It's dark in here," she whispered.

"Let your eyes adjust. There's enough light. And I'm here."

Yes, he was here. And close, too. She breathed in deeply to fill her lungs with the comforting scent of him. To her, he smelled like home—freshly cut logs and a fire in the hearth. He warmed her from the inside out.

Rafe held her gaze, his never wavering. "Just a few more steps, sweeting."

He was right. There was plenty of light in here. She could see the severity in his expression, one that told her if she had even a tiny bubble of panic, he would whisk her out of here faster than she could blink. Knowing that made her fear seem far away—a haunting memory but nothing more. The way it should have been all this time.

Their muted footsteps on the stone floor landed in perfect syncopation. The rhythm reminded her of the slow, meandering tune she'd learned on the piano. It made her wonder if this was what it would be like to dance with Rafe. Beneath her hands, his heart quickened as if he were imagining something similar while staring down into her face.

She let her hands drift down to the firm ridges of his abdomen. The shape of him fascinated her. Her fingertips traced the horizontal valleys, starting at the top of his stomach and working her way down, bit by bit. When she reached the one nearest the waist of his breeches, his flesh rippled. He let out a rush of air against her lips.

Rafe stopped walking. His grasp tightened around her shoulders as he drew her marginally closer. "Sweeting, you don't know what you're doing to me."

Hearing the rawness of his voice, she hesitated. "I'm touching you."

"Because you're afraid?"

"No, because you feel good. Different. I like touching you," she admitted, flattening her hands over him. He was entrancingly solid, so unlike her. She'd seen this part of him without clothes. She wondered what he would feel like beneath his shirt, too. Would his skin be smooth? Would that black hair on his chest and abdomen feel silken or coarse?

Marveling at these things, she moved her hands upward to his chest. When he drew in a sharp breath, she hesitated again. "Should I stop?"

"Absolutely not." He shifted closer, his boots sliding against the outside of her shoes until her knees were between his.

She lifted her face, automatically tilting it to the side when she saw his gaze dip to her mouth. "Should I kiss you?"

Rafe shuddered. While it was wonderful that Hedley wasn't quaking in fear and that she appeared to be handling this with aplomb, having her hands on him had brought him to an urgent state of arousal. He was thick and heavy with need already.

"If you kiss me and continue to touch me," he warned on a stuttered breath, "then I will start kissing and touching you too, and I'm not certain I will be able to stop."

Without guile or any coy game, she looked at him directly. "I'm not certain I would want you to stop."

He closed his eyes. She didn't know what she was saying, he reminded himself. However, telling that to a certain part of his anatomy proved futile. He wanted her with a desperation he'd never experienced, not even during his first sexual encounter. Apparently, experience and age counted for little. This desire was more than wanting to lose himself inside of her—although there was plenty of that—it was *needing* to be part of her. To be one with her. And connected in a way that he knew would change him forever. Hell, he was already changed. Forever.

"The voice of reason is telling me that you don't know what you're saying. You cannot. You are an innocent." He loosened his grip on her shoulders and trailed down to her wrists, prepared to step away. The feel of her hands was driving him mad. So then, why wasn't he stepping away?

"Believe what you like. I know what I'm saying." Hedley shuffled closer. Her lips were temptingly close. "For now, however, I'm ready to step inside of a carriage."

He hesitated. "You do realize that you are already facing your fear by merely standing here."

"I know," she said softly.

Rafe let out a deep breath. The decision was Hedley's, and yet…"If you show the slightest bit of terror"—he cupped her face—"I'm dragging you out of there."

"Agreed," she said quickly, tilting up on her toes to press her lips against his. "But not a moment before."

His knees went weak. She was going to kill him.

The carriage was on supports. Two large beams served as braces where the wheels would have been. Since it was a landau, there was still a step up, and Rafe went in ahead of her to make sure it was safe. Other than a layer of dust over the floor and cushions and a few missing buttons from the tufted red upholstery, it was in decent condition.

He peered out of the carriage door to where Hedley stood, her arms folded over the other as if she were warming them. Her gaze drifted to the carriage. "This is much larger than the one we were in that day," she said.

"Mr. Tims told me that this once belonged to the previous owner of Fallow Hall and that he'd attempted to hide it from debt collectors."

"Surely it is sturdy enough for two passengers."

"Aye." He'd never spoken a more ominous word in his life. Shrugging out of his coat, he draped it over the seat.

Refusing to listen to any more inner warnings, Rafe extended his hand. Hedley reached out but hesitated at the last moment. He did not press her, or lower his hand. She held his gaze as if drawing strength from it. Then gradually, she slipped her hand into his. Lifting her skirts out of the way, she climbed inside and settled herself on his coat. Her fingers clenched tighter around his as she took in her surroundings.

After a while, she looked at him again. The light from the open door to the carriage house barely caught the glistening of tears in her eyes. "Thank you. I needed this more than you'll ever know."

"One battle at a time," he said, repeating the words she'd once said to him.

"A quiet victory but no less potent." She released a slow breath.

They sat in silence for a few minutes. He thought of that day he'd found her standing by the road. So much had changed since then. Not only in her, but in him as well. He never wanted to see that terror claim her again. Yet she was right. Facing her fears was helping her move forward, and he was honored that she'd chosen him.

"Rafe," she said after a moment. "I need a new memory from inside a carriage. Can I kiss you now?"

He couldn't deny her. Perched on the opposite seat, his legs spread to flank hers on either side. Seeing her rake her top lip with her teeth sent a fresh surge of blood to his groin. He'd wanted to kiss her since...well, since shortly following their last kiss.

Holding her hand, he pulled her to the edge of her seat as well. The action caused her skirts to bunch in her lap and sent his mind on a foray into erotic journeys this kiss could take. However, he brushed those aside and did his best to think of a proper, chaste kiss.

Then her mouth touched his. Only her mouth. Yet in that instant, he forgot all about being chaste. He dove in. His hands drew her closer—one at the base of her neck and the other at her waist. Those berry-stained lips offered him their sweetness even as her hands reached out with purpose. She made a sound—a hungry, needy whimper—that drove him over the edge. He had no chance of withdrawing now.

He wanted more. All of her. Everything. Her tongue tangled with his in a sensuous slide that teased and invited him deeper. He pulled Hedley closer, nearly unseating her in the process. Catching her against him, he leaned back against the squabs, letting her take control. Minutes rolled by. Perhaps even hours. Her lush body draped over his, her hands in his hair, her mouth losing inhibitions by the second. She twirled her tongue around his and flicked the underside before suckling the very tip. Rafe nearly convulsed.

Taking hold of her hips, he drew her skirts up so that she could straddle him. On a groan, he arched off the seat and rocked against her.

"Mmm…" she purred, murmuring her approval. Her kisses turned more urgent. Before he even realized that her hands were no longer in his hair, he felt her pull his shirt free of his breeches. And then her hands were on his flesh. She made another sound of assent as she caressed his abdomen and chest.

Rafe was losing control. Or perhaps he'd lost control already. He couldn't think. And he couldn't have slowed down if he'd wanted to. He had the buttons at the back of her gown unfastened and her stays unlaced before he thought about the consequences. And then, once he thought about them, he no longer cared. This moment was the only thing that mattered in the world.

With a tug, her heavy breasts spilled out of her dress and into his hands. Her flesh was milky smooth, perfect and warm, the ruched flesh of her nipples velvety soft. He brushed his thumbs across them at the same time.

Breathless, Hedley lifted away from the kiss. She stared down at his hands on her breasts and then into his eyes. At the same time, her hips ground down on his turgid erection.

"*Rafe…*" His name left her lips on a gasp.

Unable to resist the invitation, he opened his mouth and drew on that taut peak. She moaned and bucked against him.

The violent trembling of her legs told him that her pleasure was building. The untutored motions of her hips drove him mad with need and frustration all at once. He shouldn't be this close to losing control. Yet if she continued, he wouldn't hesitate to rip open the fall of his breeches and thrust inside her blessed heat.

Shifting his hold, he settled her once more on the opposite seat and gained some distance. He was about to tell her that they should stop. But then he looked at those beseechingly drowsy cornflower blue eyes and that dewy, swollen mouth, and somehow he found himself kneeling in front of her.

He kissed her again, lingering and drinking in all of her sweetness. He couldn't stop touching and caressing her. The skin of her inner thigh, just above her stockings, was as soft as her breasts. Was she even softer elsewhere? He needed to know. He couldn't resist.

*She was.* The further he ventured, the more enthralled he became. Brushing against those silken curls, he found her deliciously wet. "You're drenched for me, sweeting."

He stroked her, abandoning finesse for simple carnal desire. Her body quaked and arched toward his hand. "Please, Rafe."

That plea undid him. She needed to find release. He wanted her to have everything and more. Ravenous, he forged a path of heated kisses over her breasts, nipping at her flesh. Lower, he circled the tender bud with his thumb as he slipped his finger inside her tight sheath. She shuddered. And so did he.

"Sweeting, I can't resist..." Shifting back on his heels, he lifted her skirts, revealing those pale golden curls, damp and glistening. Her sweet scent filled his nostrils. It wasn't possible, but her fragrance reminded him of the color pink—sweet, musky, and soft. "Let me taste you."

Her *yes* turned into a gasp as he dipped his head and feasted on her, drinking her warm nectar. Hedley's fingers twined in his hair. Sliding forward, she arched against his mouth. She was so unreserved and honest. Even with her pleasure, she didn't know how to be deceitful. And he genuinely loved that about her. He'd never known anyone like her. And no woman could ever taste as sweet.

He was lost in devouring her. Her moans turned to cries and pleas. Her breathing was fast and shallow. Her hips rocked against the flicks and suckling of his tongue. And when she came apart, he'd never known such bliss.

He didn't stop laving her, loving her with his mouth, until she was spent and her breathing evened. Then, wanting to prove that he would give her everything, unreservedly, he rose up and opened the fall of his breeches. His flesh was heavy, hot, and near bursting. And she was so wet and ready.

He slid the engorged tip down her folds and positioned himself at her core, barely able to resist thrusting inside.

Hedley spread her knees wider and reached forward to caress his cheek. Her gaze held his, a tender smile on her lips. "I love you."

Rafe stilled.

The words brought back a semblance of reality. Not because he was shocked that she would say them. He already knew she felt more for him than mere friendship.

No, the reason that reality suddenly intruded on a perfect moment was because he'd almost repeated those words back to her.

*I love you, sweeting…* The words were there, waiting.

But if he truly loved her, how could he rob her of her innocence and then send her off to marry another?

The simple answer was, he couldn't.

## CHAPTER SEVENTEEN

"No," Rafe said again as he buttoned her dress. "You don't love me."

Perturbed, Hedley fisted her hands. "Will you stop saying that?"

She'd never seen a man move faster than Rafe when he'd exited the carriage a few moments ago. He'd instantly righted his clothing. Although when she turned around to face him now, there was still a rather pronounced bulge beneath the fall of his breeches. A very intriguing one that she'd felt against her own flesh briefly. Until she'd said those words that seemed to have damned her into listening to Rafe refute it over and over again.

"I'm merely the first man you've encountered since you came to live here." Without meeting her gaze, he reached past her and into the carriage to retrieve his coat.

She swallowed down the tears that threatened and focused on her irritation instead. "Actually, the first man I encountered was Mr. Tims. Am I in love with him too?"

Seeing there was a great deal of dust on his coat, she assisted by patting his shoulders, somehow resisting the urge to put force behind her efforts as if to knock sense into him.

Rafe adjusted his cuffs. "What about Montwood?"

"We are not—*absolutely not*—returning to that conversation." Standing in front of him with her hands on her hips, she glared at him until he met her gaze. "Are you trying to tell me that I don't know my own mind? Or perhaps you're saying that I couldn't because I've spent so much of my life as the family lunatic?"

His dark eyes turned warm and tender as he reached out and caressed her cheek. Then, on an exhale, he let his hand fall to his side. "I'm saying that you are innocent, and I've introduced you to a great deal more than I should have. The kind of emotion that you're talking about takes time. It doesn't happen like this."

But it does. *It has.*

Was that fear she saw in his expression? She wasn't certain. This look—his furrowed brow, the tender but almost pained apprehension in his eyes—was new to her.

She moved forward to twine her arms around his neck and fit her body to his. Yet he shook his head and took a step back. She tried to swallow down this rejection as well. And tried not to remember how she *hadn't* seen him shy away from the laundress in the marketplace.

"Why do you want to talk me out of loving you? It does you no harm," she asked, her voice raspy with stemmed emotion. "Or is it because there are scores of others you'd rather have?"

"Not you, Hedley—"

A high-pitched laugh sliced through the air between them, cutting off Rafe's words. The sound was far away and yet still too close. It came from somewhere outside. The unmistakable cackle could only come from one person—Ursa.

Rafe and Hedley turned toward the vacant doorway of the carriage house. That sickeningly familiar laugh filled Hedley with dread. Her sister had returned. There was no telling what news she brought in so short an absence.

Stepping outside, the sun shone brightly, high above them. It was afternoon now, yet when they'd stepped inside it had still been morning. Two or more hours had passed. Yet now, it seemed so fleeting. And in that time, so much had changed, but not everything for the better.

Leaving one problem behind and heading into another, Hedley followed the path toward the rear of Greyson Park.

Rafe placed a hand on her arm, stopping her. "Don't rush in when you have no notion of what you'll find."

"I'm not afraid anymore," she said and looked pointedly into his gaze. "Not of anything."

He didn't respond, but she heard him all the same. *Not you, Hedley.* He'd said those words with such vehemence that she'd realized he would rather have *anyone else* admit to loving him.

What had seemed like a perfectly natural progression of love and desire moments ago, now—after Rafe's rejection— made her wonder if she'd imagined more between them than was actually possible. At least for him. Essentially, he was telling her that he wasn't in love with her. Then again, how could he love the sister of the woman who'd left him at the altar? How could he love the woman who stood in his way of owning Greyson Park?

The simple—the *sane*—answer was that he couldn't.

She was, after all, a Sinclair and a reputed lunatic, kept locked away for her own good. And he'd been with her in the carriage solely to help her. Foolishly, she'd believed down in her very soul that there had been more between them.

*Not you, Hedley.*

Just then, Mr. Tims rushed through the kitchen doorway. For the first time, she felt a little conspicuous about her appearance. Looking down, she wondered if the wrinkles in her dress were indicative of what she'd done with Rafe in the carriage, or if they looked like perfectly innocent wrinkles. Was there such a thing as a *wanton* wrinkle? If there were, she was certain to have them all over her.

Out of breath and hunched over, the caretaker stopped in front of Hedley and Rafe. "I tried to stop them. Couldn't find you."

Swallowing down a sudden rise of shyness, she made an absent gesture to Rafe and hoped that his clothes were in order—though she dare not look directly at the fall of his breeches for fear of drawing attention. "Mr. Danvers was kind enough to escort me back from Fallow Hall."

"Your sister and her husband are here, making a mess of things," Mr. Tims said, apparently not concerned that Rafe had escorted her and that she had wanton wrinkles on her dress. Likely, he didn't imagine Rafe could love her either.

Hedley pushed aside those maudlin thoughts and focused on the matter at hand. Ursa and Mr. Cole were here and *making a mess* of Greyson Park. Knowing her sister, the path of destruction would be great.

Turning to Rafe, she met his gaze with surprising calm. "Thank you for your generosity, sir. I must bid you *good day* as I have family matters to attend."

Rafe gave her a hard look before he addressed Mr. Tims. "What has happened?"

"They arrived not long ago, but Mr. Cole brought a maul the size of his head," the caretaker said, mopping his brow with a red kerchief. "They bashed in the cellar door and searched every inch, looking for that treasure. I tried to stop them before they made more holes than Greyson Park can stand. There was an awful groaning of the house when they left the cellar. Now, they've worked their way up to the main floor, but the rest won't be long, I'm sure. Miss, I warn you, it's a frightful sight."

Hedley ran past Mr. Tims and rushed in through the kitchen doorway but stopped at the edge. A sob escaped her before she could stifle it. Her kettle and the rest of her cups were smashed on the floor, the chest of tea crushed. The larder door had been broken. It hung awkwardly by a single iron hinge.

"I'm going to kill that bastard," Rafe said from behind her. "Hedley, go to Fallow Hall, and I'll see to this."

"No. *I* will see to it. This is my home…for the time being." At least, she hoped it was. However, there was no telling what Ursa had discovered. Hedley might very well be homeless this instant.

Rafe stepped in front of her, blocking her view of the destruction. Lifting his hand, he tilted her chin up until she looked at him. "No matter what you might think, we are in this together. I won't let you face this—or anything—alone."

A beautiful sentiment, but they both knew the truth.

Before she allowed her heart to turn slushy, she reminded herself that the only reason he said this was because of her promise to go to London on his behalf. This was about Greyson Park and his legacy. Nothing more.

A crash sounded from deeper in the house. Without a word between them, Hedley and Rafe took the steps in tandem until they stood in the archway of the parlor.

Hedley covered her mouth with her hand. The fireplace mantel lay in ruins on the floor. The hearth was missing a few stones. Her stiff-backed chairs lay in broken pieces on the floor. The sofa she'd painstakingly stuffed with new straw and reupholstered was now listed to one side, the curved wooden legs missing. And the low table was nothing more than a heaping pile of splinters.

Ursa clapped with glee as Mr. Cole reared back, prepared to take another swing.

Rafe charged in and grabbed the handle of the iron-headed maul. As it arched over Mr. Cole's head, Rafe ripped it from his grasp. "Destroy one more thing, Cole, or even knock a loose pebble with the toe of your boot, and this hammer will find your head."

"That belongs to me," Cole barked, shoving Rafe with his barrel chest. "Whoever you are, you have no rights here."

Rafe shoved back. "I have every right!"

"That is where you are wrong, Mr. Danvers," Ursa spat.

Mr. Cole folded his arms over his chest and smirked. "Danvers, eh? I've heard about you. Say, you'd better put down that hammer before you hurt yourself."

"Be careful, darling." Ursa smiled and sauntered over to slip her arm through her husband's. "The mad have difficulty understanding reason. You may be forced to prove your point by humiliating him."

Hammer in hand, Rafe strode across the room to stand beside Hedley. "This is your sister's home. You've no right to destroy it."

Ursa didn't even bother to look at her. "That simple creature standing there has not reached her majority and therefore is still beneath her family's care. Greyson Park, whatever is left of it, also belongs to the Sinclairs. Which is my family, Mr. Danvers, not yours. And not your concern."

"You call destroying Greyson Park taking care of your family? You wouldn't understand the meaning of it." He turned to Hedley and said in a low whisper, "I am at your command. If you want me to throw them out, I will."

Startled that he would ask her permission, as if he truly did see Greyson Park as hers, her heart gave into a poignant squish. "Thank you, but no. I will show them out."

Ursa scoffed. "How dare you suggest such a thing. We don't need to be shown out by you. I meant what I said—though you may not be able to understand it—you hold no true right over Greyson Park."

"Then prove it. In writing. I should like to see the document that erased my inheritance," Hedley challenged. She'd learned quite a bit in the recent weeks and had a fair understanding of the society to which her sister belonged. And that there were rules to follow. "What if the *ton* were to discover how the Sinclairs have treated a member of their own family? Think of the scandal."

"No one even knows about you." Ursa released a haughty laugh and dismissed Hedley with a flick of her fingers before addressing Rafe. "And if you have thoughts of interfering, you might want to abandon those as well. After all, do you imagine, even for a moment, that society would believe a Danvers over a Sinclair? Why concern yourself with such a property, for that matter? I'd never understood why you wanted this estate in the first place. But when I heard the story of treasure, I realized that it *must* be true."

Now, Rafe laughed, a low, hollow sound as he shook his head. "You believed the story of treasure, because I'd asked to have Greyson Park as part of your dowry? You've given me much credence. The truth is far simpler. This estate once belonged to my family. I'd merely wanted to return it to its proper ownership."

"All this time and at such lengths." Ursa clucked her tongue. "Do you take me for a fool?"

"Perhaps." Rafe shrugged. "After all, how can it say much for your wits if you've spent any time at all believing the ravings of a Danvers? We are all quite mad, Mrs. Cole."

That statement seemed to hit the mark. Ursa blinked. Her smug grin fell. "Are you saying...that there is nothing here? No treasure?"

Rafe set the hammer on the floor and rested the handle against the doorframe. "Am I so mad that I wouldn't have absconded with it by now?"

It was almost comical to see how dejected Ursa looked in that moment. Her steadfast Mr. Cole settled an arm around her as she turned into his embrace with a sniff. "No treasure."

Hedley stepped forward, trying not to be envious of the familiarity her sister and her husband openly shared. "That leaves the matter of Greyson Park. If it is as you say, and I am still beneath my family's care, then who will repair the damage you have inflicted on my home?"

Ursa lifted her face—one completely devoid of tears—and narrowed her eyes. The hatred within those black pools was palpable. "We both know that the only part of you that is a true Sinclair is the ink on the register of your baptism. Greyson Park, and its inhabitant, is of no real concern to the family."

"Unless of course you had something to gain," Hedley replied, her voice faltering. She looked down at the toes of her red shoes, feeling invisible for the first time in weeks. She had no family. No clothes of her own. And the man she loved did not want her.

"Hmm…No. Not even then." On the arm of Mr. Cole, Ursa crossed the room and swept past Hedley and Rafe. At the front door, she paused to issue one more cutting remark. "You have never been anything other than a burden to all of us. It's a shame that you weren't the one who died in the carriage accident that day. But I suspect you know that."

In two strides, Rafe crossed the foyer and slammed the door closed behind them. The action made Hedley aware of the hole in the center of the door. Through it, she could see Ursa climb into her carriage and Mr. Cole follow. Gradually, the driver set off, and soon there was nothing to see, other than the ironical brightness of the sun during such a dark moment.

Returning to her, Rafe drew her against him, wrapping his arms around her and stroking her back. "What she said about the accident, pay no heed. Your sister enjoys tormenting people."

*But it was true.* Hedley allowed herself to enjoy his embrace for a minute before she pulled away and walked toward the center of the parlor. Kneeling down, she began to put the pieces of her table into one pile.

Rage scorched Rafe. The heat of it filled his stomach and chest as if he himself were a furnace hot enough to melt sand and soda ash into glass. He'd never been this furious in his life. He'd never felt such complete and utter hatred. Not even when Ursa had left him at the altar. And not even when Lord and Lady Fitzherbert had given his father the cut direct.

This was new to him, and he didn't know what to do with this all-encompassing need to right all the wrongs that had been done to Hedley. Including what *he* had done. Some of his anger was directed at himself for how he'd left things unsaid between them. And that he'd missed his opportunity to tell her when they'd been in the carriage house.

Now, with the ruin of the parlor all around them, he knew it was the wrong time to unburden the tumult of emotions burning through him. In this moment, it shocked him to realize that he would sacrifice anything for her. Everything.

Yet still, that rage was inside him, roiling together with a love so raw and powerful that it frightened him.

Rafe paced from the parlor to the foyer, his breathing audible, as if he'd finished running up and down the stairs a dozen times. "I will fix this, Hedley. Greyson Park will outshine any manor in Lincolnshire. I'll make a chandelier for every room, dripping with crystals. I'll—"

"No, you won't," she interrupted and stood to face him. "You've done nothing to destroy Greyson Park, and it isn't your place—or in my best interest—for you to fix it. I will have Mr. Tims drive me to London, where I'll meet with the family's solicitor so that I can see what my rights are. Afterward, I will meet with your antiquarian society and make sure that the Danvers family gets complete credit for the legacy that is here. I assume it is in the locked attic?"

"It is." But the legacy was the last thing on his mind. Rafe raked a hand through his hair. "You cannot stay here."

"I will call upon Calliope this afternoon," she acquiesced. "But not yet. I plan to stay here for a while. And I should hurry. Mr. Tims is likely waiting for me in the cellar to see what can be salvaged."

*I plan to stay here for a while.* In other words—*alone.*

Yet he understood her need to remain. This was her home. And he was going to help her reclaim it, any way he could. He was sure to find laborers in the village.

Rafe hesitated, one foot pointing toward her and the other toward the door. He didn't want to leave her. "Not long," he said, already worried about her being here without him.

She offered a short nod, her expression full of a determination that rivaled his own.

## CHAPTER EIGHTEEN

**R**equiring an outlet or else running the risk of truly going mad, Rafe headed for the market. His first stop was Lynch & Twyck, where he paid nearly four pounds for a perfume cask that contained six bottles and no stoppers. He could have haggled, he supposed, but the truth was, he would have paid any price. Hedley's needs, her happiness, and her hopes were his priority now, and he respected her enough to give her the space she required.

Leaving that shop, he went directly to the laundress. As was his usual arrangement with the widow, he walked to the back door.

**B**y the time Hedley and Mr. Tims sorted through the rubble that was once the cellar, she realized that her dream of living here at Greyson Park was just that…a dream.

There was no way she could come back from this level of destruction and rebuild. She had little enough money for food, let alone repairs of this magnitude. Besides that, who would do the work? Mr. Tims? Right now the caretaker was wheezing as he made his way up the cellar stairs.

While she might have been insane enough to believe that Rafe could have loved her despite her family, she was not going to delude herself about Greyson Park. Not any longer.

Brushing the dirt from her once-beautiful muslin dress, she drew in a breath of resolve and hoped it would help her keep the heartache inside. "Mr. Tims, there is nothing for us here. Nothing of the cellar can be salvaged, and I fear that the foundation walls are crumbled to the point of being unsafe."

"Right you are, m'girl. I fear for this old place. Without a foundation beneath this corner, there's no telling what might happen next." His dust-roll eyebrows flanked his sorrowful gaze. "Perhaps it would be better if you stayed with your friends at Fallow Hall until something can be done."

Nothing could be done—not by her, anyway. She exchanged a look with Mr. Tims, who seemed to share the sentiment. "Before I go, would you allow me to fix you a pot of tea in your cottage and perhaps share a cup with you?"

He reached out and patted her hand. "I'd be honored."

They both knew this would be the last time.


Rafe placed the coin in the widow Richardson's waiting palm. "I'll be sending a footman for soda ash in the future."

"You've said but two words in the same number of minutes since your arrival. Won't you come inside for a proper greeting and then stay for a fare-thee-well?"

Rafe shook his head but smiled to soften the refusal. Their affair had been the longest one he'd had thus far. There'd been no expectations. No promises. No pretense. Just two people who enjoyed physical pleasure. During all that time, it had been enough. Now, he realized, he wanted more. He wanted what Rathburn and his sister had found, and what Everhart had discovered.

"As a fellow hunter, I would not wish to make an enemy of your new husband," he said to her. "The butcher is a good man. I hope you find contentment with him."

"Listen to you," the widow said in a singsong manner. "Since when do you care about contentment? I thought such rubbish beneath you, but now"—she tilted her head to the side to study him—"you look like a man in love."

Rafe laughed. He wasn't *in love*. What he felt for Hedley was too intense and raw to be compared with a mundane, flowery sentiment. The blistering, roiling mass of emotion that filled his entire body was a great deal more than love. It went soul deep. So deep, in fact, that he knew he could not draw another breath on this earth unless Hedley was part of it.

"Pity that," the widow said on a sigh and let her gaze roam over his form. "But if you change your mind..."

"I won't."

She sighed again. "No. You're not the type who does."

After her lengthy visit with Mr. Tims, which included preparing a stew for his dinner, Hedley went back into Greyson Park to gather a few items of clothing. When she returned, however, she saw that the kitchen door was opened. It had been closed before, hadn't it? Then again, how could a broken door remain closed?

Thinking that it was nothing more than the wind, she went inside.

Hedley knew she could not live at Greyson Park, nor could she return to Sinclair House. And she *would not* impose upon her friends at Fallow Hall. Walking up the stairs that now creaked and groaned beneath each step, her options felt limited and restricting. It wasn't until she reached the top that she realized what she *could* do.

She still planned on going to London to meet with her solicitor and also with the gentlemen from the Society. So why not look for employment while she was there? A large city must have hundreds of opportunities. While the village here had wanted only an experienced *modiste*, she was certain there must be shops that could use her skills.

And then perhaps…

Hedley stopped cold when she reached the door to her bedchamber. This door had been knocked off its hinge as well. The trunk that Calliope had sent over with the day dresses and underclothes lay open. Torn strips of pastel muslin draped over the sides of the portmanteau and littered the floor. Even the plum-colored walking dress lay in shreds. Ursa had been here as well.

Staggering into the room, Hedley reached out with one hand as the other held back a choking cry. "I thought they hadn't gotten this far. I thought they'd only destroyed the downstairs."

Thoughts like that were pointless now. It was obvious that Ursa and Mr. Cole had come upstairs. *Upstairs—*

Hedley whipped around and rushed into the hall, sprinting around the corners until she reached the short stairway leading to the attic door. Rafe's legacy was the only thing on her mind.

At the top of a short staircase, the attic door was open. Nails protruded from the doorframe where it had once been fastened to the door. Beyond it, she could only see darkness. An icy chill slithered over her skin, making her feel clammy and cold.

She hated attics.

Still, she held her ground at the base of the stairs. The need to make sure Rafe's legacy hadn't been destroyed overrode her desire to turn and walk away. After a peek down at her shoes for courage and a quick check of her hair to ensure that all her pins were in place, she mounted the stairs.

At the top, she was careful to stay away from the nail tips surrounding the frame. She was wearing the only dress she had left and would need it in order to go to London. Which seemed an absurd preoccupation when her pulse was pounding in her ears, and she couldn't draw a full breath.

Once she'd left Sinclair House, she'd sworn never to return to an attic. And now, here she was, standing alone in the darkest room of Greyson Park. In the light that reached her from the hall at her back, she couldn't see any ruin or objects laid to waste on the floor. In fact, the floor was quite tidy, albeit dusty. There wasn't any furniture up here, or crates, or anything. Whatever had been here was gone now. *Oh, Rafe. I'm so sorry.*

"I knew you'd find your way here, simpleton," Ursa hissed from the hall behind her.

Hedley turned with a jolt to see her sister looming in the hall outside the attic. "I thought you were gone. I thought you'd given up the idea of the treasure."

"And take your word for it?" she scoffed, coming up the stairs. Closer. The tapping of her shoes echoed around them. "Mr. Cole and I drove nearly halfway back to my aunt's before I realized that you probably wouldn't know the treasure if you were sitting on it every single day. As you can see, we were very thorough this time."

Hedley held her breath. "Did you find something, then?"

"No. You and your poor excuse for a home are still every bit as disappointing." Ursa had the audacity to reach out and brush dust from the edge of Hedley's shoulder.

Hedley swatted her hand away. She'd had enough. She'd *endured* enough over the years. And after making new friends and seeing how they treated each other and how they treated her, she knew she deserved better. Hedley had allowed Mother, Ursa, and everyone at Sinclair House to look through her. She'd allowed herself to become invisible. No longer.

"Not nearly as disappointing as you."

"*What* did you say?" Ursa asked, enunciating every syllable. Her eyes narrowed, and her nose wrinkled as if her entire face had been pinched.

"You are not the only one who has longed for a different sister," Hedley confessed. "If I had been given the choice between having a sister like you or being locked away in an attic for the rest of my life, I never would have chosen you."

"Why you little ingrate! If it wasn't for me, you never would have had any clothes. Not to mention a nice *easy* life at Sinclair House. I'm the one who talked Mother out of sending you away to a workhouse. If I hadn't reminded her of the fact that you might reveal your family to other people and risk exposure to us, then you wouldn't even be here. You should be thanking me."

Her sister's tone sounded accusatory. It was almost comical, in a way that reminded Hedley of what she'd said to Rafe about the laundress...

Then it hit Hedley—a long-awaited epiphany. "You were *jealous*. All this time, and I never understood until this moment. You were jealous of me and all the attention I'd received."

"From having fits? Hardly." Ursa offered her best glare.

"No, from before then," Hedley corrected. "Although it has been many years since, I do recall Mother brushing my hair and telling me that it was bright as sunshine." That had been one of the only moments of kind attention she'd ever offered.

Her sister's mouth parted on a gasp. "You were her disgrace. Her punishment. You didn't look like us. And soon, it was obvious. Then, after the accident, everyone knew it too."

"And you never let her forget it." Hedley felt pity for her sister and for the jealousy that had taken over her life. "I'm sorry, Ursa. I'm sorry that you never liked yourself enough. One thing I can say—after years of my own company—is that I do like myself. And I don't need fancy clothes or money to tell me what I'm worth."

Ursa reached out to shove her, but Hedley grabbed her wrists and batted them down. Appalled, Ursa backed away. "I hate you. I've hated you since the moment you were born. The riding instructor's basta—"

Ursa's insult carried out on a cry as she tripped over the train of her dress. Losing her balance, she stumbled backward toward the stairs.

Hedley stepped forward, reaching out. At the last moment, Ursa's hand clasped the doorknob. She flailed with one arm while the other held fast to the door until it slammed shut with force enough to shake the floor.

On the other side of the door, Ursa landed with an audible thump. At first, it sounded as if she was crying, but then the sound turned into unmistakable laughter.

"You get your wish after all, simpleton. The doorknob broke." She cackled. "At last, I've managed to grab a piece of Greyson Park that I will cherish forever."

Frantic, Hedley fell to her knees in front of the door. Automatically, she withdrew two pins from her hair and clumsily pushed them into the keyhole. Years ago, when she'd learned how best to use her hairpins, she'd vowed never to be locked in an attic again.

"Ursa, don't you dare leave me here."

Her sister's laugh receded down the hall.

The insistent thrumming of Hedley's heartbeat rushed in her ears. This wasn't happening. Not again. She refused to be powerless.

Hands damp and clammy, she turned the knob. But it fell apart in her hands. Looking down at it, helpless tears blurred her vision.

Rafe left Frit on the far side of the path leading to Greyson Park. Even though Hedley had started a fine leg of her journey to conquering her fears, he didn't want to push her by having his horse too near. She knew her own mind, and she would tell him when she was ready for another encounter with Frit.

Now that he'd settled a few matters within himself, he needed to apologize for how he'd left things between them.

He should have told her everything. Instead, he'd made her believe that he wanted her to marry Montwood.

Rafe would never allow that to happen.

On his way to the front door, Mr. Tims hailed him from the small cottage at the edge of the property, and Rafe altered his course.

"Miss Sinclair thought it best to stay at Fallow Hall for a time," the caretaker said before coughing into a red kerchief. "Greyson Park was in bad shape before, but now it's *unsafe*. The walls in the cellar have crumbled, and that *Mr. Cole* put too many holes in the rest of house."

Rafe nodded in agreement. "I've inquired in the village, and there are many laborers who would appreciate the employment. If I'm able to persuade the owner of the house to accept the offer for assistance, that is."

"She's a might stubborn, that one," Mr. Tims said fondly, smiling.

Rafe grinned as well. "That she is, though I hope to return to you on the morrow with good news for Greyson Park and its neighbor."

Then, with a final glance at the façade of the house, Rafe whistled for Frit, ready to head to his workshop to complete the gift he had in mind for Hedley. He needed to begin right away if he wanted to present it to her before nightfall.

And then, he hoped to lose a sizable wager...but gain so much more.

*This is only fear*, Hedley told herself. *Fear can be overcome.* It was time to face it like she had the others.

And yet, with each creak and groan of house around her, those words didn't bolster her confidence. She set the knob back in place, hoping that if she placed it just so, the door would open.

It didn't. Over and over, she tried. She was determined, after all. But each attempt earned her the same result. That was when she noticed the nail tips protruding from the door. Apparently, when Ursa had fallen, the force of the slamming door had buried the nails into the wood once more.

Still, Hedley refused to give up. In the very least, someone would hear her calling out. Someone would notice her.

She didn't want to be invisible again.

## CHAPTER NINETEEN

**R**afe whistled down the stairs, his steps light. It had taken the better part of the day, but he'd managed to finish the gift for Hedley. He hoped she liked it. More than that, he hoped she loved it...and loved him still.

Giving the cask a pat for good luck, he strolled into the map room for a drink before dinner. Montwood was already at the sideboard, pouring three glasses, and Boris lay in front of the fire.

"What tune is that?" Montwood asked, turning to hand him a whiskey. His jaw was no longer swollen, but a faint purplish bruise lingered.

Rafe lowered the cask to the table and took the drink with a shrug. "Just a random melody."

The cardsharp studied him. "You're inordinately happy for someone who is about to lose a wager."

And so he was, Rafe thought with a grin.

"Did I hear mention of someone losing the wager?" Everhart asked from the doorway, escorting his bride on his arm. "Do you see, my love, these matters tend to sort themselves out."

"I never doubted it for a moment." Calliope beamed, her gaze alighting on Rafe and then down to the box on the table. She let out a pleased gasp. "It's Hedley's cask. I'm so glad you purchased it. That horrible Mr. Lynch refused to give her a mere crown she'd asked for it, but only gave her half."

"I paid considerably more, though I would not wish her to know." Rafe kept his voice down and looked past Calliope and Everhart toward the doorway. "Where is she, by the way?"

Calliope gave him an odd look. "At Greyson Park, I imagine."

"No, that is not possible." He shook his head, lowering the glass to the table. They were teasing him, surely. But as he looked around, he saw no mockery. "She is supposed to be here. Did she not pay a call?"

"No," Calliope said. "Valentine made no mention of her arrival when we saw him a moment ago."

It did not make sense. Hedley should be here. "Mr. Tims said she'd come here."

"Is something the matter?"

"Her sister and brother-in-law destroyed much of Greyson Park today. The house is unsafe. Are you saying that she never came here?" Panic surged through his heart, yet he felt sluggish and weighted. Rafe headed for the door, though he felt as if he were walking through waist-high mud. *Please, don't let it be true.*

Calliope clutched his arm. "She did not. Where do you think she could be?"

"The house."

"If Greyson Park is unsafe," Montwood said from beside him, "then we must hurry."

Boris let out a yawp and leapt to his feet. He was out the door before any of them. Everhart called out instructions to Valentine. Montwood headed for the stables for Quicksilver and Frit. Rafe started running.

The mire of dread within him gave way to terror and added an urgency to his strides that he'd never known before. Rafe raced across the acreage that separated their estates.

He whistled for Frit. By the time he was halfway there, his horse was beside him. Taking hold of his mane, he leapt onto his back. Montwood was a close second.

"Everhart and Calliope are bringing a carriage, just in case!" Montwood shouted.

By now, they all knew of Hedley's fear, so the *just in case* would mean that they expected the direst of circumstances. Or perhaps they were hoping against it, as he was. They all loved Hedley. In such a short time she'd become part of their small family.

Greyson Park was dark. No smoke came from the chimney. The final glimmering light of day had disappeared beneath the horizon, leaving a faint purplish glow. He leapt off Frit and rushed to the door, kicking it open.

"Hedley!" He waited in the foyer for any answer. Any sound. But there was no response, only the creaking and groaning of the house. From what he could see, the small bench in the foyer was now broken in half, and there was a hole in the wall behind it, revealing the complete darkness beneath the stairs. Ursa and her husband must have returned to finish the job they'd started.

He cursed himself. He never should have left Hedley alone.

Montwood came in behind him and with an oath as well.

"Keep Calliope outside," Rafe said. "It isn't safe."

Boris tore into the house and howled. Running toward the stairs, Rafe followed him, more by memory than by sight. There was scant light, enough to see that a few of the treads had been smashed and the railing torn away.

Boris turned down a hall and then stopped, sniffing the floor. Rafe opened the door and saw a bedchamber in disarray. Hedley wasn't here. When he saw a trunk lying open, he realized that the mess around the room was the dresses from the crates at Fallow Hall. Now they littered the floor in torn scraps of fabric.

Ursa wouldn't be satisfied until she took everything from her sister. *Everything*…

"Hedley!" he shouted again, panic seizing his heart.

Montwood was just coming up the stairs, shielding a taper with his hand. "You don't think they took her, do you?"

"If they did, then I will need your help in covering up a murder."

Boris turned toward the hall, ears quirked. In the next instant, he tore off in a scraping of claws against the hardwood. Rafe ran after him.

The servants' passage had completely collapsed. The door splintered beneath the weight of the house.

Boris disappeared around the corner and released a low, mournful howl that turned Rafe's blood to ice. The dog pawed at the attic door. *The attic*…

The knob was missing, leaving a hole behind.

"Hedley!" Rafe pounded on the door. There was no answer. He rammed it with his shoulder. The door wouldn't budge. Of course, because he'd nailed it shut. Yet the fractured wood and a few exposed nail tips told him that someone had opened it recently.

Mad with desperation, he kicked in the door. It crashed open, hitting the wall behind it with a loud crack.

It was so dark that he didn't see her at first. Not until Montwood came behind him with the candle. And then, she was standing just inside the doorway, tears streaming down her face. The most beautiful face he'd ever seen. She was alive.

Rushing in, he hauled her against him. "I shouldn't have left. I'm so sorry, sweeting. It won't happen again. I won't let them take Greyson Park. They might believe they've destroyed it, but I'll repair it brick by brick." He would stand guard outside each day to make sure she was safe. He would never let them hurt her again.

"They won't come back," Hedley rasped, her voice nothing more than a raw breath. Lifting her hand to her throat, she tapped her fingertips against it. "Lost my voice...calling for you."

He pressed his lips to her forehead to keep her from seeing the hot moisture stinging his eyes. She'd been calling for him, and he'd failed her.

Never again. "Then I'll make sure that I'm never more than a whisper away," he vowed.

She smiled at that, as if she thought he was teasing. He was prepared to correct her, but not with Montwood behind them. Even then, Rafe refused to let her go.

Montwood paused at the nails protruding from the doorframe. "What have they done—I'm going to kill them."

Not if Rafe got to them first.

Hedley shook her head and let out something of a laugh as she lifted her hand for Montwood. "Not...worth it."

"Don't speak, sweeting. Save your voice." Rafe had an important question for her...but it would have to wait until she could put this behind her. He didn't want to overwhelm her.

She offered him a look of *it's too late for that.*

And together they left for Fallow Hall.

After one of the longest days of her life and a soak in a steaming tub at Fallow Hall, Hedley donned a night rail and wrapper before curling up in the soft blue chair by the fire. She stared at the flames licking over the logs on the iron grate. While the heat of the fire touched her face and hands, it didn't penetrate deep down inside her where she felt coldest.

Rafe's words haunted her. *"I won't let them take Greyson Park. They might believe they've destroyed it, but I'll repair it brick by brick."*

His main concern was Greyson Park. Of course, she'd known that all along. He'd never hidden it from her. So it made sense that he wanted to repair it and preserve his legacy. She understood his reasons. Especially now that she had seen, with her own eyes, what he strived so hard to keep safe.

Yet foolishly, her heart broke, knowing that he cared more for the house than he did for her.

Earlier, after trying for hours to open the attic door, she'd gone about searching the room as thoroughly as she could, hoping to find a secret panel that would lead her to a servants' staircase. Unfortunately, she'd found nothing of the sort.

It wasn't until the sun reached the west side of the house that she noticed the peculiar colored light slipping through windows. She'd thought they'd been boarded up. And they had...but not—as she assumed—for a lack of a window. No, they had been concealed on purpose.

Using all her strength, Hedley had managed to slip her fingers between the window casing and the warped board, where a nail had worked loose. With a screech of wood and metal, she'd succeeded. And then she stared, dumbfounded, at what she'd revealed.

Beautiful stained glass in a prism of bold, rich colors. A scene depicting a white-winged seraph placing a golden crown atop a bearded man's head formed the center. Beneath it, letters spelled out *Edward the Confessor*. In that instant, she knew this was Rafe's legacy. This window had once been part of King Henry III's Painted Chamber. And what a legacy it was. His family were respected artisans, so valued that their work had been preserved all this time.

Now, it was a matter of proving it. Whether or not her love was unrequited, what mattered most to her was ensuring that Rafe's ultimate goal was realized.

A soft knock sounded on the door before Calliope peered inside. "I hoped to catch you before you went to sleep."

"I'm not likely to do that for some time. I'm too relieved to be here, among friends, to close my eyes"—*and return to the darkness*—"just yet." She tried to suppress a shiver.

Calliope smiled as if in understanding. "You've been through a terrible ordeal, which is why I thought you could use a little cheer."

Hedley blinked several times as she watched her friend lift a familiar rosewood box into view.

"My grandmother's cask?" Her voice was still nothing more than a rasp. "But how did you—I hope you did not let that Mr. Lynch cajole you into paying a full crown for that, or I should be very cross. No matter how fond I am of you for the gesture."

"It wasn't me," Calliope said, beaming with a secret smile as she placed it on Hedley's lap. "It was Danvers. And I hope you don't mind, but I peeked inside."

Inside? Hedley stroked the fine wood grain before she lifted the tiny latch. Her breath caught in her throat. Six perfume bottles *with* stoppers. And not just any stoppers but beautiful crystal-clear glass that caught the firelight. Each one was in shape of a carnation.

"They're...exquisite." She touched the delicate blossoms gently with her fingertips, marveling over the detail, down to the clustered centers where the petals folded against one another.

"They're his finest creation so far, in my opinion." Calliope stood beside her, resting a hand on Hedley's shoulder as they both gazed into the cask. "Then again, I believe artists create their finest works when inspiration comes from love."

Hedley nodded absently. "He does love his work and rightfully so."

"No, silly. You," Calliope corrected with a laugh. "You are his inspiration. Surely you knew that already. Anyone can see it."

That cold sadness spread through her. *Not you, Hedley...* "He may care for me, but he loves Greyson Park."

"My dear sweet friend," Calliope said as she patted her shoulder. "Remember, a gentleman's heart is much simpler to understand if you listen to the things he *doesn't* say."

## Chapter Twenty

Hedley needed to know if Calliope was right. She needed to know if Rafe truly loved her, or if Greyson Park was still between them.

Later that night, Hedley opened the bedchamber door. Preoccupied, she didn't expect to find Boris in the hall. Sitting up, he tilted his head and wagged his tail, as if he'd been patiently waiting for her. She reached out and scratched him behind the ears. "You are a matchmaker, aren't you?"

He answered with a low *woof*.

"If that is true, then you are waiting outside the wrong door." She already knew her own heart. Now it was a matter of discovering what was in Rafe's.

As if he understood her perfectly, Boris stood and traipsed down the hall without even bothering to look back to see if she followed.

A moment later, she was standing at Rafe's door. She gave Boris one last pat before sending him on his way. Then, drawing in a deep breath, she turned the knob.

Rafe was sitting against the dark headboard of a massive bed, his knee elevated beneath a dark green coverlet. His shoulders, arms, and chest were bare, and he held a glass of amber liquid halfway to his mouth. But it remained there, arrested, as his gaze met hers.

"Hedley." Her name came out on a breath. His chest rose and fell like a bellows igniting a fire.

"I don't want you to speak. I want to be able to hear what you're *not* saying." With a shake of her head, she pressed her index finger to her lips and backed up against the door until she heard the soft click of the latch. "Unless you want me to go..."

She waited for what seemed like an eternity. Trepidation rose, causing her to tremble. Then, Rafe slid his free hand down to pull back a corner of the bedclothes for her.

It was all the invitation she needed. Now, something other than trepidation made her tremble. Yet somehow she managed to walk across the chamber. His gaze never left her. It roamed over her unbound hair. It followed her hands as she slid the wrapper from her shoulders. Then it turned dark as she bent to pull the hem of her night rail over her head.

She let the gauzy cotton drop to the floor and stood before him, naked. His breathing was audible, his lips parted. The night air caused her nipples to draw tight. When he swallowed, his Adam's apple rose and dipped in his throat. It was the same way her stomach felt, only hers settled much lower. She pressed a hand below her navel and took the remaining steps to the bed.

She was taking all of this as a good sign. He hadn't told her to leave. Not only that, but that glass was still paused halfway to his mouth. Reaching out, she covered his fingers with hers and drew the glass to her own lips.

The sip was cool, but burned all the way down her throat, warming her stomach. She wondered if that was the reason he drank it—because he'd felt cold all the way to his marrow too. If so, then she sought to remedy that.

When she released his hand, Rafe drank the last swallow before setting it down on the bedside table. The folded corner of the coverlet exposed the lean, sinewy length of his body, from his shoulder all the way to his knee. He wasn't wearing a stitch of clothing.

She'd already seen him in nothing but his breeches. Now, she would see him without even those. A wanton thrill shot through her. "I'm going to make love to you," she said as her fingers curled around the edge of the green velvet. "But first, I want to see you."

Rafe groaned in the same moment that she stripped away the bedclothes. Likely, she should lift her gaze to his face and inquire about the source of his groan. But at the moment, she couldn't. He was put together in such a way that…well, she never would have expected a man to look so…so *hard* everywhere. The dark hair covering his chest and tapering down into a line along his abdomen did nothing to make him appear softer—even though she knew from experience that those hairs were soft. Yet they were deceptive, because his chest and abdomen were as hard as fieldstone.

She imagined the same could be true of the thick shaft of flesh jutting up from the thatch of dark hair between his thighs and laying in column toward his navel. While she had seen his flesh exposed and in his grip—had even felt it prod against her—her attention had been more on the euphoria she'd experienced in the moments before, when his mouth had been on her.

She let out a shuddered breath. Just the thought of it made her feel warm and damp. Raking her teeth over her lip, she slid her fingertips over the mattress, following the indentation of his body. Would he feel the same type of euphoria if she put her mouth on him? As if his thick flesh had heard her thought, it leapt up in a quick nod.

Listening to what Rafe's actions were saying, Hedley climbed onto the bed. On her knees, she faced him. His eyes were dark and intense, but she saw more than desire. She knew there was more between them.

"I love you, no matter what you choose to believe," she whispered. When he opened his mouth to respond, she silenced him with a kiss. A low sound rumbled in his throat. The warm caress of his lips beneath hers, the rapid pounding of his heart beneath her palms gave her the only answer she needed.

His hands threaded through the waves of her unbound hair, holding her close. He breathed her in and welcomed her tongue past his lips. Falling against him, her breasts pressed against his chest as her hands splayed over the breadth of his shoulders. This was where she belonged, here with him. His kiss warmed her far more than any sip of whiskey could.

She settled over him, half draping her body over his and half straddling him. The scorching length of that column pulsed against her stomach. This position reminded her of falling on him at Greyson Park that first day. Yet she far preferred having no ice beneath them and no clothes between them.

Feeling his thigh shift between hers made her want to move even closer. Lifting her knee, she shifted and straddled him in earnest. He groaned anew.

His hands found her hips and guided her to slide against him as he arched upward. The kiss altered, heated. Her stomach dipped low, throbbing insistently. He was as hot as a glassmaker's furnace. When his hands cupped her breasts, and he rolled her taut nipples beneath his thumb and forefinger, she nearly convulsed as she had in the carriage. And she wanted to. But first, she wanted to taste him the way he'd tasted her.

She broke from his lips and trailed kisses down his throat, dipping her tongue into the hollow. He let out a ragged breath. His chest hair was soft against her lips. She breathed in his scent as her fingertips floated down those hard ridges…until she held that hot, unyielding column in her grasp. His hips arched off the bed.

Eager, she moved lower and wrapped her lips around the broad, fleshy tip. A low guttural groan tore from his throat. She took that as a good sign. He tasted slightly of salt and radiated heat. Against her tongue, smooth veins and ridges intrigued her, bidding her continued study down the length as far as she could go. Mouth watering, she swallowed, suckling him in the process. That earned her another groan. Tingling with pleasure, she hummed in response and repeated her actions.

Rafe's hands brushed the fall of hair away from her face. When she looked up at him and sucked harder, his hips rocked. Then, without warning, he lifted her away. Hauling her up his chest, he kissed her, breathing hard and heavy. "Hedley, I—"

She put her finger against his lips. "No words."

A devilish gleam lit his eyes as he grinned at her.

Slowly, deliberately, as if she'd issued some sort of challenge, he drew her finger into his mouth. A gasp escaped her when his tongue glided over her finger. She felt the sensation at the apex of her thighs.

Taking her hand, he sucked on each one of her fingers until she was panting and restless. She wanted to move her hips over him, but he held her still. Then, he lowered his mouth to her breast and did something with his tongue that made her body clench and quiver. She clutched his head. "Oh, Rafe—"

"No words," he said against her nipple and blew on it before he moved on to the other. At the same time, his hands shifted. Fingers on her hips, his thumbs slid between her thighs and stroked between her folds. The quivering that pulsed deep within her now centered on the mesmeric sweeping motions. She felt as if she were filled with molten glass. The heat inside her expanded and contracted, threatening to fracture. The pleasure overwhelmed her. Her head fell back. Her hips bucked, sliding against the length of him—

She shattered. Completely. Disobeying her own rule, she cried out his name over and over again as the euphoria washed through her.

And when at last she caught her breath, she was beneath him. Rafe gazed down at her with that dark fierceness she'd grown to love. Tenderly, he brushed the hair away from her face and kissed her. She felt every word he wasn't saying, and she believe them more than ever before.

He loved her.

This time when she felt the heat of him nudge the entrance of her body, she knew it wouldn't end abruptly. He wasn't going anywhere. Instead, he guided her knees up, one and then the other, and slowly wedged inside her.

The unexpected pain shocked her. Her breath caught. Her body tensed. All she knew of intimacies were the bawdy words she'd overheard from the servant girls in the kitchen at Sinclair House. She didn't recall any of them mentioning pain.

Rafe let out a staggered breath and went still, her pain mirrored in his gaze.

"It won't hurt anymore," he promised with another kiss, coaxing her to return to the fervor of a moment ago. But even if it remained painful, she would do it all over again, simply to feel him deep inside of her, filling and stretching her. They were one person now. Making love. Creating love. Breathing love with each breath they shared.

Gradually, he moved within her, withdrawing and then edging inside. The pain disappeared, leaving only the craving to have him fill her body again each time he withdrew. As if he knew, he began to thrust faster, plunging deeper until neither of them could catch their breath. Their mouths broke apart. Above her, Rafe held her gaze. She tried to hold his, but as the sensations grew stronger, she arched her neck, pressing her breasts against him and tilting her hips.

This time she was eager for the euphoria to wash through her. She craved it. Seeking it, she pressed her heels into the mattress and met his thrusts until she shattered once again. Rafe moved faster, drawing out her shudders, until his hips jerked hard. He went still, releasing a low guttural groan as a flood of heat filled her body.

He held her tightly, his cheek damp against hers. "No words," he breathed.

She smiled and pressed a kiss to his shoulder. Words weren't needed between them. He'd already told her everything.

## Chapter Twenty-One

The sound of the wind woke Hedley from a contented sleep. Lying in Rafe's arms was far better than any feather pillow or mattress. She could stay here, like this, forever. Closing her eyes to do just that, she sighed in utter bliss. His deep, rhythmic breaths stirred the hair on top of her head. And the hair on his chest tickled her nose.

It wasn't until she heard the growl of thunder that a sense of alarm grew within her. During the last storm, she hadn't heard it while inside Fallow Hall. This manor was quite sound and sturdy. Only within her beloved but ramshackle Greyson Park had she heard every breeze blowing through the windows and walls.

*The windows.* Instantly, she thought of Rafe's legacy.

No. Hedley had removed the boards from the windows. For all she knew, it was their only protection. Now, they were at risk of being destroyed by the wind—or worse.

*"I will rebuild it brick by brick..."*

But he wouldn't be able to replace his legacy. She had to do something.

She nudged Rafe. He didn't stir. Her second, third, and fourth attempts didn't wake him either. In fact, he was sleeping quite soundly.

Slipping out of bed, she found her night rail on the floor. However, seeing the parcel on a chair nearby, she decided it would be better to wear actual clothes, in case she encountered one of the servants.

Untying the strings, she dressed and then crossed the room once more to press a kiss to his mouth. Rafe slept on without a care. A flash of lightning revealed a devilish grin on his lips. She hoped he was dreaming of her.

Rafe was in the middle of a rather erotic dream of Hedley's berry-stained lips when a loud crash of thunder woke him. However, when he reached out to pull her to him, he found the bed empty.

Sitting up, the blankets fell to his lap, revealing the state the dream had put him in. Even so, the dream was nothing compared to the full sensual reality of Hedley. She loved him with a fierceness that rivaled his own. She held nothing back.

Looking around the room, he found it empty as well. There was no reason for alarm, he told himself. Likely she'd returned to her chamber in order to keep their secret from being discovered. But it wouldn't be a secret for long. He grinned. Peeling away the bedclothes, he decided that now was the perfect time to ask her—

Lightning flashed, illuminating a puddle of white on the floor. *Her night rail…* His pulse quickened. His gaze drifted to the chair to see the open parcel of clothes.

A rumble of thunder rattled the windows. Suddenly, he knew she wasn't in her chamber either.

Rafe tore out of bed, yanking on a shirt and breeches as he headed out. Down the hall and around the corner, he charged into her room.

She wasn't here. To be certain, he searched behind the dressing screen and the window alcove and—

Lightning flashed again, drawing his gaze out the window. Through the slashes of horizontal rain on the glass, he saw a shape moving across the lawn toward Greyson Park.

Hedley broke through the path between the trees. Wind and rain plastered her hair to her face. She was soaked, drenched to the soles of the red shoes. She'd donned them before leaving Fallow Hall. And now, they were in tatters, hanging off her feet, tripping her. She would have to leave them behind.

Lifting one foot and then the other was all it took to slip out of them. Her red shoes had been through so much with her. However, now they were beyond mending. Not only that, but she no longer needed them to feel visible. She knew who she was.

Looking straight ahead, she saw Greyson Park. The wind howled around her. Lightning illuminated the façade, revealing a broken parlor window with the brick casing crumbling around it. The house had shifted in the storm. A terrible groaning of timber roared from within it.

If she didn't hurry, she would be too late. Yet even now, she didn't know if she could save the windows in the attic. If Rafe hadn't been able to remove them without damaging them, then how could she?

Yet her inner drive and determination would not allow her to give up. If she had to, she would return to Fallow Hall for help.

"Hedley!"

She whipped around to see Rafe rushing up behind her. His shirt was transparent and molded to his body. He raked a hand through his hair, revealing the furrows on his brow. "What are you doing? You can't possibly go inside. Look at it."

"I have to, Rafe." She had to shout over the wind. When he started to shake his head, she lifted her hand to his face, brushing her fingertips over his cheek. "You don't understand. I removed the boards from the windows. Your treasure—*your legacy*—it isn't safe."

There wasn't time to argue. She turned to go, only to have him block her path again.

Taking her by the shoulders, Rafe hauled her to him. He pressed his lips against her temple. "Don't you know by now that you are my treasure, Hedley? Our children will be my legacy." Then he took her face in his hands, the rain peppering down on her cheeks. "I love you."

He didn't smile at all when he said it. Instead, his expression was fierce and raw. Hedley forgot about the rain, the wind, the treasure, and Greyson Park.

"You love me." Had she heard him correctly? But she knew she had. Still, she had to make sure. "What about the wager?"

"Devil take the wager."

She smiled. "But I'm supposed to marry Montwood."

"No." That fierceness of his grew even more intense. "You're supposed to marry me."

"Am I?"

Instead of answering, Rafe claimed her mouth in a kiss.

## EPILOGUE

*One month later*

Hedley pressed her cheek against the cool windowpane in her bedchamber at Fallow Hall. She felt hot and shivery at the same time, and her stomach churned most unpleasantly. "I do wish this travel sickness would end."

It wasn't fair that she was still feeling ill. They'd returned from London a few days ago.

"For your sake, I do too," Calliope said, rubbing small, comforting circles between her shoulders. "No bride wants to be ill during her own wedding breakfast. Of course, I was rather late arriving at mine. Everhart had the driver take us on a detour through the park."

At the wistful sound in her friend's voice, Hedley turned to catch Calliope blushing. "It must have been a lovely detour."

"It was, indeed." Her friend beamed and settled her hand over her middle, where a nearly imperceptible bulge resided. "Though we did marry in haste, and for good reason, I wouldn't have had it any other way."

"I wish Rafe and I had married in haste. Waiting for the bans to be read for three Sundays felt like an *eternity*." Hedley said the words with such exasperation that she felt her stomach roll over. She turned her face back to the windowpane. "*Ugh.*"

They'd spent more than two weeks in town, staying with Rafe's parents. And during that time, it had been impossible to find any time alone *together*.

At last, their separation was at an end. They were married in the village this morning. And if not for her queasiness, she would have sprinted down the aisle to him. He'd seemed just as eager when he'd taken her hand.

"*I'm glad you're here,*" he'd whispered.

She never would have let him stand at that altar alone. "*Did you doubt it?*"

"*Not for a single instant.*"

Hedley smiled at the lovely memory.

Right now, Rafe was below stairs with their guests—a small party that included his parents, Calliope's family, and Mr. Tims. Unfortunately, Montwood had had urgent business to attend, which kept him in London, but he sent his "*many felicitations*" in a missive, in addition to a gift for Hedley. Inside a slender box, a single white taper lay with a note that read:

> So that you will never endure the dark again.
>     Your friend forever and always,
>     M

It was a tender gesture, from a man she thought of as more brother than a mere friend, even in the short time of their acquaintance. While Rafe might feign jealousy and tease about being eager to have Montwood marry, Hedley knew her husband wanted Montwood's happiness just as much as she.

Calliope returned to rubbing her back in small circles. "You know, I've been thinking. When we first went to London, I don't recall you suffering from travel sickness. In fact, it started while we were already there."

At first, Hedley had imagined that it came from the lingering effects of her fears. But in truth, she no longer thought about that day in a way that seized her with panic. It was a memory now. A heartbreaking memory but nothing more.

"Likely because I was not used to the odors of London." Even thinking about the sewage and horse manure in the streets made her feel a bit green. She was certain her coloring in this moment did not complement her lovely pink satin gown. "If it wasn't for the many shops and shoes, I don't believe I'd want to return."

Hedley now possessed a great deal of shoes, and they all fit her perfectly. They came in an assortment of styles, from slippers to half boots, in a myriad of colors.

While they were away, they'd accomplished far more than shopping. Now that Greyson Park was in ruins, Mother no longer desired to have it as part of the Sinclair estate and had had the solicitor amend the stipulations of Hedley's inheritance. It was the most generous thing Mother had ever done for her.

Of course, with Hedley's name recognized in society, doubtless Mother wanted to save face. Nonetheless, now Hedley had her own property—one that would never revert to the Sinclairs.

As for Ursa, she was on a ship with Mr. Cole and likely wouldn't return for another six years or more. And for that, Hedley was grateful.

"But what if it isn't travel sickness at all," Calliope said in a whisper, even though they were the only two in the room. "What if it's another sickness altogether—"

The door of the bedchamber opened, and Calliope stopped speaking.

Celestine Danvers, Rafe's mother, bustled in with a tea tray. Her vivid cerulean blue gown stood out in sharp contrast against the red, brown, and silver tones of her hair but matched the vibrancy of her character. She was a whirlwind of brightness.

Without a word, she settled the tray on the foot of the bed, poured a splash of tea into a cup, added a generous amount of sugar, and then walked straight over to Hedley. "Drink this, my dear, and you'll feel more like yourself again."

Hedley hated to refuse her, but the thought of putting anything in her mouth seemed like a dire mistake. "I'm not certain I should. At the moment, I'm rather…" She dare not finish.

"We Danverses have a bit of a sweet tooth." Celestine smiled and reached up to tuck a lock of hair behind Hedley's ear. "And I suspect that you are, now, even more of a Danvers than you are aware."

"I'm not sure I know what you—" Hedley's words cut off when her mother-in-law's gaze drifted down as her brows went up. *Oh.* Then, over Celestine's shoulder, Hedley saw Calliope press her lips together and nod eagerly.

The soaring of her heart made her lightheaded. Hedley sank down onto the window seat and gulped her tea. The brew was shockingly sweet and yet...comforting. She took another sip, and before she knew it, she felt remarkably better.

"Very much a Danvers." Celestine smiled, her eyes misting over as she brushed her fingers against Hedley's cheek. "I can't wait to put this face in clay."

Then, with those parting words, she whisked out of the bedchamber, leaving the door ajar.

"If I didn't know that your mother-in-law was a sculptor, that statement might have given rise to my overactive imagination." Calliope laughed.

"Do you think it's true?" Hedley asked dreamily, her hand straying to her middle.

"If it is, then Fallow Hall will require a new name, don't you think?"

Hedley grinned. "Fruitful Hall?"

"Abundant Hall," Calliope added with plenty of cheek. And by the time they arrived at *Virile Hall*, they were both breathless with laughter.

"Feeling better, sweeting?" Rafe stood outside the door, his expression at once fierce and worried. Hedley's heart went slushy. He looked quite handsome in his fine gray coat, and the pristine white of his cravat made his features darker. She grew warmer just looking at him, imagining that *soon* they would be together. As if he sensed her thoughts, his gaze heated.

Her stomach bobbled but not unpleasantly this time. "Much better now."

Calliope reached over and took the forgotten cup out of Hedley's hand. "As much as the two of you would like to be alone...I'm afraid you still have a wedding breakfast to attend."

After picking up a hatbox from the hall, Rafe stepped into the room. "Surely, one moment more won't be too long. A man has the right to give a present to his bride, doesn't he?"

*Bride.* Hedley felt the word wash through, warming her. So much had changed since he'd first called her *armless girl*. So much was about to change, if they truly were going to have a baby. Yet after seeing him hold his nephew when they'd visited his sister in London, she knew he would be the perfect father. And she would be the mother she wished she'd had.

"I'll take the tray out into the hall, but I'm leaving the door open," Calliope warned with a grin.

Rafe placed the box on the bed where the tray had been and then lifted the peach silk gown she'd laid out. He let it glide through his fingers as he looked at her hungrily, as if he were imagining the way it would feel *and taste* against her flesh. "Mmm…this is nice."

Hedley blushed. Then, unable to resist the urge, she drew closer to him. Her hands drifted naturally to his shoulders, and his to her waist. She inhaled his scent, feeling perfectly at home. Not to mention, eager to close the door—no matter how many people waited for them downstairs. "It's uncanny how the gown and organdy sheath make it appear as if I'm wearing nothing at all. I was planning to wear it to dinner this evening."

Pulling her flush against him, he released a low growl. "Then we'll be dining in our rooms."

"I was hoping you would say that," she whispered, rising up on her toes for a kiss.

"*Don't forget about your guests,*" Calliope singsonged from the hallway.

On an exhale, Rafe pressed his forehead to hers. "Our guests. Do you suppose they'll notice our absence?"

"Perhaps after the first hour," Hedley teased. "Shall I open my gift, then?"

"Yes. I think you'd better, or else I will find an excuse to lock the door."

Turning slightly—though with Rafe's arm still draped around her waist—she untied the pink ribbon from the striped hatbox and lifted the lid. Her hand flew to her mouth on a gasp.

There, on a swath of red silk, sat a pair of glass shoes. The morning light coming in from the window glanced off the surface, making them appear as clear as water.

"Oh, Rafe. They're…they're absolutely beautiful." She was in awe. Tentatively, she reached out to touch them and found them perfectly smooth and cool. "And they look just like my red shoes."

"I made a cast from those shoes," he admitted. "Well, *after* I had a little help from Calliope to stitch them back together. I knew they were important to you. And…since they were the shoes that brought you into my life, they're important to me as well."

A sob threatened to escape. But instead of falling apart into a soggy mess, she threw herself into his arms and kissed him in earnest. She would never forget the steps she'd taken to find happiness, friendship, and love.

At the door, Calliope coughed, reminding them that they weren't alone. Not yet.

Regretfully, Hedley drew back. "I have a gift for you, dear husband, as well, but it will have to wait until we have more time…alone."

His brows lifted and a grin curled his lips. "You could tempt the very devil himself, sweeting. However, you have already given me a gift—the sole surviving window at Greyson Park."

Miraculously, the seraph window in the attic had survived. Montwood, Everhart, and even Mr. Tims had helped to rescue it from certain destruction. She glanced over at the crate sitting in the corner, prepared for a trip it never took.

"Yet when I garnered an agreeable response from one of the fellows at the antiquarian society, you declined their visit," she said, still puzzled by his decision.

Rafe brushed a fingertip across her lips before lifting her chin to his gaze. "You helped me realize what's truly important. The window's rightful place is in Greyson Park, where the Danvers family—*our family*—will reside for the rest of their days. It doesn't belong in a museum, for the sake of vanity."

She smiled up at him, loving him more with each passing moment. "Then perhaps, when we rebuild Greyson Park, the window could go in the parlor? And beside it, a glass-front cabinet..."

Her list continued as she threaded her fingers with his. Together, they walked to the hall and joined their patient friend.

"As long as Montwood marries, and I don't have to hand over five thousand pounds, then we can make Greyson Park as grand as you wish," Rafe said with a wry laugh.

Hedley knew he was teasing, because he'd already hired the laborers to clear away the rubble. *Men and their wagers*, she thought.

Boris greeted them near the top of the stairs. One of Calliope's sisters—likely Tess—had fashioned a flower chain around his neck. He didn't seem to mind the adornment. Or at least, he *tolerated* it with minimal fidgeting.

"Poor fellow," Rafe said, giving him a hearty scratch that soon earned happy tail thumps against the runner. "It's a good thing you weren't part of our wager, or I suspect you'd be married by now to those Pekingese."

Boris gave a *woof* of understanding.

Hedley tsked. "Rafe Danvers, are you blaming the wager for your current married state?"

"Of course not. I give you *all* the blame for that, sweeting." He grinned and pressed a swift kiss to her frowning lips. "If not for you, I'd have been a lonely old bachelor all of my days—a doddering fool looking around for the other half of my heart, like a pair of spectacles I'd left in the other room."

Hedley forgave him in an instant. Calliope sniffed and surreptitiously dabbed her eyes while pretending she hadn't overheard. Then with Boris's escort, they walked down the stairs.

"My parents have a wedding gift for you as well," Rafe explained as they entered the drawing room. "Though I do not know what it is."

Everhart was standing in front of the sofa, blocking a large shape behind him. Cuthbert and Celestine Danvers were near the glass-front cabinet, admiring their son's work. When they saw Rafe and Hedley's arrival, they turned in unison.

"I'm glad you're feeling better, my dear," Celestine said with a secret smile.

Cuthbert drew an unlit pipe from his mouth and pointed to Everhart. "Gabriel, if you please."

Everhart stepped to the side, revealing a rather large, gilt-framed portrait, propped up against the sofa.

Hedley stared in disbelief. It was *her*...and yet, not quite her. The dimple in her chin was missing. But it was the same face, with wide blue eyes. The same widow's peak of hair pulled into a chignon. The same figure, although the shimmering silken gown and heaps of lace were far more elegant than anything she would ever wear.

"Uncanny likeness, isn't it?" Cuthbert asked, shifting the pipe to his other hand.

Rafe stepped closer, squinting. "This isn't one of yours, Father."

"Right you are. It is not one of mine at all."

Hedley didn't understand. Neither did Rafe, for that matter, because he asked, "Then how did you come by such a likeness of my wife?"

"Artists are part of a small community. At the mention of your betrothal, an old friend shared with me a portrait from his gallery." Rafe's father shrugged as if it were a matter of happenstance. "Apparently, the subject of the portrait had a rather illustrious career as an opera singer. Caused quite the scandal, back in her day."

Then Cuthbert turned fully to her and bowed. "Hedley, my dear daughter-in-law, I would like to introduce you to your great-grandmother, Edwina Sinclair."

Hedley gaped, unable to form words. Her great-grandmother *Sinclair*? On her father's side. "That means...*she* was my grandfather's mother."

So then, Hedley was a Sinclair after all.

"Perhaps that was why he gave you Greyson Park," Rafe said softly. "He knew who you were all along."

She didn't even realize she was crying until her husband lifted a handkerchief to dry her tears. When another thought occurred to her, she looked up with concern. "That means you married a *Sinclair* after all."

And he hated the Sinclairs.

"This changes nothing. I already knew who you were." His fiercely tender gaze returned, making her heart beat in that odd cadence. "From the very first moment, you were *mine*."

## Acknowledgments

I'd like to thank Cindy C. for going to the ends of the earth to find the perfect books for me and for being the best librarian ever.

Innumerable thanks go to Chelsey and the entire Avon Impulse team for another dream realized. I'm so grateful for the chance to tell Rafe's story.

Thank you to all the amazingly talented glass artists who've posted your videos to YouTube. You've provided me with valuable research, in addition to a lifelong appreciation of your craft.

Thank you to Cyndi for being my first reader and my biggest fan. I love you.

And most of all, I thank God for the blessings and lessons in my life.

Vivienne Lorret's steamy new series continues!

Keep reading for a sneak peek at the final book in her

Rakes of Fallow Hall series:

# The Maddening Lord Montwood

Coming July 2015 from Avon Impulse.

## An Excerpt From

## THE MADDENING LORD MONTWOOD

*Lucan Montwood is the last man Frances Thorne should ever trust. A gambler and a rake, he's known for causing more trouble than he solves. So when he offers his protection after Frances's home and job are taken from her, she's more than a little wary. After all, she knows Lord Montwood's clever smile can disarm even the most guarded heart. If she's not mindful, Frances may fall prey to the most dangerous game of all—love.*

Frances moved closer to the desk. A blank page waited on the surface with a quill resting in a stand beside a pot of uncapped ink, as if prepared to attend to business matters. Out of the corner of her eye, she saw a shadow cross in front of the door and automatically turned, expecting to see Lord Whitelock.

Yet, it wasn't he at all. It was Lucan Montwood instead.

She started. "What are *you* doing here?"

"I live here, Miss Thorne." He moved into the room and lifted one hand in an absent gesture, as if the matter were of little importance. Wearing a hunter green tailcoat over a gold waistcoat and a pair of snug buttery breeches buttoned at the knee above his boots, his self-assured gait bordered on brazen.

She tried not to notice the way each step accentuated each shift and clench of his muscles. Her throat went dry. "You live here?"

That hand—those long fingers—stroked the line of his jaw as one corner of his mouth curled up in a smirk. "I'm afraid that I must admit to subterfuge. You see, this is Fallow Hall, and *not* Whitelock's residence. His estate is a few miles further north."

The words registered slowly. A pulse fluttered at her throat. "You've abducted me?"

That grin remained unchanged. "Not at all. Rest assured, you are free to leave here at any time—"

"Then I will leave at once."

"As soon as you've *heard* my warning."

It did not take long for a wave of exasperation to fill her and then exit her lungs on a sigh. "This is in regard to Lord Whitelock again. Will you ever tire of this subject? You have already said that you believe him to be a snake in disguise. I have already said that I don't agree. Therefore, there is nothing more to say unless you have proof."

"I have the same proof against him that you hold against me," he challenged with a lift of his brow. "You have damned me with the same swift judgment that you have elevated Whitelock to sainthood."

*What rubbish.* "I did not set out to find the good in his lordship. The fact of his goodness came to me naturally by way of his reputation. Even his servants cannot praise him enough. They are forever grateful for his benevolence."

"Perhaps he wants your gratitude," he said, his tone edged with warning. "This entire series of events that has put you within reach of him reeks of manipulation. You are too sensible to ignore how conveniently these circumstances turned out for him."

"Yet, I suppose, I'm meant to ignore the *convenience* in which you abducted me?"

He laughed. The low, alluring sound had no place in the light of day. It belonged to the shadows that lurked in dark alcoves and to the secret desires that a woman of seven and twenty never dare reveal.

"It was damnably hard to get you here," he said with such arrogance that she was assured her desires would remain secret forever. "You have no idea how much liquor Whitelock's driver can hold. It took an age for him to pass out."

Incredulous, she shook her head. "Are you blind to your own manipulations?"

"You are putting your faith in the wrong man." His charmer's grin was absent now and something akin to irritation flashed in his gaze. "Perhaps those spectacles require new lenses. They certainly aren't aiding your sight."

"I wear these spectacles for reading, I'll have you know. Otherwise, my vision is fine," she countered. "I prefer to wear them instead of risking their misplacement."

He gave a small cough of disbelief that irked her to no end. "You wear them like a shield of armor."

"Preposterous. I've no need for a shield of any sort. I cannot help it if you are intimidated by my spectacles, and by my ability to see right through you." She narrowed her eyes as he stepped closer, watching him as he slid the blank parchment toward him and withdrew the quill from the stand.

Ignoring her, he dipped the end into the ink and wrote something on the page.

Undeterred, she continued her harangue. "Though you may doubt it, I can easily spot those *snakes*—as you like to refer to members of your own sex—quite easily. I come to an understanding of a man's character in moments of introduction. I am even able to anticipate his actions."

He handed the parchment to her.

*"As soon as you've finished reading this, I am going to kiss you."*

## About the Author

USA *Today* best-selling author **VIVIENNE LORRET** loves romance novels, her pink laptop, her husband, and her two sons (not necessarily in that order…but there are days). Transforming copious amounts of tea into words, she is proud to be an Avon Impulse author of works including *Tempting Mr. Weatherstone*, The Wallflower Wedding Series, and the Rakes of Fallow Hall Series.

Discover great authors, exclusive offers, and more at hc.com.

Give in to your impulses . . .
Read on for a sneak peek at four brand-new
e-book original tales of romance
from HarperCollins.
Available now wherever e-books are sold.


# CHANGING EVERYTHING
## A FORGIVING LIES NOVELLA
*By Molly McAdams*


# CHASE ME
## A BROKE AND BEAUTIFUL NOVEL
*By Tessa Bailey*


# YOURS TO HOLD
## RIBBON RIDGE BOOK TWO
*By Darcy Burke*


# THE ELUSIVE LORD EVERHART
## THE RAKES OF FALLOW HALL SERIES
*By Vivienne Lorret*

An Excerpt from

# CHANGING EVERYTHING
## A Forgiving Lies Novella
### *by Molly McAdams*

Paisley Morro has been in love with Eli Jenkins
since they were thirteen years old. But after
twelve years of being only his best friend and
wingman, the heartache that comes from
watching him with countless other women
becomes too much, and Paisley decides it's
time to lay all her feelings on the table.

## Paisley

I fidgeted with my coffee cup as I tried to find the courage to say what I'd held back for so long. Twelve years. Twelve years of waiting, hoping, and aching were about to come to an end. With a deep breath in, I looked up into the blue eyes of my best friend, Eli, and tensed my body as I began.

"This guy I met, Brett, he's—well, he's different. Like, he's a game changer for me. I look at him, and I have no doubt of that. I have no doubt that I *could* spend the rest of my life with him." I laughed uneasily and shrugged. "And I know that sounds crazy after only a few weeks, but, honestly, I knew it the first day I met him. I don't know how to explain it. It wasn't like the world stopped turning or anything, there was just a feeling I had." Swallowing past the tightness in my throat, I glanced away for a moment as I strained to hold on to the courage I'd been building up all week. "But there's this other guy, and I swear this guy owns my soul."

Eli crossed his arms and his eyebrows rose, but I didn't allow myself to decipher what his expression could mean at that moment. If I tried to understand him—like I always did—then I would quickly talk myself out of saying the words I'd been thinking for far too long.

"Eli," I whispered so low the word was almost lost in the chatter from the other people in the coffee shop. "I have been in love with you since I was thirteen years old," I confessed, and held my breath as I waited for any kind of response from him.

Nothing about him changed for a few seconds until suddenly his face lost all emotion. But it was there in his eyes, like it always was: denial, confusion, shock.

I wanted to run, but I forced myself to blurt out the rest. "I've kept quiet for twelve years, and I would've continued to if I hadn't met Brett. These last few weeks have been casual, but I know he wants it to be more. But if there is a chance of an us, then there would be absolutely no thoughts of anything else with him."

Eli just continued to stare at me like I'd blown his mind, and my body began shaking as I silently begged him to say something—anything.

After twelve years of being his best friend, of being used by him as a shield from other women, of being tortured by his pretending touches and kisses . . . I was slowly giving up on us. I couldn't handle the heartache anymore. I couldn't stand being unknowingly rejected again and again. I couldn't continue being his favorite person in the world for an entirely different reason than he was mine. I couldn't keep waiting around for Eli Jenkins.

This was it for me.

"Eli, I need to know." I exhaled softly and tried to steady my shaking as I asked, "Is there *any* possibility of there being an us?"

An Excerpt from

# CHASE ME
## A Broke and Beautiful Novel
*by Tessa Bailey*

Bestselling author Tessa Bailey launches the
Broke and Beautiful trilogy, a fun and sexy
New Adult series set in New York City!

Roxy Cumberland's footsteps echoed off the smooth, cream-colored walls of the hallway, high heels clicking along the polished marble. When she caught her reflection in the pristine window overlooking Stanton Street, she winced. This pink bunny costume wasn't doing shit for her skin tone. A withering sigh escaped her as she tugged the plastic mask back into place.

Singing telegrams still existed. Who knew? She'd actually laughed upon seeing the tiny advertisement in the *Village Voice*'s Help Wanted section, but curiosity had led her to dial the number. So here she was, one day later, preparing to sing in front of a perfect stranger for a cut of sixty bucks.

Sixty bucks might not sound like much, but when your roommate has just booted you onto your ass for failure to come through on rent—again—leaving you no place to live, and your checking account is gasping for oxygen, pink bunnies do what pink bunnies must. At least her round, fluffy tail would cushion her fall when her ass hit the sidewalk.

See? She'd already found a silver lining.

Through the eyeholes of the bunny mask, Roxy glanced down at the piece of paper in her hand. Apartment 4D. Based on the song she'd memorized on the way here and the swank interior of the building, she knew the type who would answer the door. Some too-rich, middle-aged douchebag who was so bored with his life that he needed to be entertained with novelties like singing bunny rabbits.

Roxy's gaze tracked down lower on the note in her hand, and she felt an uncomfortable kick of unease in her belly. She'd met her new boss at a tiny office in Alphabet City, surprised to find a dude only slightly older than herself running the operation. Always suspicious, she'd asked him how he kept the place afloat. There couldn't be *that* high a demand for singing telegrams, right? He'd laughed, explaining that singing bunnies only accounted for a tenth of their income. The rest came in the form of *strip-o-grams*. She'd done her best to appear flattered when he'd told her she'd be perfect for it.

She ran a thumb over the rates young-dude-boss had jotted down on the slip of paper. Two hundred dollars for each ten-minute performance. God, the *security* she would feel with that kind of money. And yet, something told her that once she took that step, once she started taking off her clothes, she would never stop. It would become a necessity instead of a temporary patch-up of her shitstorm cloud.

*Think about it later. When you're not dressed like the fucking Trix Rabbit.* Roxy took a deep, fortifying breath. She wrapped her steady fingers around the brass door knocker and rapped it against the wood twice. A frown marred her forehead when she heard a miserable groan come from inside the apartment. It sounded like a *young* groan. Maybe the douchebag had a son? Oh, *cool.* She definitely wanted to do this in front of someone in her age group. Perfect.

Her sarcastic thought bubble burst over her head when

the door swung open, revealing a guy. A hot-as-hell guy. A naked-except-for-unbuttoned-jeans guy. Being the shameless hussy she was, her gaze immediately dipped to his happy trail, although, on this guy, it really should have been called a rapture path. It started just beneath his belly button, which sat at the bottom of beautifully defined ab muscles. But they weren't the kind of abs honed from hours in the gym. No, they were natural, I-do-sit-ups-when-I-damn-well-feel-like-it abs. Approachable abs. The kind you could either lick or snuggle up against, depending on your mood.

Roxy lassoed her rapidly dwindling focus and yanked it higher until she met his eyes. Big mistake. The abs were child's play compared to the face. Stubbled jaw. Bed head. Big, Hershey-colored eyes outlined by dark, black lashes. His fists were planted on either side of the door frame, giving her a front-row seat to watch his chest and arms flex. A lesser woman would have applauded. As it was, Roxy was painfully aware of her bunny-costumed status, and even *that* came in second place to the fact that Approachable Abs was so stinking rich that he could afford to be nursing a hangover at eleven in the morning. On a Thursday.

He dragged a hand through his unkempt black hair. "Am I still drunk, or are you dressed like a rabbit?"

An Excerpt from

# YOURS TO HOLD
Ribbon Ridge Book Two

*by Darcy Burke*

In the second installment of Darcy Burke's
contemporary small-town saga, the black
sheep of the Archer family is finally home,
and he's not looking for love . . . but he's about
to find it in the last place he ever expected.

Kyle Archer pulled into the large dirt lot that served as the parking area of The Alex. He still smiled when he thought of Sara coming up with the idea to name their brother's dying wish after him. It only made sense.

The hundred-plus-years-old monastery rose in front of him, its spire stretching two hundred feet into the vivid blue summer sky. The sounds of construction came from the west end of the property, down a dirt lane to what had once been a small house occupied by the head monk or whoever had been in charge at the monastery before it had been abandoned twenty-odd years ago. It was phase one of the project Alex had conceived—renovating the property into a premier hotel and event space under the Archer name, which included nine brewpubs throughout the northern valley and into Portland.

Alex had purchased the property using the trust fund left to each of them by their grandfather, then set up a trust for each sibling to inherit an equal share of the project. He'd planned for everyone to participate in the renovation, assigning key roles to all his siblings. And he'd made his attorney, Aubrey Tallinger, the trustee.

She'd endured copious amounts of anger and blame immediately following Alex's suicide because to all of them it had seemed unlikely that she'd established the trust without knowing what Alex had planned. But she insisted she hadn't known, that Alex had told her he was simply preparing in the event that he died young, something he'd convinced her was likely with his chronic lung disease.

However, things hadn't quite worked out the way Alex had envisioned. Not everyone had been eager to return to Ribbon Ridge, least of all Kyle. He shook the discomfort away. He'd fucked up. A lot. And he was trying to fix it. He owed it to Alex.

While Alex had been tethered at home with his oxygen tank and debilitating illness, the rest of them had gone off and pursued their dreams. Well, all but Hayden. As the youngest, he'd sort of gotten stuck staying in Ribbon Ridge and working for the family company. His participation in the project should've been a given, but then his dream had finally knocked down his door, and he was currently in France for a year-long internship at a winery.

Kyle stepped out of Hayden's black Honda Pilot. He'd completely taken over his brother's life while Hayden was off making wine—his car, his job, his house. Too bad Kyle couldn't also borrow the respect and appreciation Hayden received.

He slammed the car door. It wasn't going to be that easy, and he didn't deserve it to be. He should have been driving his own goddamned car, but he'd had to sell it before leaving Florida so the same shit that had driven him from Ribbon Ridge wouldn't also drive him from Miami.

But hadn't it? *No.* Things hadn't gotten as bad as they had four years ago. No one had bailed his ass out this time. He'd learned. He wasn't the same man.

An Excerpt from

# THE ELUSIVE LORD EVERHART
## The Rakes of Fallow Hall Series
### *by Vivienne Lorret*

Vivienne Lorret, the *USA Today* bestselling
author of *Winning Miss Wakefield*, returns
with a new series featuring the three roguish
bachelors of Fallow Hall. Gabriel Ludlow,
Viscount Everhart, was a fool to deny the depth
of his feelings for Calliope Croft, but the threat
that kept him from her five years ago remains.
Now he must choose between two paths: break
her heart all over again or finally succumb to
loving her . . . at the risk of losing everything.

"Surely you've heard of the Chinese medicinal *massage*," Gabriel said, attempting to reassure her. Yet the low hoarseness of his voice likely sounded hungry instead. Slowly, he slid his thumbs along the outer edges of the vertebrae at the base of her neck.

"I don't believe I have," she said, relaxing marginally, her voice thin and wispy like the fine downy hairs above her nape teasing the tops of his thumbs.

"Taoist priests have used this method for centuries." His own voice came out low and insubstantial, as if he were breathing his final breath. As it was, his heart had all but given up trying to lure the blood away from his pulsing erection. *This was a terrible idea.*

He was immensely glad he'd thought of it.

His fingertips skirted the edge of her clavicle. Hands curled over her slender shoulders, he rolled his thumbs over her again.

Calliope emitted the faintest *oh*. It was barely a breath, but the sound deafened him with a rush of tumid desire. As if she sensed the change in him, she tensed again. "Are you trying to seduce me, Everhart?"

"If you have to ask," he said, attempting to add levity

with a chuckle, "then the answer is most likely *no*." Yet even he knew differently. The *most likely* was said only as a way of not lying to himself. He wanted to seduce her, slowly and for hours on end.

For five years he'd wanted to feel her flesh beneath his hands. For a moment this evening, he'd even thought this one touch would be enough to sate him. He hated being wrong.

Those pearl buttons called to him. He feathered strokes outward along the upper edges of her shoulder blades, earning another breathy sound. Only this time, she did not tense beneath the heat of his hands.

"I've read—*heard* stories," she corrected, "where the young woman is not certain of seduction until it is too late."

Gabriel caught her quick slip and was not surprised. Her penchant for reading was another aspect of her character that drew him to her. Earlier today, in fact, he'd spotted her disappearing through the library doors.

Unable to control the impulse, he'd found a servant's door off a narrow hall and surreptitiously watched her from behind a screen in the corner. Browsing the shelves, she'd searched through dozens of books. Yet her method fascinated him. She only viewed the last pages of each book. When she found one she liked, she clutched it to her breast and released a sigh filled with the type of longing he knew too well. He had little doubt that she sought the certainty of a happy ending. All in all, it had taken her over an hour to find three books that met her standards. Yet, instead of being bored, he'd been enthralled by every minute.

And now, here they were . . .

Under the spell of his massage, her head fell forward as

she arched ever-so-slightly into his hands. Rampant desire coursed through him. Even so, he was in no hurry to end this delicious torment.

"I cannot imagine that a woman would not suspect an attempt at seduction in some manner." He leaned forward to inhale the fragrance of her hair, the barest scents of rosewater and mint rising up to greet him. "Aren't all young ladies brought up with the voice of reason clamoring about in their heads?"

His gaze followed the motions of his fingers, gliding over her silken warmth, pressing against the supple flesh that pinkened under his tender ministrations. He'd always wondered . . . and now he knew she felt as soft, if not softer, than any one of his dreams.

"Curiosity has a voice as well," she said, her voice faint with pleasure. "And are we not all creatures put upon this earth to learn, just as you have learned this *exquisite* medicine?"

And sometimes curiosity could not be tamed.

It was no use. Did he truly imagine he could resist her? "Well said, Miss Croft."

Unable to hold back a moment longer, Gabriel gave in to temptation, lowered his head, and pressed his lips to her nape.